An Excerpt from
Dark Control

Who was he? Where was I? *What had I done?*

Memories of the night before darted through my aching brain: a trip from Fort Greene to my ex-Dom's neighborhood, to his favored BDSM club. I'd lingered beside the bar while I watched for him, ordering cocktails for courage. I'd drunk too much too fast, hating myself every moment, knowing I shouldn't have been there. I'd wandered outside, not knowing what to do, or how to feel better. And then...

Nothing. Blank space. I didn't know.

I pulled on the cuffs, trying to clear the bleariness from my eyes. The man beside me turned over and blinked, awakened by my frenzied pulling. His lips parted in a yawn and then closed again as our gazes held. I forgot my headache and dry throat, and opened my mouth to scream.

He lunged before I could do it, clapping a hand over my lips. His muscular body settled half on top of mine. I shook my head while making urgent mewls against his palm. *Please, please don't kill me. Please let me go.*

"Calm down," he said, and his voice was as gravelly and scary as I expected it to be. My senses were heightened as I took in his expression, his dark hazel eyes, his angular jaw, his slightly curved lips. His hand tightened over my mouth, and I understood something with terrible clarity: He liked that I was about to pass out from fear...

Copyright 2017 Annabel Joseph

This book is a work of fiction and fantasy. Names, characters, places, and incidents are products of the author's imagination or are used fictitiously. Any resemblance to actual events, locales, or persons living or dead, is entirely coincidental.

This book contains edgy forms of sensuality that should not be attempted by the uneducated or inexperienced. In other words, don't try this at home.

All characters depicted in this work of fiction are 18 years of age or older.

Dark Control

Dark Dominance Book One

Annabel Joseph

Chapter One: Fort

I never patronized touristy Manhattan BDSM clubs, especially Underworld, but my friend Devin had ducked inside, so I waited with my other friend in the courtyard, watching pseudo-Doms and glitter subs flirt with each other in the line.

"Waste of time," Milo grumbled. "None of these chicks are Gallery material."

I turned my head to see if his low voice had been overheard. Unlike Underworld, The Gallery was a secret, extremely exclusive BDSM club, and we weren't supposed to spread the word, lest we find our private play space overrun with gawkers, wannabes, and the safety police.

A moment later, Devin emerged. Like us, he was dressed in a suit, fresh from a late dinner at Coleman's. He grinned, his blue eyes rueful in the dim light. "Found a hot one, but she's a Domme."

"Wow," Milo drawled. "Good work, Dev."

"She offered to lock my dick in a trap." He grabbed his crotch with a leer. "So we're not compatible. Nice ass, though."

I nodded toward the door. "How are things inside?"

"Stupid. Crowded. Worst music I've ever heard in a BDSM club."

Milo gave him a dark look. "That's why we don't come here."

I rubbed my forehead, then shoved back a drooping curl while the two of them bickered. This whole scene was bullshit. I wanted action, wanted to beat on some masochistic, cowering sub who was into the game. A real sub, not the posturing, pretty club mavens milling outside Underworld. Unfortunately, The Gallery wasn't open tonight.

I wasn't sure where my sadistic urges came from. I'd grown up in a safe, loving home with two younger sisters I adored. Sure, my parents had battled through a wretched divorce when I was a teenager, but I'd been into the idea of pain and passion long before that.

I drifted away from the courtyard and noticed a girl in the shadows, slumped against the corner of the adjacent building. Her forehead rested against the brick, her fingers splayed on the wall for support. Her face was covered by messy, shoulder-length hair, but I could see that she wore a collar. Maybe that was why I headed toward her. Kinky people had to stick together. I might be a sadistic Dominant, but I was also a decent human being, and she was alone and distressed in a not-so-great area of the city.

"Hey, Fort, where you going?" Dev called.

"There's a girl over there."

"Yeah, and she's going to mug you when you ask if she needs help," Milo said. "How long have you lived here?"

I slowed when I got closer, trying to figure out what was wrong with her. She was dressed in a short, dark dress with gray over-the-knee socks. Beautiful legs. Curvy, not too skinny.

God, she was shitty-drunk. I could smell alcohol on her from five feet away. She looked at me sideways with large, kohl-rimmed eyes. Her dark lipstick was smeared, and one hand clutched her stomach.

"Don't." She extended her other hand shakily in my direction. "Don't mess with me."

"I'm not going to mess with you. Do you need help?"

She turned unsteadily from the wall, her face bunched up with tears. "I...need... I'm fucked... Fucked up."

"I see that." I took a step closer, trying not to look threatening despite my height and dark features. "Bad night? How much have you had to drink? What are you doing out here?" She was too clean to be a street person, and too unconventional-looking to be a prostitute. The dress, the eyeliner, the marled, beribboned socks. "It's not safe to wander around here in the middle of the night," I told her. "Where are your friends?"

"I'm...here..." She waved a finger in the air, as if her explanations had to be caught from the space around her. "I came here..."

"What's your name?"

"Je-wels. Jewels."

Artsy name for an artsy-looking chick. "Okay, Jewels, my name's Fort. Are you ready to go home? Is there anyone here who can help get you home?"

She shook her head, suddenly angry. "No. Not with... I'm done. Not him."

"Who's him?"

"There's...no him. Don't know... How..."

She was sober enough to stay vertical, but not sober enough to make any sense. I turned back to my friends. "What should I do?"

"She's cute," Milo joked, "but you're not supposed to fuck the drunk ones."

I scowled at him. "We need to help her." I lowered my voice. "She's one of us. See her collar?"

"I doubt she's one of us," said Devin. "I'm sure she belongs in there." He pointed to Underworld's crowded courtyard. "Just lead her back inside."

I had a feeling this woman's situation was more complex. "Who are you with?" I asked again. "Do you have a way home? Do you have money? Identification?"

She patted her pockets, reached over her shoulder for a ghostly bag that was no longer there. She turned to look on the ground behind her. Jesus, had some lowlife already stolen her shit?

I thought about what to do. Call the police? With no ID and little ability to speak, she'd probably end up in the drunk tank. Should I take her into Underworld to try to find the person she'd come with?

"Did you come here with someone?" I asked, brushing my fingertip over her collar. "Do you have a Dominant? A Master somewhere inside there?"

She burst into tears again. "He's bad. I hate him."

"Who?"

She didn't answer, or couldn't answer. She was distraught. Her eyes were pools of pain.

"Did someone hurt you?" I checked over her skimpy dress for signs of a struggle.

"Really?" Dev said. "You're going to play therapist?"

"Shut the fuck up and look at her. She's a mess. Something might have happened to her. What if she's been drugged?"

"What if she took drugs? What if she's a junkie?"

"She's drunk, not high," I snapped.

She slid down the building and wrapped her arms around her knees. Her shoulders shook with sobs.

Milo sighed. "What do you plan to do, man? Drop her off at a hospital?"

"No," said Devin. "They'll turn her over to the police."

"I have to go home," she sobbed, squinting up at us. From this angle, I could see how blue her eyes were. "Have to...get there."

"Home? Where's your home?" asked Milo.

"Blackwall. Please."

"The Blackwell." Milo turned and punched my shoulder. "You live in the Blackwell, Fort. She's all yours. Take her home."

"Do you live in the Blackwell?" I asked, kneeling beside her.

She nodded. Okay. Fuck. I tried to catch her wavering gaze. "Hey, listen, Jewels. Do you want me to take you home? I live in the Blackwell, too."

She nodded, poking the front of my suit jacket. "Blackwall."

"Jesus, you're fucked up." I turned to my friends. "Are you going to come with us?"

"Dude." Milo held up his hands. "You're the one that got a fucking hard-on to help her. You take her home."

"Come on. Dev?"

"Nope. Sorry, man. Allie just texted me." Dev held up his phone, showing a stream of messages littered with emojis. "She's invited us to hang out at her place tonight."

Allie. Damn it. One of those masochistic, cowering subs I'd been craving for days. I stood and turned to Milo, but he was looking at his phone, thumbing through Allie's messages. In his head, he was probably

8

already rigging her to her personal bondage rack. Meanwhile, "Jewels" continued to sob at my feet.

"Drop her off at the Blackwell and meet us at Allie's," said Milo. "We'll save a little piece of her ass for you, if you don't take too long."

"Fuck." I looked down at the top of Jewels' head, wondering why I'd chosen tonight of all nights to play the superhero. "Fine, I'll meet you there as soon as I can. But before you go, help me get her into a cab."

* * * * *

The woman fell asleep as soon as the taxi rolled into traffic. The ten-minute ride to the Blackwell building stretched to twenty minutes because of an accident, and she slumped against my shoulder, her unkempt curls tickling my chin.

At least she'd stopped crying. I couldn't deal with female tears, unless they were sexual-masochist tears, and then I wanted to bathe in them. *Yeah, don't think about that now. Wait until you're at Allie's.*

We pulled up at the Blackwell, and I half-helped, half-carried her into the lobby. "Any idea where this one belongs?" I asked the doorman.

"No, Mr. St. Clair, don't recognize her."

"Fuck." I lifted her as she started sagging. "She told me she lives here."

"I don't know, sir. I can't say I know everyone in the building."

I wanted to ask if I could leave her in the lobby until she perked up, but the doorman's expression was already telling me no. This wasn't the type of building that allowed passed-out club girls to sleep it off on the sofas, even if she lived here.

"I guess I'll take her up to my place until she's a little more with it," I said.

"That sounds like a good idea, sir."

"If anyone asks after a woman named Jewels, give me a call."

"You got it, Mr. St. Clair."

You're an idiot, Mr. St. Clair. That's what his tone communicated, and he was right. I was bringing an unknown woman to my penthouse in the middle of the night. Neighbor or not, she might wake up and accuse me of anything. She might go on a rampage and murder me in my apartment before she jumped out of my fortieth floor window. She might be anyone, or do anything in response to my act of kindness.

As soon as I got her in my apartment, I laid her on a couch in the living room. I'd already checked her clothes in the cab for pockets, ID, a phone. Nothing.

I sat back on my heels, staring at her, trying to think. Fawn-brown hair, smooth skin, but older than I'd originally thought, now that I saw her in the light. Who was she? Had I ever seen her in the elevator? She had gorgeous legs, and I had a weakness for legs, so I probably would have remembered her. I pulled the top of one of her socks to make them even, and let my thumb drift over the bare skin above it before I let go. *No, we don't fuck the drunk ones.*

I took off her shoes instead, because they looked clunky and uncomfortable, and she curled into my sofa. She looked a little less vulnerable now, even though her mouth was half-open, and her eyelids twitched as if she was having a nightmare. I brushed aside her hair to find the back of her collar so I could unbuckle it.

She turned her head as I pulled it off, but she didn't wake. I'd hoped there might be some tag or label, or identifying words written on the inside. No such luck. I turned it over in my hands, inspecting the hardware. It was a novelty store collar, pleather with crap stitching, nothing a serious player would use.

A serious player. I sounded like an elitist asshole, but in the BDSM world, there were people who dabbled, and people who swam in the deep end. I belonged to the latter group, as did the perverts I hung out with. I played in the world where consent and force started to blur—with willing partners, of course, when I could find them.

And when I found them, I didn't adorn them in cheap pleather painted brass novelty store shit.

I tossed the collar on the end table and went to the kitchen, shedding my suit jacket and loosening my tie. I rolled up my sleeves and ran cool water on a dishtowel, soaking it through and squeezing it out. Damn, the perfect way to spend a Friday night, with someone's messed up submissive who might or might not throw up on my favorite sofa. If I could go back in time...

If I could go back in time, I'd still help her.

"Wake up, little subbie," I said. "Where do you live? Someone's probably looking for you."

Her eyes tried to open, but didn't quite manage it. "Good luck," she said.

"What? Stay with me a minute, Jewels. What unit do you live in?"

"Blackwall." She rubbed a hand over her face, smearing more eyeliner. "Blackwall."

"We're at the Blackwell. What's your apartment number?"

"Good luck. Boundless."

I sighed. "I need to get you home. How are you feeling? Are you going to be sick?"

I showed her the bowl, but she ignored it, snuggling deeper into my couch. "So tired. Call good luck."

She tried to sit up, then laid back down again. I dabbed her head with the cool towel, but she was falling back to sleep. "Tomorrow," she said on a quiet breath. "Good luck." A minute later, her eyelids resumed twitching as she relaxed into dreamland.

Great. Because of my heroics, I was going to miss my much-needed stress release with Allie. I texted my friends that I wouldn't be showing, then stood over Jewels with my hands on my hips. The dark look in my eyes would have sent any of my Gallery submissives into a panic, but the woman on my couch took no notice. Her fingers fell open beside her messed-up curls as she let out a faint snore.

CHAPTER TWO:
JULIET

I woke slowly, reluctantly, with sore eyes and a throbbing head. I reached to rub my temple but my hand wouldn't move. Oh God, neither hand would move. A large, dark-haired man shifted beside me at the same moment I realized my hands were cuffed to an unfamiliar headboard.

Who was he? Where was I? *What had I done?*

Memories of the night before darted through my aching brain: a trip from Fort Greene to my ex-Dom's neighborhood, to his favored BDSM club. I'd lingered beside the bar while I watched for him, ordering cocktails for courage. I'd drunk too much too fast, hating myself every moment, knowing I shouldn't have been there. I'd wandered outside, not knowing what to do, or how to feel better. And then...

Nothing. Blank space. I didn't know.

I pulled on the cuffs, trying to clear the bleariness from my eyes. The man beside me turned over and blinked, awakened by my frenzied pulling. His lips parted in a yawn and then closed again as our gazes held. I forgot my headache and dry throat, and opened my mouth to scream.

He lunged before I could do it, clapping a hand over my lips. His muscular body settled half on top of mine. I shook my head while making urgent mewls against his palm. *Please, please don't kill me. Please let me go.*

"Calm down," he said, and his voice was as gravelly and scary as I expected it to be. My senses were heightened as I took in his expression, his dark hazel eyes, his angular jaw, his slightly curved lips. His hand tightened over my mouth, and I understood something with terrible clarity: He liked that I was about to pass out from fear.

"Deep breaths," he said. His gaze was intent, direct, and unsettling. "I'll let you go, but you can't scream. I'm a friend."

A friend? I stared at his face, but I didn't know him. His body was still pressed against mine, and his fingers flexed over my lips.

"Can I let you go now?" he asked.

I shook my head yes, then no. I was too scared to think.

"For real, calm down," he said, watching my eyes dart back and forth. "I'm telling you the truth. I'm a good guy. No screaming and thrashing, okay?"

So he'd noticed my legs poised to kick him off me. I noticed something too—my socks were still on, as well as my underwear and clothes, and he was dressed also, in a t-shirt and sleep pants. I did a quick body check, and besides my splitting headache, I wasn't hurting. He hadn't done anything bad to me—yet. Maybe he wasn't a serial killer.

Please don't let him be a serial killer. His eyes looked too human for that. My panicked panting slowed to reasonable breaths, and I nodded to let him know he could stop holding me down, that I wasn't going to scream. My mouth felt so dry, I didn't think I could scream even if I wanted to, and I couldn't attack him, because both my wrists were cuffed to his bed. He slowly moved his hand from my mouth, and when I didn't start shrieking, he eased sideways and sat up.

"Who are you?" I asked, pulling again at the cuffs. They were actual, real bondage cuffs, constructed so I couldn't fumble open the buckles. That amused glint came into his eyes again, as he saw me realize my plight.

"My name's Forsyth St. Clair." He shook one of my cuffed hands. "I know, most pretentious name ever. My friends call me Fort. So, is your name Jewel, or Jewels? You were hard to understand last night."

That made sense, considering I had no memory of our conversation…or anything else that might have occurred. "My name's Juliet. Jules is a nickname."

"Oh, J-u-l-e-s. Short for Juliet. I was picturing diamonds and rubies, those kinds of jewels."

"No. Like Romeo's Juliet, with one t." I fell silent, wondering why I'd volunteered that information. What was I doing here? And why the hell hadn't he uncuffed me yet?

I pushed down adrenaline. He wasn't attacking me. I didn't know him, but despite his size and his very effective wrist cuffs, I had no reason to believe he meant me harm. Still, there was a question I needed answered.

"Can you tell me what I'm doing in your bed, Fort? Did we…last night…"

"No. I'm not that kind of person, and this isn't my bed, it's the guest room bed."

"Oh."

"I'm sorry about the cuffs." He didn't actually look very sorry. "I put them on you last night before I fell asleep, because I didn't know what you'd do when you woke up. And you're in my guest room because I didn't know where else to take you, aside from a hospital or police station. You were drunk last night, breaking down outside Underworld. Do you remember that?"

"Yes. Vaguely." I pushed back my hair. "Not really. I mean, I remember that I was there." I watched him as I spoke, scrutinizing him for any break in his expression, any lapse in his pleasant personality that might signal a maniac underneath.

Meanwhile, everything came back to me: the shots I'd done at home to shore up my courage, the trip on the subway, the dread and hope that I'd see Keith at Underworld and entice him back into our relationship. Why? So he could tear out my heart again? "I shouldn't have gone to Underworld. I realize that now."

"No one should ever go to Underworld," said Fort. "But you don't seem like a psycho, so I'll set you loose." He started to undo the cuffs, and when I frowned at him, gave a half-shrug. "I did find you outside a BDSM club. I didn't think you'd freak out about the restraints. Would you rather I'd used rope?"

"No." I rubbed my wrists when he released me, and tried to sit up, then collapsed again when the room spun.

"Take it easy." He unwound the cuffs' chain from the headboard and backed off the bed, standing to his full height. "I'll get you some water and ibuprofen."

"You don't have to."

He pointed at me on his way out the door. "Stay there."

Spoken like a true Dominant. It wasn't a coincidence that he'd found me outside a kink club, or that he owned the serious kind of cuffs. In a less hungover situation, I would have been drooling over his alpha-male posturing and muscular physique, but right now, I was just trying not to cringe from the sunlight bleeding through his window shades.

By the time he returned, I'd managed to sit up, drawing my legs under me. I felt gross and awful, embarrassed, stupid, everything. I was thirty-two years old, too old to be waking up hungover in some stranger's guest room. He presented me with a tumbler of ice water and two pills, and I took them, because he was acting dominant and I was feeling submissive and defeated as hell.

"I'm so sorry about this," I mumbled.

"Drink as much water as you can. It'll help the headache and dry mouth."

He was right, the water was heavenly. I drained the tumbler and asked for more, and by this time, I'd woken up enough to watch him leave. Tall, thick, dark hair, gorgeous ass. What was his name again? Fort? He was built like a fort. I'd never seen him at Underworld, but if I had, I would've considered him out of my league.

By the time he got back, I'd crawled from under the covers and perched on the edge of his bed. He sat beside me, leaving some space between us, and watched while I guzzled most of the second glass.

"Feeling any better?" he asked.

"A little." *Not that I deserve to.* "Thanks for rescuing me last night. Seriously, I appreciate it."

"You're welcome, but you need to be more careful. Don't go clubbing alone, and..." He clicked into lecture mode. "Don't drink. You're not good at it. You were so wasted, you couldn't even tell us where you lived."

"Us?" I darted a look toward the door.

"My friends aren't here now, but they were with me last night. They can vouch for me, that you were mumbling and sobbing, leaning against the Caraway hotel. You're sure nothing happened to you? You seemed pretty upset."

I looked down at my clothes, and my slightly rumpled, but still intact, gray over-the-knee socks. "I don't think anything happened, but thanks for stepping in to help me. Most of last night is a blur."

He studied me, his hazel eyes narrowed with concern. "Did you play last night in the club? In Underworld?"

"No." A blush crept into my cheeks. "I was just watching."

"Whose collar were you wearing?"

I couldn't meet his gaze. This was so humiliating, especially since he was obviously kinky, obviously a Dom. "It was no one's collar. I mean, it was from an old relationship. A failed relationship. A relationship I need to let go."

He looked away. "Sorry, I shouldn't pry. The collar's downstairs, by the way."

"I don't want the stupid collar." I finished the last of the water, swallowing against my tears. "I'll never do anything like this again."

"You mean the drinking?" His eyes flickered. "Or the collar?"

What a question. The truth was, I always, *always* got involved with the worst jerks and players, convincing myself I could change them and make them love me if I put up with enough of their shit. I'd been born into a poor, dysfunctional family with an absent father, so my behavior wasn't unexpected, just hard for me to overcome. It was an endless cycle of self-deprecation and heartbreak, made worse by my submissive tendencies.

"I don't know that I'm cut out to survive either thing," I said, summing up my issues. "I'm sorry you had to get involved, but thanks for not leaving me on the street."

"You're welcome. You said you lived here at the Blackwell, so I figured, in the morning—"

"The Blackwell?"

He blinked at me, fighting irritation. "You told me several times that you lived at the Blackwell. I guess someone stole your shit at Underworld, or outside Underworld, because you didn't have any identification on you." He grimaced. "You might want to cancel your cards."

Damn. My wallet. My phone. Now that I was fully awake and functioning, I felt like I'd been hit by a car. Ice picks were stabbing my brain. "I live in a place called the Black Wall," I told him. Tears welled in my eyes again.

"The Black Wall?" He smacked his forehead. "The Black Wall. That stack of shipping containers in Fort Greene. The artist colony. Are you an artist?"

"No, but I work for one. Goodluck Boundless." At his confused expression, I clarified. "Goodluck Boundless is his actual, legal name."

To my surprise, Fort started to laugh, the rich sound filling the bedroom. "Last night, you kept telling me 'good luck, good luck.' You started up with the 'boundless,' and I gave up on trying to understand you."

He laughed so hard that I had to smile too, which was better than crying. "Yeah, Goodluck's my boss, and my friend. We both live in the Black Wall."

He gave one last chuckle. "Sorry I didn't put Goodluck Boundless and the Black Wall together. I'm not big into the art scene. So what do you do for Goodluck Boundless? You're a model?"

Nice of him to ask, but I was twenty pounds overweight, with short legs and intractable, mousey-brown hair. "I'm not a model. I'm his business manager. I plan his shows, coordinate with sales agents, that kind of thing. He got me an apartment in the Black Wall so we can work together more easily. Three other artists live there, too."

"And it's got a big mural on one side, right? They paint a new one every few weeks?"

"Yes, it hasn't been a black wall since the beginning. Right now it's a huge plaid rabbit playing a violin."

"I'd like to see that." He took the glass from me. "If you want I can drive you home, unless..." He turned the glass in his hands. "Would you like some breakfast first? Some coffee?"

I looked at him, thinking how easily he could become my next pathetic, hopeless crush. He didn't just set off my Dom radar, he exploded it, smashed it to pieces. I rubbed my wrists in an unconscious gesture that became much more conscious when he looked down at my hands.

One cup of coffee, more time to talk... Who knew what might develop?

No, too masochistic, even for me. I turned away and tugged at one of the bows on my socks. "I've already put you to too much trouble, Mr.—what's your name again? I'm sorry."

"It's okay. St. Clair. Fort St. Clair."

"Fort, yeah. Sorry. I can take the subway. It stops right by my place."

"The subway? You're sure?" He slid a look over my wrinkled dress and day-old makeup. "So, just reminding you that you don't have any money, although I can give you money if your heart's set on the subway..."

Shit. My purse, my phone, my money. I covered my face with my hands. "This is fucked up. Okay, I'll accept a ride, but I feel so bad about all this."

"It's all right. I've never seen a plaid rabbit playing a violin before." He stretched and stood, and I thought, *he is too fucking gorgeous for words.* "We can leave whenever you're ready. Oh, and there's a guest bathroom there if you want to use it. I should have told you that before."

He pointed to a door on the other side of the room and left.

Okay, Jules, pull yourself together so you can get out of this man's hair, and maybe make a long-overdue appointment with a therapist.

I got up and limped over to the bathroom, and stepped into a window-walled chamber of sun overlooking the city. Jesus, how high up was Fort's apartment? He had to live near the top of the Blackwell, in one of the shiny glass penthouses.

I backed away from the view, my stomach churning, and turned to the mirror. I looked awful. Silly, to entertain thoughts of Fort and me, when I was lying in his bed looking like a sad, hungover clown. The eye makeup I'd painstakingly applied last night was smeared up into my eyebrows and down my cheeks. All that remained of my lipstick was an outer lining of uneven burgundy. My eyes were swollen and red, and my curly hair looked like a ransacked bird's nest.

All of this contrasted with his spotless marble and teak bathroom, making me feel worse. I turned on the burnished gold faucet and used his French-milled hand soap to wash off what makeup I could. My mouth tasted like death, but a timid pull of the nearest drawer revealed packaged toothbrushes and travel-sized tubes of toothpaste. I brushed my teeth and debated taking a quick shower, because the fancy, rainshower spout looked so inviting. In the end, everything was too clean and perfect, and I didn't want to sully his spotless white towels.

At least I looked *slightly* more presentable when I walked out of the bedroom and down the hall to his living room. He acknowledged the change in my appearance with a quick once-over. A sign of interest? Should I let him know I was submissive and available?

God, no.

I was finished chasing after cool and unattainable men. Last night was a low point. Waking up cuffed to a bed in a stranger's home—even if it was a gorgeous stranger and a gorgeous home—was a wakeup call I couldn't ignore.

"You ready?" he asked. He'd cleaned up too, although he hadn't shaved off his stubble. His navy sweater and well-fitted jeans almost stole my resolve, but I collected myself and nodded.

"I'm ready. Thank you."

As I expected, his car was sporty, fast, and loud. A uniformed valet brought it up from his private parking area under the building. Although I worked for one of the preeminent artists in the city, I wasn't used to such ostentatious displays of wealth. Goodluck was filthy rich, but he didn't have a car because he lived more like a hobo than a millionaire.

Even if Goodluck had a car, he wouldn't have driven it like Fort, so smoothly and confidently, his hand working the gearshift in stop-and-go traffic like he didn't even have to think about it. He kept up a polite stream of conversation about the New York art scene and my experiences as Goodluck's manager. He told me he worked at his father's company, Sinclair Jewelers, a global luxury firm. That explained the penthouse and flashy car.

When he stopped outside the Black Wall, we admired the rabbit mural for a moment together, but I didn't invite him inside or make any overtures to keep in touch. He didn't make any overtures either, just smiled one last time as I left his car to do my walk of shame to the lobby door. I pulled it closed behind me, letting the clutter and kitschiness of the Black Wall's communal ground floor surround me.

I belonged here in this colorful, comfortable place. The marble penthouse was a fantasy...and so was Fort St. Clair.

Chapter Three:
Fort

I hadn't told Juliet, but I'd started my kink life in clubs like Underworld. I wasn't ashamed of it, but I'd quickly moved on to harder places, and harder types of pain. I'd met Devin soon after I graduated college, at a Manhattan munch—I used to go to those, too—and recognized a kindred spirit. Dev introduced me to Milo through a submissive partner they shared, and Milo was the portal for both of us into The Gallery.

Since then, The Gallery was my standing Saturday night date.

The Gallery wasn't your typical BDSM club. It was a kinky stronghold you could only join through word of mouth, a stone clock tower and dome at the top of the Bridgeport building, which was, incidentally, half owned by Milo's family, who were famous Italian instrument makers.

The original Gallery owners banded together to buy the undeveloped clock tower when it came on the market, meaning to use it as a private men's club. They renovated it Versailles-style, did it up with rococo sculptures, fleur-de-lys carpets, and carved, gold-painted doors. A circular staircase twisted up to the dome, into a stone chamber where the early members had established a dungeon-like sex chamber.

Now the whole three-floor establishment was kinky as fuck. There were twenty to thirty members at any given time, as privileged invitees joined or drifted away. It cost a small fortune to become a member, but for me, it was money well spent. Membership was restricted to Dominant males, and each member was allowed to bring in any woman he liked, as long as that woman agreed to be discreet, follow the rules, and adhere to the dress code: exhibitionist lingerie and a collar that marked her as communal property. The Gallery was about as gothic and perverse as a legal, private BDSM club in New York City could be.

So it was strange that I was sitting on the sidelines in the middle of prime time, during the height of screams and scenes, thinking about last night's encounter with Juliet.

Encounter, was that even the word for it? Why had I noticed her, and felt so strongly that I had to help her? Her ruined makeup and tangled hair had triggered something protective in me, to the point where I'd let her spend the night in my guest room. *Yeah, and you brought out the cuffs, even though you had no real reason to think she needed to be restrained.*

Fine, I'd had a little fun with her. It must have been because she was new and different. All kinds of women came to The Gallery as guests of their sponsors, but all of them were a certain type—wild, fearless, and masochistic.

They were also all very familiar to me.

As for myself, I hadn't sponsored any women in a while. The last woman I'd invited hadn't enjoyed the experience, and threatened to report all of us to the police, which would have been grounds for getting my ass permanently banned from the club. Dev still teased me about it, but it wasn't funny. My bad taste in subs was becoming a thing.

Maybe that was why I'd felt drawn to Juliet last night. Maybe she seemed safe, since she was an Underworld kind of submissive. No risk of entanglement, since she had very little to offer me. The whole Black Wall thing, her artist boss, it made her interesting, but it didn't make her a hardcore sub. If an Underworld Dom could reduce her to tears and drunkenness, that was a bad sign for our compatibility.

Dev came over and greeted me, interrupting my thoughts. A thin, blonde sub trailed him, preening in her Gallery uniform and leash. We were both in uniform, too—dark suits and ties. Our gentlemanly attire was part of the power imbalance, a contrast to the scanty, slutty garments the slave girls wore.

"Hey, man," he said, sitting next to me on the couch. "I didn't know you were here."

"Yeah. Haven't gotten started yet."

Across from us, a woman wailed through a flogging, dancing on her toes. In the bench area, a bent-over submissive's mouth and ass were being plowed by two Doms.

"You never made it to Allie's last night," he said over the flogged woman's screams.

"I wanted to, but I couldn't. I just said goodbye to last night's 'good deed' a few hours ago."

"What? You kept that chick with you all night?" He blinked. "You didn't sleep with her?"

"Do I usually sleep with drunk, emo subs from Underworld?"

He chuckled, giving me that one. "What was her deal?" he asked.

I looked around The Gallery, and at Hanna, the girl at Devin's feet, and decided I didn't want to talk about Juliet here. "She didn't live in the Blackwell," I said, summing up. "Turns out she lives in a place called the Black Wall."

"The Black Wall? Never heard of it, but it sounds awful."

"It's an artists' complex in Fort Greene, built out of shipping containers. I saw it when I dropped her off this morning."

He gave me a look. "How chivalrous of you to drive her home."

"She didn't have any money for the subway. Don't be a dick."

"Wait, let me get this straight. You kept the sobbing Underworld refugee at your apartment all night? She slept there and everything?"

"Yes, in my guest room. She passed out." I didn't mention that I'd slept beside her after cuffing her wrists to the headboard. Dev was the type who'd never let something like that go. I changed the subject. "You and Milo had fun with Allie?"

He picked up the new topic of conversation with gusto. "You missed out, my friend. She was in high spirits. Nothing we did to her was too much. All she wanted was pain, and for us to hurt her pussy." Dev's eyes sparked with perverse pleasure. "Milo got out that thin cane she likes and used it on her fucking clit."

"No way."

"I know. She was screaming and coming like crazy, with the tears, and the black lines running down her cheeks..."

He made a guttural sound, miming mascara trails. I didn't get off on smeared makeup as much as Dev, but yeah, I could see it in my mind.

"We had her in clamps and restraints, the whole deal. Then I fucked her ass while Milo jammed his cock down her throat, and every time she gagged, she clenched around my dick. You know how they do that? And every time he let her up for air, she's crying *more, more, more...*"

I gave an appreciative nod, but the story made me uncomfortable more than it turned me on, and here's why: I didn't want my partners to be begging for *more, more, more*. That killed it for me. I preferred a woman crying *stop, stop, stop,* and truly wanting me to stop, but letting me have my way anyway. I knew that was edgy and fucked up. That was why it was hard for me to find someone compatible at The Gallery—because all these women were thrilled to be in the company of sadists. They were all hardcore humiliation freaks and pain sluts.

But women who weren't humiliation freaks and pain sluts were hard to entice into the fold.

"So after all that," said Dev, "Allie wanted us to put hot sauce on her caned-up clit. And Milo's like, 'no, because I don't feel like listening to you squeal for the next two hours.' But in the end I did it for her, and tied her face down on the bed so she couldn't rub the pain away. We both fucked her ass while she screamed like a banshee, trying to buck the heat from her clit onto the sheets." He shook his head with an evil grin. "Too bad you weren't there, man. You could have stopped up her mouth with your cock, and we could have had some peace and quiet."

I could picture all this, including Allie begging for them to be rougher, to fuck her ass harder. "I'm sorry I missed it." But not that sorry. I'd gotten a pretty deep thrill from carrying Juliet's unresponsive body to my guest room and cuffing her to the bed. I didn't want to think about why.

"When we finally untied Allie, she freaked about the hot sauce and started clawing at her clit," Dev continued, "so Milo made her sit in an ice cold bath until the hot sauce wore off, but he wouldn't let her wash it off herself. It had to soak off while she shivered in the water. She came twice more from Milo twisting her nipples and yelling at her not to touch her pussy."

"What were you doing through all this?"

He rubbed his crotch. "Dude, I was beating off. You know how I get when girls lose their shit."

"I'm surprised no one called the cops." Allie was a screamer, and being a professional vocalist, she had an ear-splitting voice.

"Her neighbors are used to it by now, I think."

"She's not here tonight," I said, looking around.

"No, we told her she wasn't allowed to show up tonight. Her pussy needs time to heal. Hot sauce sounds fun and kinky until it's burning into your mucous membranes."

"Ugh." I shuddered, giving him a look. "How do you know what hot sauce feels like?"

"I never do anything to my girls that I haven't done to myself first, for experimental purposes. Well, more or less. Actually, there's a ton of shit girls ask me for that I'd never do to myself, but the hot sauce, yeah, I tried it once. Put it on my balls. It doesn't feel good." He shuddered, stroking his cock through his pants. "Anyway, sorry you missed out on Allie. You should go upstairs and find someone to play with." He indicated the second-floor play space, which sounded even more active than the first. "Make it up to yourself. There's a good crowd here tonight."

"I'm not sure I'm going to play tonight." There was plenty going on, but none of the women made me want to hurt them. "I'm in a weird mood."

"What, you going soft on us?" Dev asked.

No. I think I'm going too hard to the other side. I want something harder and more authentic than The Gallery, and that worries me. I was notorious for getting involved with the wrong women, but maybe the crux of the problem was me.

"I should just go home," I said.

Dev looked down at his slave, who'd been pretending not to follow our conversation.

"Hanna, why don't you try to relax my friend here with your whore mouth? He's had a trying weekend."

I waved him off. "She doesn't have to."

"She doesn't mind," said Dev. "Look at her face. She's been dying to give you a blowjob. She's a hungry little slut."

She did, in fact, look excited to be nudged over in front of me, so I made room for her between my knees and let her roll on the condom that Dev provided. A blowjob wasn't what I'd come here for, but it would take the edge off.

I rested my head back against the couch and stroked Hanna's hair while she took me in her mouth. Dev had been training her for a couple of years now, and she'd learned a lot about giving head. As she licked and sucked, my cock started to cooperate, but I wasn't thinking about Hanna. I wasn't thinking about Allie or rough sex, or pinning a struggling girl under me. I was thinking about Juliet.

Which was stupid, because she was emotionally sketchy, possibly alcoholic, and not kinky enough. Case in point about the kink: her amateur collar.

But what if you taught her about better collars, and showed her the pleasures of harder scening? What if she was the one kneeling in front of you, taking you in her mouth?

Hanna's straight, glossy blonde hair was supermodel beautiful, but my fingers wanted to feel Juliet's unkempt curls. I'd only touched them once last night. Why was I thinking of that now? Why had she left me with this heightened, almost violent, surge of sexual energy?

I couldn't release that energy on Hanna, who was doing me a favor. I couldn't push her back on the floor and jab into her throat while holding her down by the hair. She wasn't my slave, so I had to let Devin be part of this scene, and in that sense, I could only go so far.

But I controlled the blowjob, varying my rhythm and the depths of my thrusts to throw her off whenever she got comfortable. She went along with whatever I did, but I wanted something less generous and more...dubiously consensual.

Like cuffing a passed-out woman to my guest room bed.

Chapter Four:
Juliet

I sat up late in the Black Wall's communal lobby, an art-filled dump of chairs and beanbags that covered the entire ground floor. My favorite chair was in the corner, set beneath an amber, recycled-glass chandelier. The cushy seat was round and bowl shaped, perfect for curling up in order to think or sleep.

But sleep eluded me, because Goodluck was sprawled beside me, talking quietly to himself about esoteric stuff. I tried to catch the strings of his thoughts, adding them to the maelstrom in my brain. I'd done way too much thinking in this chair, thinking about Keith and why I'd let him manipulate me, and wreck my self-esteem for his kinky pleasure. Then there was the Dom before that...and, sigh, the Dom before that. I also thought about Fort St. Clair, who'd come to my rescue on one of the darkest, most miserable nights of my life.

After our limited time together, I'd been intrigued enough to do an Internet search, and I'd gotten a barrage of results. Businessman, playboy, oldest son of the wealthy St. Clair family. I'd been about to start a folder for digital clippings and photos of him—God, he was *so* photogenic—but then I remembered that I'd done the same thing with power-realtor Keith. I had a habit of mistaking money and prestige—and dominance—for redeeming qualities. Lots of guys in this city were rich, especially the kinky ones. I needed to get it through my skull that it didn't make them worth my time.

So I forgot about Fort St. Clair as well as I could, and threw myself back into work. Goodluck was riding an inspirational high, and neither of us knew when he'd crash, so I scheduled gallery shows, tracked down prospective models, and sourced discontinued varieties of film and darkroom chemicals so he could achieve the grainy, overexposed prints his collectors liked.

On top of business and artistic needs, my job involved managing Goodluck's personal craziness, his artistic ups and down. It was mentally exhausting work, but I didn't mind too much, because my boss wasn't a Dominant or a soul-crusher, or even a romantic prospect. He was a friend. At twenty-nine, Goodluck Boundless was three years younger than me, but pretty much timeless.

And often a little unhinged.

"Here's the thing," he said, turning to me mid-mumble. "What do eagles dream about? Why do they deserve our support?"

I thought a moment. "Why *don't* they deserve our support? I like watching them fly."

Goodluck's eyes went hazy. He opened his mouth and closed it, then made some mysterious centering gesture with his hand. "In the beginning, the amoebas flew in a liquid dream of existence. Every day, all day, the waves in the ocean fly along the earth's shores." He sat up a little straighter, grabbing my knee. "Babies fly in their mothers' wombs as they wait to be born, floating and weightless and full of promise." He clapped his hands on either side of his head in awed discovery. "We are eagles in our hearts."

"Absolutely." Sometimes the best thing was just to agree with him. "Your photos fly too, Goodluck. I think people feel your work in some deep, primeval part of themselves, the part that remembers that they once flew."

The word "primeval" probably gave him a boner. Not a boner to use on me. We were platonic, although people loved taking pictures of us together. We looked weirdly similar, with the same wild brown hair and bright blue eyes. Rumors surfaced now and again that we were an incestuous couple. But no, he wasn't my brother or my boyfriend, and I'd never had sex with him. I was pretty sure the only sex he ever had was masturbating to the striking, blurred images he created.

"Precision. Effort. Patience," he said, lying back again. The amber chandelier sparkled above us, lit by colored bulbs. "Nothing worth doing is easy."

"That's true."

"Sweat creates magic, but the sweat is not magic. What's in your mind is magic. Your emotion, your will, your inner spark of expression, all this magic makes the swirl and flow of an eagle's flight."

Sounded like an eagle-themed portfolio was in the works. "Do you want to take a trip to Mongolia?" I asked. "There are lots of eagles there, flying across a huge blue sky."

"There are eagles in New York. Don't edit nature, friend. Ask yourself, why is Mongolia the first place you associate with eagles? You should ask instead, what gift do eagles bring to our lives? To the world?" He made an expansive gesture. "There are so many gifts in the world if you're open to receiving them. Sometimes you seem like an eagle to me." He touched my face, looking at me fondly. "But more often you seem like a grieving meteor streaking across the sky."

"Wow."

"I understand your power, friend, and I recognize your pain." He sobered. "But I think you need to move on. You're still caught in your ex-boyfriend's orbit, aren't you? You were too good for him. You're made of the dust of the ages. That's a fact."

Maybe he wasn't moving into eagles next. Maybe he was going to try outer space photography. Either way, I was just along for the ride.

He took my hand between his, his wide, blue eyes painfully sincere. "Don't waste your dust, beautiful friend. You need to be a comet, not a meteor. Don't let his transgressions drag you to earth, a flaming, destructive force that—"

"I haven't spoken to Keith in five months. I don't even think about him anymore," I lied.

"You should meet someone new, someone who soars like an eagle. The last guy was more of an armadillo."

It was a relief to laugh about Keith, to get to the place where I could do it. Bless Goodluck for taking me there. It had definitely been good luck when I met him at one of his early showings, when I was a business major fresh off the bus from Tennessee. He liked my small-town roots, and his metropolitan success made me feel like I was accomplishing things, even though my social life was dead in the water.

"Don't change, okay?" He hugged me, his long, frizzy hair tickling my cheek. "You inspire me. You're magical, Starcomet."

"Juliet."

"We've talked about this. I think you should change your name to Starcomet. It holds more power."

"I'm not doing that." He suggested this to me almost every week. "I mean, it's a nice idea, but no."

"It can change your entire universal dynamic. It works, friend. You must call out what you want in this world, and cry and shriek and scream until the power of the universe responds to you."

I wanted a healthy, non-excruciating relationship, not the power of the universe. "I don't have the energy to shriek and scream right now," I said.

He held up a finger in rebuttal. "Your body shrieks and screams at me every day. Your eyes scream like a jeweled phoenix striving to rise from the ashes of your soul's conflagrati—"

"Goodluck." I buried my face in my hands until I felt calm enough to look up again. "Thanks for the advice. I'll figure things out, okay? You should be concentrating on your art, not my personal life."

"Everyone is their own nectar," he said, pouting a little. "Even you."

I was afraid to ask what he meant by that. "Well, boss, I'm going to bed." I leaned up, hauling myself from the chair. "We can work on your 'Evergreen Life' catalog tomorrow, if you feel up to writing the descriptions. The show's next month."

"Oh!" He snapped his fingers. "I forgot to tell you. Some watch company wants to use my work in some ad campaign. I didn't want to touch it, you know, because ads are corporate and capitalistic, but my agent said it might broaden my international scope. I was thinking about, you know, using eagles in the pictures." He drifted a moment, thinking. "But they wanted some of the prints from my 'Graceful People' portfolio."

"An ad campaign? That's new. Can you forward me the email?"

"Sure. They said the ads will run in sixty-eight countries, everywhere they sell these Montclair watches."

"And they're mentioning your name in the ad copy?"

He waved a hand. "I don't know. I don't care either way. Do you know what watches mean to me? Sadness. Watches mean slavery to time. They mean a shackle you wear on your wrist, to tell the world that you must be somewhere, even if you don't want to be. Anyway." He closed his eyes and curled back into a ball. "Sleep tight, Starcomet. May the dream world glisten with your light."

"Same to you," I said.

I left the lobby and took the outside stairwell to my apartment on the third floor. Just before I went in, I took a moment to lean on the railing and take in the city. The Black Wall only had windows at the opposite end, so I rarely got to see this view, not that it was especially breathtaking. Nothing in New York had seemed breathtaking to me for a while. I scanned the sky for eagles, but I only saw light pollution and smog.

"Everyone is their own nectar," I repeated.

If only that made sense.

* * * * *

I'd accompanied Goodluck on countless business meetings during our ten years together, so I didn't think much about the following week's appointment with the watch company until he forwarded me the email from their advertising director.

It turns out it wasn't *Mont*clair watches, as Goodluck had told me. It was *Sin*clair watches, produced by Sinclair Jewelers, Fort St. Clair's family enterprise. After doing more research, I learned that people were willing to shell out ridiculous amounts of money for a Sinclair watch. Their exclusive line was manufactured in Switzerland, crafted of precious, responsibly mined materials, and renowned for keeping flawless time.

Timex was more my speed when it came to wrist shackles, so I hadn't known any of this.

It was stupid to imagine there was any connection between my embarrassing interlude with Fort, and Sinclair Jewelers' recent decision to use Goodluck's art in their advertising, but I still wondered. How involved was Fort in the advertising side of his father's business? Would he be in the meeting room when we convened to talk about which photographs to use in the campaign?

I took a little extra time to get ready that morning, just in case. I applied careful makeup and put up my hair, but when we arrived at the Park Avenue offices, a company rep named Angela was the one who welcomed us with a handshake and a smile. She was an older woman with avid brown eyes.

"Mr. Boundless, we're so glad you could be here today," she said. "As you know, Sinclair Jewelers prides themselves on their world-famous watches, notable for their sleek and elegant design."

"Do you know what I believe about watches?" said Goodluck.

I cut him off with a warning look and followed the two of them into a sumptuous wood-and-glass boardroom. Then I sucked in a breath, because Fort was sitting a few feet away from me, surrounded by a couple other suits, and a scruffy guy who was probably the art director.

"The elder St. Clair couldn't be with us today," explained Angela, "but his son agreed to sit in on our meeting so we could come to a consensus on the vision of this campaign. Mr. Boundless, I'm pleased to introduce Forsyth St. Clair."

Fort rose from his chair at the head of the table. "How do you do?" he said, extending a hand to Goodluck, who gave him a limp shake. Fort wore a dark gray suit and narrow black tie that accentuated everything powerful about him, from his broad shoulders down to his long, muscular thighs.

I tried to compose my expression as Angela introduced me next. "This is Juliet Pope, Mr. Boundless's business manager. They've accomplished extraordinary things together, judging by his success."

He held out a hand, fixing me in his gaze. "I'm pleased to say we've met. And I'd expect nothing less than extraordinary from her."

His hand was warm and encompassing as he shook mine. Nothing less than extraordinary? Was he being sarcastic? Last time we'd met, I'd been about as far from extraordinary as a trashed idiot could be.

"How wonderful that you already know one another," Angela enthused. She introduced the rest of the people around the table, but my mind was taken up with Fort's closeness, and his power-businessman persona. Goodluck bit a nail, unimpressed.

"Let's begin by looking through some mockups designed by our art department," Angela said.

"I need coffee," Goodluck interrupted. "Fair-trade organic decaffeinated coffee, if you have it."

"Of course," Fort agreed in a smooth voice. "We should have had it waiting. Angela?"

The woman stood and scurried from the room. A moment later, Goodluck exited after her, leaving me to face the confused looks of everyone else.

"I'm not sure he's coming back." I felt a blush spread across my cheeks. "He has a short attention span for everything but photography, but we've discussed which photos he'd be willing to contribute to the campaign, if you'd like to take a look?"

Fort smiled, and something about that smile reminded me of ghostly leather cuffs. His eyes were lion's eyes, dark hazel and gold, even more intense under bright boardroom lights than in his guest room. I hid my hands under the table before I was tempted to rub my wrists.

"Thank you, Ms. Pope," he said. "Let's stick to business. And if you'd like some irresponsibly sourced, caffeine-infused coffee, there's some right next door."

A wild chuckle escaped me. "Irresponsibly sourced?"

"Grown in Antarctica and harvested by endangered rhinos."

I shook my head, trying to be the sober business manager. "I don't drink coffee, but thank you for the offer. Before I show you the photos, can you show me the mockups, and some samples of the watches you're hoping to advertise?"

Forty-five minutes later, I'd been schooled on what distinguished a plain watch from a fine watch, and a fine watch from a luxury timepiece. I'd tried on some Sinclair watches and brainstormed about them in conjunction with Goodluck's images. I'd conferred with Sinclair's talented art director on the mockups' tiniest details. I thought Fort might leave at some point, but he stayed, contributing measured and intelligent opinions, making my heart race with unprofessional lust.

There were several ads planned, and the amount of money they intended to invest in the campaign floored me. The clear, focused way they worked floored me too, since I was used to decoding Goodluck's wispy thought trails whenever I needed to get anything done.

As I'd suspected, Goodluck never returned to the Sinclair boardroom, even after Angela showed up with the fair-trade decaf. Their marketing director agreed to send the final contracts to Goodluck's lawyer, and we were done. As everyone stood and filed out of the conference room, Fort turned to me.

"We're grateful that Mr. Boundless agreed to take part in our 50th anniversary advertising campaign. Thanks for your help in making it happen—and thank you for staying after he disappeared."

"You're welcome." I stared at his textured, pressed suit and dotted silk pocket square. "So, you take a pretty active role in the Sinclair business?"

"Yes. I oversee public relations, product presentation, and corporate branding for my father." He smoothed a hand down the front of his suit, a casual gesture that made me even more aware of his body. "I see you do the same kind of work for Goodluck."

"It's nothing like this." I glanced around the gleaming room, then gestured toward the window, slipping by him. "Wow. Look at your view."

I had to distract myself, to remind myself why I needed to walk away from this meeting and forget about Fort St. Clair, no matter how professional and charming he was. He followed me to the window and stood behind me, looking over my shoulder. It felt weirdly proprietary, the way he stood so close.

"You can see the top of the Black Wall from here," he said, pointing.

"Is that why you thought of Goodluck for your ad campaign?" I asked, turning to him.

"Yes." He hesitated a moment. "No. Not really. After I met you, I did some searching online." He cleared his throat. "I wanted to learn more about Goodluck Boundless, the Black Wall, those kinds of things. The idea for the watch ads came out of that research."

"Oh, that's great."

Holy crap, he'd Internet-searched me just like I'd Internet-searched him.

"I'm glad to see you looking better," he said. His gaze skimmed down my body, then ended up somewhere in the area of my neck. Was he thinking about the collar he'd taken off me? What had he done with it?

"It must be a relief to see me acting like a normal human being," I said, trying to sound breezy.

"Normality is overrated, don't you think?"

Smooth voice, white teeth, those crazy-sexy lips. Was he flirting or just being nice? I didn't know what he wanted from me, didn't even trust myself to guess. I couldn't fall for him, which meant I couldn't stay here a moment longer.

"Well, it's been great to see you again," I said. "I should probably...get going..."

Before I could slink around him, he held out an arm, trapping me where I was. "Are you busy right now, Ms. Pope? Are you doing anything for lunch?"

"Actually, I have to go find Goodluck. I can't really—"

"How about dinner, then? We should catch up."

I saw Angela almost enter the room, then back out when she saw us at the window. "Catch up on what?" I asked. I didn't mean to be snarky. It was more like self-defense. "What should we catch up on? Whether I've gotten falling-down-drunk again in the last couple weeks? Because I've tried not to."

"That's good." His smile deepened. "Come on, I hate eating alone."

I stared at him, not believing for a second that he ever ate alone, not if he wanted company. A filthy rich jewelry heir. A serial seducer, no doubt, but the attraction crawled all over me, like a nagging insect trying to burrow under my skin. Knowing he was a Dominant made the temptation so much worse.

"I think—maybe..." I squinted at him through the light from the window. "It might be awkward to have dinner. I mean, I've been cuffed to your bed, and now we're working on this ad campaign together..."

"That's why it'll be so fun. There's this new place I've been wanting to try. Have you been to the Ivy yet?"

He looked embarrassed when he said it, as embarrassed as a rich, gorgeous man could be, because everyone knew the Ivy was impossible to get in to. I didn't bother to ask if he could get reservations. I didn't blurt out *"that place is ridiculously expensive!"* the way I wanted to. I just stammered, trying to think up an excuse before I foolishly agreed to go with him.

"I don't know. Not sure if I'm free tonight."

"Another night?"

I turned away, biting my nail.

"You're hurting my feelings," he said. "Fine. Maybe I can convince Goodluck to go to the Ivy with me. He seems like interesting company." He took out his phone. "I'll have to call first and make sure everything on the menu has been responsibly sourced."

"Okay, I'll go to the Ivy with you." I blamed this cave-in on Angela, who was too far away to save me from this carnal pheromone bomb, with his dark, curly hair and disgustingly attractive suit. "But I don't understand why you'd want to take me to dinner. I didn't make the best first impression when we met."

"I doubt I made a good first impression either, so why not try for a second impression? A better one this time?"

I glanced down at his crotch. I was sure he noticed. Why did he make me think so much about sex? The deep voice? The confidence? The bold way he looked at me? His gaze dropped to the front of my blouse. I hoped he couldn't see my nipples, because they were hard. I crossed my arms over my chest as his lips twitched into a panty-melting smile. He knew I was in pain, and he liked it.

"I'll pick you up at the Black Wall tonight at seven-thirty. You don't even have to dress up," he said, leading me to the door. "It doesn't have to be a date. I'd just like to learn more about what makes you tick."

That was a watch joke, from a watch heir. It took me a moment to get it because he scrambled my brain whenever he smiled at me. That was the only reason I was agreeing to go out with him—brain-scramblement. How was I supposed to survive dinner at the Ivy without falling even harder for him?

"Come on," he said, touching my arm. "I'll walk you downstairs and make sure they get you a car."

Chapter Five:
Fort

I shut my office door and paced for the next half hour. Dinner? Nope. Fuck. Not what I'd intended.

Okay, it was what I intended, but why? Why had I suggested Boundless as an ad partner so I could see her again? Why had I waited anxiously for her to arrive at the conference room door?

And when she showed up, why did she have to be so damned enticing? So fucking different and new?

There were no over-the-knee socks today. She'd been dressed more conservatively, for business, but she still struck an erotic chord. Maybe it was her dark-lined blue eyes, the way they widened whenever she bit her lips, or the slow, sweet way she talked. Maybe it was the way she wore her hair in a loose chignon that begged to come down, or maybe it was the way that chignon bared her neck.

I'd wanted to bite her fucking neck in the middle of the meeting. I wasn't usually one to obsess over biting women's necks, but Juliet Pope made me go vampire. She'd even made me ask her out to dinner.

Bad idea.

She wasn't a seductress. She wasn't ballsy and crazy like Allie, and she didn't strike me as particularly strong or confident in her sexuality. There could be no after-dinner hookup, no matter how much I ached to bite her. It would take me approximately four-point-three seconds to shock her sensibilities if I was stupid enough to unleash the sexual urges she inspired in me. There was no path forward for Juliet Pope and me.

But I'd stood behind her in the conference room as she looked out the window, and stared at her nape like I was hypnotized. I'd done my damndest to memorize her scent like some kind of stalker. When she'd turned around and looked at me, her blue eyes even more striking in the sun's light, I'd had to work to not physically react to her gaze, to keep talking like we were only having a friendly encounter. I'd decided to work with her artist boss because I'd wanted to see her again—out of curiosity, I told myself—but now I was hooked on her eyes and neck and lips, on her freaking scent.

I had to cancel the Ivy, tell her I couldn't get reservations tonight because they were booked. I'd leave her hanging on a follow-up date, tell her I was headed out on a trip and wasn't sure when I'd be back. Devin could fly me somewhere, anywhere, to get her out of my head. I had her phone number from the ad campaign contact sheet, so I could text her. No need to hear her light, halting voice again, and fall for her soft southern accent.

My fingers hovered over the screen, but I didn't send the text I started. ***Hi Juliet. As it turns out...***

As it turns out, we were having dinner at the Ivy, even though it was a terrible idea.

Chapter Six:
Juliet

I went home and took a shower, shaved everywhere, plucked my brows, painted my toenails, and tried on fifteen different outfits, then sat on my bed with my head in my hands. A minute later, I picked up my phone and composed a text.

Hi Fort. Sorry for the late notice, but I can't meet you tonight.

As soon as I finished typing the words, I deleted them carefully so I wouldn't accidentally send them. Then I retyped them.

Hi Fort. Sorry for the late notice, but I

Delete delete delete delete delete. I wasn't strong enough to duck out of this dinner, not after I'd spent three hours getting ready, fantasizing about staring into his intense eyes from across the table. I went into rationalization mode. *It's not an actual date. He told me we could keep things friendly...*

So I got up, put away my phone, and tried to dress in a friendly way. When Fort knocked on my door at seven-thirty, I was wearing an understated burgundy shift dress with a cropped matching sweater, and a layered glass-bead necklace. I'd done my hair in two loose French braids so it wouldn't look like I was trying too hard. Then I let him in, and all my self-protective intentions fell away. He was perfection: sexy and handsome in a dark blue three-piece suit and a blue, diamond-patterned tie.

"Good evening, Juliet." He reached out and touched the side of my waist, below my sweater. The contact was unexpected, and he quickly moved his hand away. "You look beautiful. I love that color. Are you hungry?"

"Starving."

"Good. Get your coat."

I was halfway to retrieving it when his tone of command registered. I took my coat from the back of my couch and started to shrug into it. He was suddenly behind me, helping me put it on. I turned to him as I buttoned the front, but he was looking around my small apartment. It wasn't a glossy penthouse, that was for sure. It was messy and utilitarian, furnished with eclectic furniture.

"It's chilly out," he said, taking a step back toward the door. He waited with a smile while I got my matching flower-embroidered clutch, and did a last minute check for lipstick, tissues, and apartment key. He didn't touch me as we descended the stairs, but it felt like he was touching me, because he stood so close and he was so big.

He informed me that he'd hired a driver tonight so we wouldn't have to bother with parking. I bit my lip against vapid, flattering comments as he ushered me into the sleek sedan. Yes, we were going in a private car to have dinner at the most expensive and exclusive restaurant in Manhattan. It was a big deal for a girl who'd been raised on the poor side of Knoxville, but I didn't think he'd want me to fawn all over him about it. Instead, we talked about real estate and traffic, and how cold it was for the middle of October, even in New York.

When we arrived at the Ivy, the driver got out to open the door for Fort, then Fort turned to assist me like I was the Queen of England and he was one of my guards. He did it so naturally, so easily, taking my hand with the perfect amount of pressure to help me out of the car. When he put a hand at the small of my back to lead me toward the restaurant, I felt that touch between my legs.

Was he interested in sex, too? Did he want me? Would he make a move at the end of the night? He had to know I wasn't rich or suave, or as experienced as he was in the BDSM lifestyle.

"Reservation for St. Clair," he said to the maître d'.

"Of course, Mr. St. Clair. Right this way."

I barely caught a glimpse of the intimate, ivy-covered foyer before we were whisked past other waiting couples into the main dining room. I think I made a sound when we entered, a startled *ooh* or *ahh*. I'd heard about the unique atmosphere, the interior woodland decor, but it was something else to see it in person, to walk through branchlike bowers into intimate dining spaces bedecked with trailing ivy and fresh bunches of flowers in low, warm light.

"This place is... Wow..."

He took my arm before I walked into a table. "It's beautiful, isn't it?"

Beautiful wasn't the word for it. The Ivy was magical, so magical even Goodluck would have been impressed. Vines of glossy leaves delineated dining areas of varying sizes, some already filled, some waiting for the rich clientele who had the clout to reserve a table. Lights twinkled from within the vines and flowers, tiny, delicate pinpoints of illumination. A waiter brought menus, and I scanned the gourmet offerings.

"Does anything look good to you?" he asked.

"It all looks good. Wow, this place is just..." *Wow, Jules, stop saying WOW like an idiot.*

"Would you like some wine?"

"Sure, okay." I shook myself. "I mean, no. I'm trying not to drink in stressful situations anymore, since..." I could feel the blush on my cheeks. "Since what happened that night."

He looked surprised. "Is this a stressful situation?"

"No, it's just...well...." My blush burned hotter. "I'm trying to make a better impression."

"That's right, we talked about that earlier. I won't drink, either."

"It's fine if you want to."

"I don't." He passed a hand over his face and smiled. "Not to belabor the night we met, but I keep thinking 'Jewels' when I see you."

I fidgeted with the linen napkin in my lap. "A lot of people call me Jules."

"I mean the sparkly kind. Maybe it's your eyes."

I touched my necklace, fidgeting with that too. I couldn't stop touching things. "Thanks, I'll take that as a compliment."

"I hoped you would."

He was great at this casual-date thing—hire a car, flatter the girl, don't drink wine if she doesn't want to drink wine. I tried to be classy like him. I didn't want to be the gawking, fumbling dinner companion, but I felt out of my element. It wasn't just the breathtaking dining room or the sky-high prices. It was Fort's outsize presence, his naturally dominant manner—and I wasn't the only one who noticed. Our waiter stammered as he took our order, and a woman at a nearby table looked over her shoulder at my dinner companion every thirty seconds or so.

Soon after we ordered, the manager stopped by our table, delivering crystal pitchers of water with flowers floating on top. "Didn't you find anything to your liking on our wine list, Mr. St. Clair?" he asked as he poured for us.

"The wine list was excellent, but we're not drinking tonight."

"I understand." He bowed like Fort was royalty. I had those Queen of England feelings again. "My name is Mr. Marchand," he said, taking in both of us with an ingratiating smile. "If there is anything at all I can do to make your visit better, please let me know."

I followed Mr. Marchand with my eyes. He didn't visit any other tables to simper and bow. Just ours. "How rich are you?" I asked Fort. "Seriously. Are you secretly a European prince?"

"No," he said, picking one of the orchid-like blooms from the carafe of water and holding it out to me.

I took the flower and tucked it behind my ear. "You're so rich you don't want to talk about it?"

"I was taught not to talk about it." He shrugged. "I try not to let the Sinclair name define me. My father built the company, I just help with it. Does my money make you uncomfortable?"

I looked around at the shimmering vines. "I'm sorry. I shouldn't have brought it up. I have no class, as you probably guessed from our original meeting."

"You have plenty of class." He pursed his lips, scrutinizing me with his head propped on his hand. "That night... Well, I'm assuming something went wrong."

"Ugh, really wrong." I narrowed my eyes at the gawking woman at the next table. "I just need to stop dating douchebag playboys. In my defense, I'm around a lot of them because they come to Goodluck's art exhibits."

"A lot of art collectors are douchebags," he agreed. "And let's be honest. A lot of D-types are douchebags. You know who I mean by D-types?"

"Yes. Dominant types. And I agree."

"Have you always dated Dominants? I mean, are you new to the lifestyle, or..."

"Not new. I've always been submissive, although it took me a while to work up the courage to act on it."

He studied me a moment, sending new flutters over my body. "We all reach a point where we can't deny our needs anymore," he said.

My flutters turned to flames at the edge of intensity in his voice. What kind of D-type was he? I looked at his mouth and imagined him kissing me. I knew with some submissive sense that he wouldn't be soft and gentle. I looked at his hands and pictured them hurting me, holding me down, white knuckles and force. What were his needs? He owned some pretty serious cuffs. What did he do to women under his power? I couldn't ask, or I'd start down that slippery slope where I might invite him home with me, or accept an offer to "come up for coffee" at his place.

"Sometimes..." I shifted in my chair and bit my lip, a nervous habit. "Sometimes I make really bad choices when I get to that point. You know, when my needs get really strong."

"I do the same." He flashed a sardonic smile. "But I also enjoy when my needs get really strong, so what's a pervert to do?"

"We're not perverts," I said in a quieter voice. "Lots of people want the things we want. BDSM isn't a big deal anymore."

His smile faded. "It's a pretty big deal to me."

My fantasies of force multiplied, as did the feeling I was in over my head. He was holding back words, holding secrets behind his predatory gaze. A distraction arrived, the first batch of our small plates. I turned my attention to the waiter with a sense of relief, and then the food: chipotle shrimp, braised Brussels sprouts, some creamy brie with artisanal grapes.

"It all looks so good," I said.

He gestured with his fork. "Dig in, and eat all you want, please. We can order more. I like a woman with an appetite."

He didn't say it in a sleazy way, but all I could think of was "sexual appetite." He had to have women in his bed every day of the week, submissive women, since he was a D-type. I wondered what he did to them to satiate his "needs." My fantasy brain was going crazy, imagining undefined, sadistic acts while we sat surrounded in woodland magic.

But he moved the conversation to tamer topics as more plates of food accumulated in front of us. We talked about work, our experiences in business school, movies and music we liked. He was into rock stuff while I was more an indie-alternative gal. When we came back around to personal topics, he kept the focus on me. He wanted to know what had happened at Underworld the night I'd gotten so drunk. In some way, he had a right to know, since he was the one who'd had to deal with the aftermath. I tried to explain about Keith, and why that night felt like the end of my rope.

"He was one of those guys who have so much charisma," I said. "So much personality that you just get sucked in, you know? When he talked to me, when we played together, he made me feel like I was his whole world."

"So you did play with him?"

"Not that night." I poked at an assortment of balsamic-glazed vegetables. "We hadn't scened in months. He was done with me, but I couldn't get over him. This has been a pattern in my life, something that happens repeatedly in my relationships, and I know it's my fault for picking the hot ones."

"The hot ones?"

"The Doms with flair. The Doms every sub wants. There aren't enough Dominants who know what they're doing."

"True," he agreed.

"And when there's a Dom like that, who really has his shit together, there are fifty subs waiting in line to be with him, and each of those subs is expendable."

"Exploitable."

"Yes. Ugh." Lingering anger heated my cheeks as I tugged at a braid, twirling the end around my finger. "Keith used me, manipulated me for fun. He got off on how much I fell for him. The stupidest thing is that I saw him do it to other girls. I knew this seduce-and-conquer routine was his thing, but when he did it to me, I was sure he loved me. I was sure I was different and special. He told me I was. He whispered it in my ear."

Fort grimaced. "It's the worst when they whisper it in your ear."

"Are you making fun of me?"

"No," he said. "I've seen what you're describing. That's why I don't go to places like Underworld. It's not real kink, it's a meat market. It's where the sport fuckers go to find an easy mark. I'm sorry it happened to you."

"More than once," I said, putting down my fork. "So I can't get involved with D-types anymore. I'm not cut out for it."

He pushed a basket of bread my way. "That's it? You're done with the lifestyle?"

"I think it's for the best." I was trying to convince myself as much as him. "I'm going to focus on work for a while, maybe read some self-help books about relationships and emotional health."

"Sounds...healthy." His gaze went intense again. "But what will you do, Jewels, when your needs get too strong to ignore?"

I knew he was still calling me "Jewels," not "Jules." I could tell by the way his lips caressed the word. *What will you do?* He wanted to know about my *needs*.

"I don't know what I'll do," I said, picking up my fork again. "Where can I be submissive without being taken advantage of? Where can I meet Doms who aren't assholes?"

He tilted his head, acknowledging my frustration. "Most of the Doms I know are assholes."

I wasn't sure if he included himself in that number, but I assumed he did, and it made me feel even sadder. "Well, it doesn't matter, because I'm done with the BDSM scene. It's not worth the drama."

The waiter sidled up to the table to add water to both our glasses. As soon as he was gone, Fort took a long look around the room.

"The scene," he repeated. "It fucks up so many people. It fucked you up, but maybe..."

His voice trailed off, and he wouldn't look at me.

"Maybe what?" I asked.

He glanced at the vines above us, steepling his fingers under his chin. "Fuck. What am I doing?"

"Excuse me?"

He looked back at me. "The night I saw you leaning against that building, I..." He snapped his mouth shut and rubbed his hand across his lips. "Well, I liked your socks, the way they fit your legs. I liked them a lot."

"Oh. Thank you."

"The little bows on top..." He scanned the plates in front of us. "Do you want dessert?"

I blinked at him. "I don't...think so."

He signaled the waiter and he came running. "Could we have some coffee?"

"Certainly, Mr. St. Clair."

He turned to me after the waiter left. "Juliet, I think you're great. Your socks are great. Your hair, your eyes..." He sighed. "You're a very attractive woman, but I shouldn't be flirting with you, complimenting you, and asking you about the lifestyle. I shouldn't have asked you to dinner. Even though you're submissive, we wouldn't be a good fit as a couple."

"Oh, okay." My blush was back, scalding heat crawling over my skin. "I mean, I wasn't really asking to become, you know, involved with you."

"I know. And you shouldn't."

I glanced at the ravaged plates between us. "This was just a friendly dinner, right?"

"Right. So what am I doing?"

I looked down at my lap, as our civilized conversation unraveled and split apart. "I thought you wanted to make a better impression on me."

"I did. I wanted to, but I shouldn't. I'm not an asshole like your parade of charismatic whore Doms, but I'm not relationship material either. I can't emphasize that strongly enough."

My parade of charismatic whore Doms? I felt insulted. "You're the one who invited me here," I pointed out.

"Because there's something about you that attracts me. There are so many things about you that turn me on."

"All right. I get it." Now I was the one looking up into the vines because I couldn't meet his gaze. Also, because I was getting tearful. "You just hoped to sleep with me. You find me attractive in a sexual way."

I saw his denial in my blurred peripheral vision. "I find you attractive in a way that your...your hair is braided like that, and your eyes are so blue, and you have this weird intensity of feelings and arty-ness and..." He waved his hands, searching for words the way Goodluck sometimes did. "The problem is, this can't go anywhere." His hands moved between us and came to rest on the table with a thump of finality. "We would never work out."

"Wow." What was I supposed to say? Our friendly dinner had suddenly turned into, *You're quirky and hot but I don't want you, and I don't know why I asked you out.* Why had I expected this to go any other way but fucked up and sideways?

"Juliet. God, I didn't mean to upset you, but I know I have."

"It's okay. I wasn't even going to come tonight," I said, putting my balled-up napkin on the table. "I almost texted you. More than once. I get it, because I'm obviously..." I narrowed my eyes at him. "Obviously not relationship material either."

"I know I sound rude, but I didn't mean it that way. Honestly, I didn't. Forgive me."

His gentle apology, his sincerity only made me feel worse. I sat up very straight and spoke quietly but firmly, half to him and half to a sparkling vine located just beyond his shoulder.

"You know, I feel shitty enough about the state of my life. I spend my days in Goodluck's shadow and my nights wishing I had someone to love, to the point where I'm chasing after guys I shouldn't, and letting them break my heart. I'm a single, thirty-two-year old woman in New York City, and I agreed to come to dinner because you seemed so polite and elegant—" I swallowed the rest of the words as I stood to push in my chair. He wasn't getting compliments from me. "Anyway, I don't want to feel any more bad things, and I don't like coffee, so I'm leaving."

"Juliet, wait." He stood and took my hand. "Wait and I'll drive you home."

"I think I've let you drive me home one too many times already."

He leaned down, catching my gaze with fervent sincerity. "I'm trying to protect you from being hurt again. To protect you from me."

"Oh, that's very selfless," I said, extricating my hand from his grasp. "Thanks. Please stay and enjoy the coffee if you'd like. You deserve it for being so *protective*."

"Jewels, don't go."

Fuck him and his *Jewels*. His stern orders had no effect on me because I wasn't doing kink anymore. I wasn't doing guys anymore. They were all idiots, and this one was easily one of the worst. He was protecting me from him? What did that even mean? Why had he led me on, even flirted with me, if this was his endgame?

And if he was so dangerous, why had I been the one handcuffed to his bed?

I picked up my coat and sailed out the front door. Where was his fucking driver? There weren't any cabs to jump into, just texts from Fort to PLEASE WAIT.

I started walking, pulling my coat around me. Before I could get very far, Fort took my arm and turned me around, staring at me with a pained expression. He breathed in, his chest rising so violently I processed it as anger, although I knew it was something else.

"Let go of me," I said.

When I took a step back, he circled me with his arm, preventing escape. His other hand cupped my jaw. His scent enveloped me as he pressed his lips to mine.

My fingers opened in a panic against his chest. I hadn't consented to this kiss, this forceful possession. I hadn't asked for it, no, but I'd imagined it feeling just like this. His arm tightened, pulling me against him. Lust and violence. Hardness and heat. Was this what he'd wanted to protect me from? His lips molded to mine like he was trying to breathe me in, and I could feel his thick, hard cock pressed to my front, even through my coat. His fingers crept into my hair, tangling in my braids.

Then, as quickly as he'd attacked me, he let me go. "That's what I feel," he said when he pulled away. "And that's what I need to protect you from."

Without thinking, I slapped his face, leaving a flushed mark on his cheek. "That's what I feel. Leave me alone, Fort. I'm going to the subway, and if you follow me, I'm going to call the police."

I turned and left, barely aware of gawking onlookers. Let one of them mess with me. I was in a bad, bad mood, and fairy lights and ivy would forever be the stuff of nightmares to me.

Again? Seriously, again? I berated myself. *You let yourself fall for the hot ones, and pay the price for it every time.*

Chapter Seven:
Fort

I looked up from my phone as Devin strode into the Paris airport's private Gibraltar lounge. His steel-gray pilot's uniform intensified his blue eyes, though they still weren't as blue as Juliet's. *Stop. Don't think about her.*

"Well, if it isn't my old friend Forsyth," Dev said, wheeling his bag to the chair beside mine. "Thanks for the text. Nice to see you while we're both blowing through town. Headed to Milan?"

I nodded. "My flight's in a couple of hours."

He took in my leather weekend bag and pinstriped suit as he eased into one of Gibraltar's club chairs. I liked to travel rich, which he knew. His father was part owner of Gibraltar Airlines, so Dev and I flew wherever we wanted, whenever we wanted, as our schedules allowed.

"You look dapper," he said, with a snarky curl to his lip. "I hope you had time to torment some poor French subbie while you were in Paris." My non-response was enough of a response for him. He threw up his hands. "You have a stable here, surely."

"I used to, Dev. I don't keep up with all of them. Anyway, I didn't have time."

The old me would have made time. The new me had come to Paris to be sure the Sinclair ads featuring Goodluck's art were displayed in all the contractually negotiated places, including several large boards at the airport. It had been almost two months since Juliet Pope had slapped me outside the Ivy, and I'd managed to leave her alone, letting Angela handle the necessary business contacts.

But every time I looked at one of the damn billboards, I thought of her.

"Well?" My friend stared at me. "You know what I'm going to ask. Are you sick? Testicular cancer? Did you finally contract herpes?"

"Jesus, Dev. I just didn't feel like trolling around Paris this time."

He stretched his legs and crossed them at the ankles, and regarded me with steepled hands. "Why do I have a bad feeling about this?"

"About what?"

"I know you, man. I know that look on your face. Who is she?"

I considered denial, but Dev was right. He knew me. "She's no one," I said. "A bad idea that I'm trying to get over."

"Someone from The Gallery?"

"No."

His brows rose when I failed to elaborate. "I'm telling you this as a friend, man. Don't get messed up in any shit."

He was as careful as me when it came to relationships. We'd both grown up with everything money could buy, the world at our feet, everything under our control except women and the havoc they created when you let them get too close. I knew Juliet Pope was a storm of havoc waiting to be unleashed.

"I'll move past her eventually. It's just that she's different. She's unconventional, but sweet..." I tried to explain her lingering appeal. "And kind of effortlessly beautiful, but not in the standard way."

Devin made a dismissive sound, something between a growl and a laugh. "Let me tell you a story about a messed-up young man named Forsyth and a beautiful graduate assistant with a feminist roommate."

"I'd rather you didn't."

"Then there was the ballroom dance instructor who also had something about her."

"Enough."

"They don't all turn gay, you know. Some of them litigate. Some of them go off the deep end and start to self-harm. Some of them threaten to go to the police—"

"I said enough."

I needed no reminder that my wealth and status invited fucked-up relationships. Add in the kink, and I was in an excellent position to fail. Sometimes I thought about marriage, romance, the classic family, but it would only end up in another bitter St. Clair divorce. I rubbed my forehead with a groan.

"Jesus," said Dev. "Who is she? I gotta know."

"You don't need to know, because I'm not going to get involved with her."

"From the way you're acting, you're already involved, my friend."

I sat back in my chair, crossing one leg over the other. I had to tell someone. I had to get it out, put the frustration into words so I could get over it. "You remember the girl we saw that night? The messed-up girl outside Underworld?"

"I knew it." He clapped his hands, the sound reverberating through the quiet lounge. "I knew you slept with her when you took her home, you fucking creepo."

"I didn't sleep with her. She was drunk. Will you keep your voice down?"

"You hooked up with her afterward?"

"We haven't hooked up." My hands fisted in my lap. I tried to release the tension before Dev noticed, but he noticed everything.

"Well, I'll be." He laughed. "There's a woman in New York who doesn't want you. She a lesbian?"

"No."

"Asexual?"

I pressed the heels of my palms to my eyes, wishing I could go back in time and not text Devin that I was here in Paris. "I think it's almost time for my flight."

"Okay. So whatever's going on, you and the drunk girl aren't working out."

"Her name is Juliet, and no, we're not working out. I couldn't bring her to The Gallery anyway, so that's a nonstarter."

"It's not just a nonstarter," said Dev in a hard voice. "It's an ender. I don't know this drunk girl—"

"Juliet."

He rolled his eyes. "I don't know Juliet from Adam, but if you think she's a bad idea, then she's a bad idea. Trust your gut. Run the other way."

"Running is a shit move."

"Inviting drama is a shit move, but you do it time and time again."

"You're an asshole," I said to Devin, an understatement.

His light, direct gaze betrayed no guilt. "Just trying to save you some hassle, friend. You're the one who likes things to be neat and clean."

He was right. I craved precision and predictability, my life's events clicking together like luxury watch gears. "This is a tough one," I said with a sigh. "She has this energy. She's unconventional. She works in the art world, as Goodluck Boundless's manager."

"Whos-it whats-it's manager?"

"Goodluck Boundless. He's this famous photographer. Why don't you know anything about the New York art scene?"

"Oh, I don't know, Fort. Maybe because I'm not a pretentious jerk-off, hanging around museums and art galleries pretending ugly shit looks good. There's only one Gallery I care about, and it needs you back. If this Juliet woman knew the shit you're into..."

"She's kinky," I said, a pathetic straw-grasp. "She identifies as a submissive."

"An Underworld submissive. She's not of our world," he lisped in an affected voice.

"She might be, if she knew about it." I made a fist and hit the arm of my chair. "She's intense, you know? With this whole big, emotional world she carries around."

"Sounds horrible," Devin drawled.

I shook my head, even though he was right. With all that emotion, she'd be scarily vulnerable in our world. "It's just... I can picture her in the throes of subspace, really letting go. Imagine that energy, that physicality if I helped her tap into that part of herself."

"Jesus. If you've got it that bad for her, fuck her and get it over with."

"I can't fuck her. We're not on speaking terms."

"Good lord," Devin said, giving me a look. "I want to punch you in the face right now. Maybe that's the sadist talking."

"Yeah, thanks for listening." I blew out a breath and grabbed my bag.

"You don't have to leave," he said, putting a hand on my knee. "Don't get in a fucking mood. How long are you going to Milan for?"

Long enough to forget about her, or try to. I didn't say that out loud. Instead I said, "I hate messes. That's the fucking truth."

Devin squeezed my knee and let go. "You've always been a damned feely bastard, Fort. Do yourself a favor and hook up with some pretty, delicious sexpot in Italy, a power sub who can pull your head out of your ass."

"Yeah." I stood and stretched. My friend stood too, turning his pilot's cap in his hand. I followed the silver cording as it slid beneath his fingers.

"Remember why," he said. "Why it's important to keep your shit under control."

Leave your submissives in better shape than you found them. Don't take more than they can give. Never, ever fuck with the vulnerable. There were a lot of rules at The Gallery, but the last one was the most important.

And Devin, the most heartless Dom of my acquaintance, enforced it most zealously of all.

Chapter Eight:
Juliet

I stood in the corner of the oddly shaped Manhattan gallery. We'd chosen it based on display space, and there were plenty of walls, but the room itself felt suffocating. People stood shoulder-to-shoulder, turning back and forth to talk and point at elements of Goodluck's art. We had to be over the room's maximum allowed capacity, but the staff didn't say anything, just bustled around passing out brochures and glasses of champagne.

Goodluck was unveiling his new "Eagle on the Wing" collection. None of the blurred photographs had eagles or wings in them, but his fan base didn't care. They'd come out—hundreds of them—in sub-zero wind chill, eager to escape the January doldrums and buy something new. Goodluck was camped by the fruit bowl, picking out grapes with his fingers, leaving his agents to handle the inquiries. Collectors corralled me into private conversations, eager to get a foot in the door.

The Sinclair ads had increased Goodluck's international appeal, bringing dozens of new buyers into the fold, all of them competing for an acquisition. The price of his work was rising with each subsequent collection, reaching stratospheres previously unheard of. One of the photos in the ads sold for four million dollars at private auction, the one dubbed the "New Mona Lisa" by the press. Rather than an enigmatic smile, the model had an enigmatic form, difficult to make out in the scattered light behind her.

The photo haunted me, because I felt like that model, partly there and partly a ghost. For the past three months, I'd been looking inward, hermiting, staying at home and trying to find myself after my unproductive crush on Fort St. Clair. Now that the ad push had died down, I didn't think about him anymore...except when I did, which was way more often than I wanted to. I had too much going on to think about him tonight. I flitted around the room, decked out in a bright red dress with black over-the-knee socks, and a flower-embroidered cardigan, my signature artist-manager look.

Every photograph already had a sticker on it, an indication that a buyer was interested. Still, the crowds lingered, oohing and ahhing. I grabbed the gallery manager and asked if he could turn the heat down, and he told me he'd already turned it off. This was just the heat of clamoring human bodies. I took off my sweater even though it left my arms bare, and downed a glass of ice water.

"My beautiful Starcomet," said Goodluck, grasping my shoulders from behind in a friendly massage. "Given any more thought to changing your name?"

I leaned closer to him. The massage felt good on my knotted muscles. "Too many people know me as Juliet Pope," I said, speaking over the noise. "It wouldn't be good for my career."

"Your career?" He sighed. "'Career' is another way of saying 'cage.' Don't box yourself into a career, or a name, for that matter. Break the fetters, my friend."

"That would be a good name for me: Fetters."

He made a disapproving sound. "I can think of so many names that are worthy of you," he said, digging his fingers deeper. "I have so much trust in you. I should call you Trust."

"You do call me Trust. You call me pretty much everything except Juliet."

He stopped massaging and turned me around to hug me, pressing his cheek to mine. "It's because of that play. So tragic. Listen, I'm grateful that you're here to help me tonight. I'm grateful that you're strong and creative, and that you have glorious hair." He buried his nose in my hairline, careless of my painstakingly crafted up do. "And incredible, shining eyes that caress me with belonging. I'm grateful that you're resilient and dependable, and that you help me share my work with the world..."

His recitation went on, and I half listened, holding his hand. It wasn't that I didn't appreciate his praise. It was that he was going through a gratitude obsession right now, and I heard such recitations every day. *I'm grateful for this, I'm grateful for that.*

"I'm grateful to work for such a visionary artist," I said when he finished. "Everyone loves your new work."

"Yes, they do. But there are too many people here, so I wanted to let you know I'm going home. I want to pet my cat."

"Goodluck, no, you can't leave!"

"If anybody has questions, you can answer them, can't you? Call me tomorrow. Tell me how everything went."

I watched helplessly as Goodluck bailed on his huge opening show. All the fair trade champagne I'd ordered, all the organic canapes I'd sourced... Now that he was gone, people would leave. I sighed as a couple dozen art groupies followed him out the door.

God, since when did he have a cat?

The din in the room calmed down, and I took a breath. Everything was fine. It didn't matter. Sure, all my hard work to put this party together was wasted, but he was my boss, and he got to do whatever he wanted. I'd try to entertain everyone as best I could, although I didn't have Goodluck's ability to introduce bizarre, unrelated topics from thin air.

I felt a touch on my bare arm, soft enough to send a shiver through my body in the stifling room. I turned, expecting to hear someone's displeasure that Goodluck had already left.

Instead I saw a suit, a tie, and dark hazel eyes. His classic ghost of a smile, to match the ghost I was turning into. "Hello, Juliet."

I held my sweater tighter and stared at Fort, wondering how long he'd been here. How had I missed him? "Hello," I said. He looked the same, which is to say, he looked beautiful and powerful, a lion in this room of wildebeests. My heart pounded at his proximity. Even after all these months, after how we'd parted, adrenaline surged and my painful crush reawakened. I switched into polite-hostess mode to cope. "Thank you so much for coming to Goodluck's opening."

"I'm happy to support our business partner." He looked around, running a hand down the front of his suit. "The new photographs are beautiful."

"Did you have some champagne? It's responsibly sourced."

He clasped his hands in front of him, fidgeting with his fingers. "No. I try not to drink in stressful situations. I learned that from a friend."

His tie was embossed with gold and green vines the same color as his eyes. I looked past him into the thinning crowd.

"Are you busy?" he asked. "Do you have a moment to talk?"

"About what?" I sounded defensive, and I felt cold now that the room was emptier. I started pulling my sweater back on.

He reached to help me when I couldn't find the other sleeve. "I wanted to tell you that sales are up thirty-three percent since the ad campaign," he said.

"Wow. That's great."

"Also..." He paused and smoothed a hand over his tie. It was a nice tie. I waited for his next words but they never came. Instead he gazed at my neck, and I fingered the choker I wore. It wasn't a collar. It looked nothing like a collar, but...

The last time we'd stood this close, he'd grabbed me around the waist and kissed me, his big hand holding my face. *The problem is, this can't go anywhere.* He'd said that, I remembered his exact words. We would never work out.

I came to my senses and took a step back. "I'm glad your ad campaign was successful. It's done a lot for Goodluck's brand as well." I waved a hand toward the door. "He left early, but if he was here, I'm sure he'd thank you. And now... I really..."

"At least come and meet my friends."

He took my arm and led me across the gallery before I had a chance to refuse. His other hand settled on my back, a proprietary touch. Did he mean it that way, or was it my overwrought, regrettable attraction to him?

He stopped in front of a blond man with a dark-haired nymph on his arm. She looked like a runway model, but shorter. The man exuded the same cachet as Fort: wealth, looks, and unerring confidence.

"This is Juliet Pope," Fort said, turning to introduce me. "Juliet, this is my friend, Devin Kincaid."

I eyed the woman next, but she wasn't introduced. She stared at the closest photo, looking bored. As for Devin Kincaid, he greeted me with icy civility. His eyes were like Fort's, direct and assessing.

"Nice to meet you," he said, shaking my hand. "Interesting photos, not that I'm into art."

I stiffened at his tone. Fort made a face. "That's polite, Dev."

"What? I've never been to an art premiere before," he said, like the idea of it was ridiculous. "When I need to see art, I go to museums."

I could have explained about art premieres, sales, the importance of community, but his friend seemed like an asshole, so I just said, "Museums are great. It was nice to meet you, Devin and..." My voice trailed off because I'd never learned the woman's name.

Fort gestured toward his friends. "They're going for drinks."

"I thought you were going to join us," said Devin, scowling at him.

"I'm going to stay a while. I haven't seen everything yet."

He touched my back again, the same light, familiar caress he'd used on the way over here. My hands started to shake.

"Enjoy the artwork," Devin drawled. "We'll see you later."

Then he smiled at me, but it wasn't a nice smile. I glanced at the woman as the two of them headed for the door. I knew Devin was going to fuck her after drinks, because everything in his body language said that. He'd probably do other things to her, dominant things, since she was obviously his sub. When Fort turned to face me, I shivered.

"Dev didn't want to come here," he said in apology. "I made him."

"Why?"

He took a breath and let it out before he answered. "I wanted him to see you, to understand why I can't just..." He looked around.

"Can't just what?"

"Can't just get over you." His voice hitched and he lost a little of his confident swagger. "You're wearing over-the-knee socks again."

"I wear them a lot."

"They're black, damn it. And your hair's up...again."

I stared at him, going cold. No, not cold. Frightened. Excited. Hot like a coal about to spark.

He took my hand. "Can we go somewhere to talk? Just for a minute? Somewhere private?"

"Why would we do that?" I asked as he led me toward a corner. "You can't come up to me after months of silence and say stuff like...like, 'I can't get over you.'"

"Here's the thing." His hand tightened around mine. "I need to touch your legs, and I need to put my fingers on your neck, and if you don't come with me somewhere private, Jewels, I'm going to do it here."

I gaped at him, feeling those things as he said them, his hand on my leg, his palm against my pulse. "You said we wouldn't work. You were insistent on that point. So what do you want from me?"

"I told you." Even as he said it, he guided me toward the back of the gallery, to the corridor that led to offices and bathrooms.

"The party," I protested. "I have to stay."

"The party's over. The artist left."

He took me through a wide door at the end of the corridor, into the gallery's workshop, the room where they prepped paintings for hanging and constructed made-to-measure frames. It smelled of lumber and chemicals, and the paint-sullied walls had piles of old frames stacked against them. There was no one here, and the only light came from a weak plug-in lamp in the corner.

He backed me against the wall between two stacks of frames, hemming me in, forcing his leg between mine. He pulled one of my thighs toward him, finding the top of my sock and squeezing the skin there. I felt his hand on my neck, on my face, and then the kiss. Hot, hard, demanding. As I'd done before, I shoved him away.

"No. Fucking no."

We stared at each other, squared off like combatants, our hands in fists at our sides. The way he looked at me made my insides melt. His lips were set. He didn't give me space, and I didn't really want space. I just wanted a minute to process some anger before I fell.

The right decision would have been to leave then and there, to walk back out to the gallery and mingle with the remaining guests, but I wasn't going to do that. The wrong decision was to stay where I was, daring him to take me if he wanted me so badly. That was the decision I made, flattening myself back against the wall, squeezing my legs together because he'd already made me so wet. The gallery was out there, Goodluck's agents and caterers, his super fans, but I didn't care.

Fort came at me a second time, and this time I didn't push him away. I let him trap my hands and shove them over my head so I had to arch my back. His cock swelled against my belly as I hung there, acquiescing to his force. I never decided to give in and let him kiss me. He just took what he wanted, turned my face with his other hand and held it hard, and thrust his tongue between my lips.

Chapter Nine:
Fort

Now that I had her against me, in my power, I couldn't touch her enough. But I had to be careful. That was what I told myself: as long as I was careful, I could have her body and not do her any harm. I'd be a kind sadist. I'd be clear about our boundaries so she didn't feel used or manipulated.

Well, I'd do that later. First, I had to shove my tongue down her throat.

She responded as if she liked it, humming and pushing her body against mine. I let go of her wrists and grabbed her hair, then shoved her wrists back against the wall when she dropped them. "Over your head," I ordered, and she obeyed.

I hoped no one would discover us here. We were hidden between two piles of lumber, in the darkest corner of the room, but we'd be heard. She moaned, I growled. After I pulled her hair down from her chignon, I wrapped my fingers in it. I could hear metal hairpins hitting the concrete floor, make-out shrapnel. I left her mouth to trace a line down her neck, half kissing, half biting the tender skin. I shoved a thumb up under her chin, pinning the back of her head to the wall as I lapped at the hollow of her clavicle.

Until I saw her out in the gallery, I'd forgotten how she stole my control. I'd come to get a glimpse of Juliet, nothing more, after months of restraint and good behavior. But once I touched her, once she turned to me, all reason fled. The way her eyes widened in surprise—and a little fear. Her bare, pale arms, the hair, the goddamned socks...

I ripped off her sweater, pulling it down her shoulders, barking at her to lower her arms when she tried to keep them over her head the way I'd told her.

First things first: I used the girly red cardigan to tie her hands behind her back, wrapping it around her wrists and cinching it tightly, even though it would probably ruin the garment. I'd buy her another one. I didn't care. I looked in her eyes and saw that it was okay, that the bondage excited her even though it took away her control.

At that point, I still only meant to kiss her. I held her by the waist and ground my cock against her, running my fingers over her hips and breasts. I molested her sock-covered thighs, then took her knees and hiked her up the wall so her legs were around my waist.

"Put me down," she said. "I'm too heavy."

"You're not too heavy." I kissed her again to shut up her protests, and pulled her skirt higher so I could squeeze her ass. Jesus, a thong. I smacked her bare cheeks a few times, I couldn't help it. Her trapped fingers scratched mine but she couldn't get loose. "Stop struggling," I said. "You can't get away from me."

"Oh God."

She squirmed as I yanked the thong up between her ass cheeks. She was wet as fuck, and it was all I could do not to force my fingers inside her pussy. My hands did minor violence, squeezing her breasts, pulling her hair, scratching her thighs, but it wasn't enough. The more she arched against me, the more I wanted to be inside her. "I want to fuck you," I said, pressing her against the wall. "I want to jam my cock inside you until you hurt."

Her fingers closed around mine as she pressed her face into my neck. She clung to me with her thighs and then I did push a finger inside her, fucking it in and out. She made an animal noise that signaled *more*, but I didn't have a condom. Damn it. Damn it to hell.

"I don't have anything," I said through my teeth. I tightened the cardigan around her wrists, frustrated and disappointed. "I don't have any protection."

I could have made her come another way. She could have made me come just by stripping down to her thong and her over-the-knee socks, but her tormented gaze told me it wouldn't be enough. In this moment, we both needed a savage fuck. It had been months that I'd wanted her, fucking months...

"Listen, I'm clean," I said. "I always use protection, one hundred percent of the time."

Except now, when I was somehow willing to risk going without it. What did that mean? I gave her a shake. "Are you clean?"

She stared at me. "I haven't had sex in forever. Yes. I've been tested."

"Are you on anything? Birth control? Are you on the pill?"

"I have an IUD."

"You won't get pregnant?"

"No, I don't want to get pregnant." She gasped, then moaned as I thumbed her clit. "That's why I got the IUD, for extra backup."

"Good enough." I kissed her and shoved another finger inside her, manipulating her pussy until her hips bucked. I nicked her clit with my nail and she made a noise like she was already about to go off.

"You'll have to let me down," she said, struggling against me.

"No. I'll fuck you however I want." I made her look at me. "I'm going to fuck you now, without a condom. Is that okay?"

"It's so bad," she whispered, burying her face in my neck. "A bad idea."

"But you want it, don't you?"

She let out a sob, humping my fingers. "Yes."

"I'm going to take care of you, baby. Everything's going to be okay. You want it?"

"Yes, I want it," she cried.

"Say it to me. 'I want you to fuck me.' Look in my eyes."

She did, with hot passion. "I want you to fuck me. Please!"

Jesus hell. I pressed her against the wall and shrugged off my suit coat, dropping it on the sawdust-covered floor. I undid my pants and released my straining cock, then I took a moment to collect myself so I didn't fucking injure her. I wished I could kiss her breasts, bite her nipples, but I didn't want to take the time to rip off her dress. Later. Some other time.

I held her ass and yanked her panties to the side, twisting the thong around my finger. I felt a savage need to push inside her, but I was a big guy, so I tried to go slow. When I pressed the tip of my unsheathed dick to her pussy, a groan poured out of my throat. I looked in her eyes. They were vivid blue, sparkling like jewels.

"Everything's good, right? Are you ready for me?" I teased the head of my cock over her clit, transported by her whimpers. "I'll get tested tomorrow, I swear. I'll have my physician send you a report."

She opened her lips, then whispered three incredible words. "I trust you."

I growled and sank inside her pussy, inch by fucking inch, forcing my way into her slick tightness. I was so hard for her, so iron hard that the penetration held an edge of pain. There was so much sensation, between the intensity of her heat and her squeezing muscles. How long since I'd fucked a woman bareback? Years and years, many girlfriends ago, when I was open to fluid bonding and trust.

She said *she trusted me*, which almost shattered me. What had I done to deserve that trust? I tried to be honest with her, and I was telling the truth about using condoms. I was glad now that I'd been so fastidious, because it allowed me to have this reckless fuck with her now. Her walls gripped me, pulsing with raw, wanton need. I was already so close to coming, but I didn't want that, because I needed this to last longer. I tried to draw back, to distance myself and enjoy her gasps and moans, her thrusting hips. I fisted her thick, messy hair, bit her neck, kissed her forehead, and basked in her scent.

"Don't stop," she said. "Please…"

I didn't want to hurt her, but that *please* triggered something inside me. She was begging for more, and my body wanted more. I grabbed her hips and plowed her with my cock, driving deep, letting her know—beyond the bondage and rough kisses—that I was in charge. I was ravishing her, stretching her tight pussy with my thrusting shaft. She whined, acknowledging my dominance and her submission to it.

"You feel so fucking good." I bit the words out against her ear as I dug fingers in her hair.

She arched her neck as I tugged, but she didn't fight me. "Harder," she whispered, like she was ashamed for me to hear.

I grabbed her neck instead of her hair, squeezing the smooth column, stroking the velvet skin I'd raked with my teeth. She gazed back at me, so engaged, driving me on. She wanted this. She liked this.

And me? I'd never fucked any woman with this much intensity. *What are you doing? What do you want?*

"I'm going to come," she said. "Oh, God, please. Can I come?"

Fucking hot, that she asked me for permission. I answered by shoving a couple fingers into her mouth, then replacing them with my tongue. Something in my brutal kiss triggered her climax, and I urged her along with ragged encouragement. "That's right. Come for me. Come harder, you fucking wanton. I want to feel you squeezing every inch of my cock."

Her sensual abandon was gorgeous. Breathtaking. Her shoulders writhed, her bound fists pumping behind her back, still caught in their bondage. Her legs squeezed my waist, her heels kicking into the small of my back. A heaviness grew, expanding like a bubble inside me. I knew I was going to come soon—come hard—but for the first time in my life, I wasn't in control of it. She wrested it from me, trapping and taking me, going wild in my arms.

A few more thrusts and the bubble burst, sending pleasure along every nerve, blending with the darkness and her scent, and her hot sex shoving against me. My limbs trembled until I struggled to stand, but damn, I wouldn't drop her. I held her and rode through my orgasm with a few more violent thrusts, cupping her face and gazing into her eyes for the last ones. I couldn't say anything. The depth of my pleasure had stolen my voice.

I came to a rest, sagging against the wall. Lust-adrenaline gave way to muscle exhaustion, and I had to let her down, but I didn't let her go. She stood against me, within the cage of my body as I bowed my head to hers and murmured in her ear.

"I tried to stay away from you." I pushed stray strands of hair back from her face. "It didn't work."

She didn't answer. Fuck. All my violence fled, replaced by concern. I reached behind her to untie the cardigan and free her arms.

"Stretch a little," I said, pulling them forward. "They might feel stiff. Are your shoulders okay?"

"My shoulders are fine." She gave them a little roll, then adjusted her panties and her skirt, and leaned to pull up her slouching socks. She looked down at the floor, at the scattering of hairpins, then back up at me. "How does my hair look?"

A little laugh escaped her, too hysterical for my comfort. I shoved my cock in my pants and tucked in my shirt, and pulled her back into my arms. I could feel her trembling as I rubbed a hand up and down her back. "Are you cold?" I asked.

"No. Can you help me put on my sweater?"

It was snagged and stretched out, but I helped her put it on and then leaned to pick up my coat. I brushed off as much sawdust as I could and studied Juliet's face. "You should leave your hair down," I suggested as she tugged at her curls.

"Oh." Her arms dropped at her sides. "Yeah. Well. Okay. You really dirtied me up, though. I should probably go home."

"I'll take you."

"You don't have to."

I sighed and held her against me a second time, stroking her neck, massaging her ear. "Do you not want me to take you home because you don't want to have sex again? Because we don't have to have sex again."

"I think I'm just basically..." She paused, swallowing. "Just basically scared shitless of what we just did."

"I'm going to take you home and stay with you until you feel less scared, okay?" I forced her to meet my gaze. "Because you shouldn't feel scared. I enjoyed what we did. Did you enjoy it?"

She nodded, with another small laugh that sounded a little less hysterical. "I enjoyed it. It was just a little crazy. Like, really crazy."

"It was really fucking crazy," I agreed. "But that's okay. Are you ready to go now?"

"I have to check out with the gallery manager first. Have to check with him before I leave. Can you meet me out front?" She rubbed her forehead. "What time is it?"

I checked my watch. "Almost eleven o'clock."

She was sex drunk, rumpled and gorgeous. Anyone she talked to would know she'd just been fucked. I moved ahead of her to open the door, then checked my phone as it vibrated in my pocket. A text from Milo.

It's Sat night. Where the fuck are u?

Busy, I typed.

He sent back a trio of fire emojis. **Again?**

I muted the conversation and followed Juliet back out into the gallery—not the sex club Milo was texting me from, but the actual art gallery where I'd come to find her. I never imagined when I touched her arm earlier this evening that things would turn out the way they did.

She stopped in the bathroom to clean up, and I thought, *my cum is inside her. We fucked bareback.* She'd said that she trusted me enough to do that, and I hoped she could be trusted too. I hoped she really had an IUD, or I might be fucked.

My cock wanted to worry about that later. It stirred to life as I imagined my cum escaping her skimpy thong and running down the insides of her thighs to collect in the cuffs of her socks.

By the time she emerged from the bathroom, I'd willed the erection away. No more sex tonight, not until we pinned down what had happened between us, and agreed on whether to move forward in some kind of D/s relationship. It was important to talk things out right at the start. Or the end, whatever she decided.

No drama or misunderstandings. I couldn't bear to trudge into that territory again, especially with her.

Chapter Ten:
Juliet

I dreamed of the feel of him against me, his cock shoving inside me. I dreamed of the concrete wall and the strain of my arms bound behind my back, then startled awake in the dark as Fort stretched his long, hard body along my back. This happened several times, and each time it shocked me. Once, when I had trouble settling down again, he took my wrists in his hands and held them against my headboard, and my eyes drifted closed just like that.

We hadn't talked yet about anything that had gone down between us. We'd showered together when we got to my apartment, quietly and awkwardly, and gone to bed wearing a layer of underwear, presumably to talk in the morning.

But when I woke, harsh daylight wresting my eyes open, he was gone. His side of the bed was made up, down to the pile of ruffled pillows stacked against the headboard where he'd held my wrists.

Had I imagined the whole thing? No. I could still feel him on me, in me. All those things had happened, even if he'd stolen from my bed in the light of day. I still couldn't process what had happened between us at the gallery, might never be able to process it, so maybe it was for the best that he'd gone.

I got up and stumbled to the bathroom, and turned on the shower. Once the water was warm, I washed away the scent of his cologne and the smell of him in my hair. I shaved and slathered on scented lotion after I dried off, and dressed in Sunday morning clothes—faded gym shorts and a natty, secondhand t-shirt with the number 55 silkscreened on the back. I started to dry my hair, then gave up and corralled the mess back out of my eyes with a fuzzy blue headband.

I went down the hall to the kitchen, thinking I'd need to lock my door after Fort's pre-dawn escape, but he wasn't gone. He stood by my apartment's only window, wearing his white shirt and slacks from the night before. He turned when he heard me.

"Oh, hi," I said. I regretted putting on the weekend hangout clothes as he ran his eyes over my outfit. "I didn't know you were still here."

"We were going to talk, weren't we?"

"Yes. Of course." I padded into my kitchen. "Do you want some tea?"

"Do you have coffee?"

I sorted through my collection of brew pods. "No. Sorry."

He smiled, walking over to sit on my couch. "That's okay. I'll have some tea. Thank you."

He was being pretty obvious about keeping his distance, about not touching me. We'd had sex, and it was truly, mind-numbingly incredible, but it seemed more and more like an impetuous, one-time-only encounter. The man on my couch had dragged me into a dark room, bound my hands behind my back, and shoved his huge, hard cock in my vagina until I had the strongest orgasm of my life. That had happened, and now...

"What are you thinking about?" he asked as my brewing machine spit out the first cup of tea.

I turned to look at him. That man had done those things. I didn't know how to put my thoughts into words.

"What do you like in your tea?" I asked instead.

"I never drink tea. Surprise me."

I added milk and sugar and carried his cup over on a mismatched saucer. "I can make you some toast if you like...or..." I grimaced. "I mostly eat out. I don't have very much food."

"Don't worry about it." He took the saucer, holding my gaze. I couldn't read his expression. It wasn't morning-after pleasantry, but it wasn't an unpleasant expression either. It was something cautious, something in-between.

"If you check your phone, I've had my doctor send my most recent STI test results," he said as I headed back to the kitchen.

"You didn't have to do that."

"Yes, I did. I don't want you to worry." He took a sip of tea and blew out a breath. "Fuck, that's hot."

"It's tea. It'll be hot for a little while."

He gave me a look that said, *Don't be a smartass*. It made me shiver.

I put in my own tea pod. He watched me do this like it was utterly endearing, or ridiculous. God knew what kind of hot drink setup he had in his fancy penthouse.

"I don't have a doctor on call," I said over my shoulder. "And I haven't been tested in a while because I haven't been sexually active lately. But I go to my lady doctor once a year, if you want those records."

He looked bemused. "I won't requisition your records. You're too artless to lie."

I turned to him as more tea spit out of my machine. "What does that mean?"

"You don't know what artless means?"

I knew what it meant, and I knew why he thought I was that way, but I didn't know if he meant it as a compliment or an insult. Because Fort St. Clair wasn't artless. Oh no. He was artful, composed, put together like some luxury watch. I turned back to my tea, but I could feel his gaze on my back.

Once my tea was done, I crossed to join him on the sofa, leaving some space between us for the questions and uneasiness to fit. He put his cup on the table behind him, then reached across the space to touch the top of my knee. His fingers trailed over the place he'd grabbed me last night, lightly, nothing sexual now. He wanted to *discuss things*. A future for us, maybe.

Next, he tilted my neck, inspecting the place where he'd bit me, his touch lingering like he might still soothe the pain. "No marks," he said. "At least nothing obvious. You feel okay?"

"Yes, I feel fine." I felt more than fine. God, I felt a million things. "How do you feel?" I asked, turning the question back on him.

"Conflicted," he said, coming right out with it. "Here's the thing about last night. What I did to you up against the wall in that work room...that was me on my best behavior. That was me being a gentleman."

"Was it?" I took a sip of my tea now that it was cooler. "It felt pretty nice."

"I can be worse. I usually am when it comes to sex."

"Hmm." I took another sip of tea to process, rolling the vanilla and cinnamon flavors on my tongue. "You mean you can be even rougher?"

"Rougher, colder, more intense. I'm a Dominant, but it's more accurate to call me a sexual sadist. I like to hurt women and force them to do things for my pleasure. It's how I prefer to get off."

"I understand about BDSM."

He shook his head. "You understand mainstream BDSM, the safe, sane, consensual stuff they do at Underworld. You're into the romance of it, the slap and tickle to get off. To me, that's going through the motions. It's not real. Well, not real enough."

I met his gaze, wondering what he meant by that. *Not real enough?*

"It's hard to explain," he went on, an edge of frustration in his voice. "Especially to a BDSM baby like you."

"A BDSM baby?" I protested. "Maybe I'm a mess, but I'm not a baby. I've been submissive for years. I've done a lot of scenes, experimented with a lot of things."

"I'm not trying to insult you. I'm trying to explain. You've been with a few Doms, you've participated in the lifestyle, but at the end of the day, you're looking for pleasure, a good time." He grimaced. "I'm into something different."

"You don't like having a good time? How does that work?" I blinked in confusion. "Why do you do whatever the hell you do if it's not fun?"

"It's fun to me. Dark fun, though." He shifted, pushing back his hair. "I do BDSM for the rush and release. I like to push boundaries, and hang out with other people who like to push boundaries. Places like Underworld only scratch the surface of power exchange. I belong to a private club where people...go a little further."

"So..." I put my tea on the low table in front of us. "This is why you're not good for me? Your sadism is the reason you believe we won't work out?"

"It's hard for me to work out with anyone, Juliet. Except, you know, the women who come to the private club. I can be as rough as I want, as cruel as I want, and they want more."

I looked away from him, biting my lip, considering how to reply. "Do you think..." I turned back to him. "Do you think I didn't want more last night? Do you think I responded badly to your force?"

He held my gaze. "I think you responded wonderfully. That's why I'm sitting here on your couch, drinking tea with you, which I literally fucking hate." He picked up his cup as if to illustrate his point, pounded the rest of his tea, and swallowed with a disgusted face. "I hate tea, Jewels. More than anything in the world."

"I'm sorry."

"I'm not sorry. I only meant to say hi to you last night, but it went further than that, and now we have to decide..."

"Decide if we're going to go further still?" I looked at him from under my lashes. "How often do you go to your private club to do dark, sadistic, non-fun things?"

"Often enough," he said tightly. "And I don't always play with the same women. It's not a relationship thing, where we all pair up into couples."

"It's a sex club thing."

He shrugged. "It's scratching a mutual itch with no emotional expectations. So it's not for everyone, especially emotional types. When the wrong people get caught up in that kind of lifestyle, the results aren't pretty. That's why I've been trying to stay away from you, even though I find you painfully attractive."

"Painfully attractive." I sniffed and sipped my tea. "Can't hurt me, can't live without me."

"It's not a joke, Juliet."

"I know." If it were a joke, I wouldn't feel such lust and confusion, such horrible curiosity. "You could show me the kind of dark stuff you like to do," I suggested. "You could invite me to this club to see what goes on, and I could tell you how I felt about it."

"Spectators aren't allowed. Only vetted people are allowed at the club, so there aren't any misunderstandings."

"Oh." At this point, I understood what he was trying to say. Even after last night's scorching-hot hookup, he thought we might be terminally non-compatible.

He reached for my hand and held it hard. His deep hazel eyes hit me full force, his lips pressed in a line. "I'm trying to protect you," he said. "Since I can't..." Those eyes raked over me, leaving me feeling stripped. "Since I can't enter into any kind of..."

"Relationship," I provided.

"Any kind of relationship with you, especially the sweet, emotional relationship you probably want..."

I let out a long breath. "That's fucked up. You don't know me well enough to know what kind of relationship I want. Honest talk: I wanted sex from you from that first sober morning I met you, and I got it." I stood with my cup and saucer, carrying my tepid tea over to the sink. It had too much sugar. It was too sweet, like me. "I don't have any judgment about your...your thing. Your sexual sadism, your private club, your playboy ways."

"Playboy ways," he repeated in an amused mutter.

"At the same time, I think you're kind of an asshole. If you don't want a relationship with me, don't ask me to dinner at the Ivy. Don't invite my boss to be part of your ad campaign, and then drop by his art show to fuck me against a wall after weeks without contact."

"I tried to call you after the Ivy. You blocked my number, Sparkles."

I glared at him from the kitchen. "*Sparkles?*"

"To go with *Jewels*. To go with your eyes when you get really emo and intense."

I picked up a dishtowel and started aggressively wiping invisible spots on the counter. "I had to block your number, Fort. No offense to you personally. I'm just at the point where I have to be more careful about the men I let into my life."

"As you should be." He stood to bring me his cup, his expression turned serious. "I try to be careful too. I try to maintain boundaries when I think someone might be easily hurt."

My eyes widened. "Me? You think I'm some fragile flower? I'm just super sensitive to bullshit right now."

He didn't reply, only watched me with his lofty, level gaze. A sadist? Definitely. He could hurt me in so many ways, and those were only the ways I knew about.

"Come here, Sparkles," he said from across the counter.

"My name's not Sparkles."

"Come here, Juliet."

I wanted to say no. I wanted to make some more hot tea and dash his most-hated mixture in his face.

No, I wanted to go to him. His expression was kind, if resigned. His arms opened for me. I walked around the counter and let him embrace me. He pressed his cheek against my forehead and stroked my back.

"You'd hate it," he said. "You'd hate what I'm into."

"I didn't hate it last night."

"I was careful with you last night." He tilted my head back and brushed fingers across my temples and through my hair. "We have this rule at the club: never fuck with the vulnerable. We're not allowed to hook up with women who are emotionally or physically complicated, women we might damage. We can't even bring them into the space. It's like an honor system."

I tugged my chin from his fingers and looked away.

"I figured out why I like you," he went on. "I figured out why I want you so much. It's because you're all on the surface. Your emotions are right there, plain as day, all the time. You don't give a fuck about saying what you feel and being who you are. You have this open expression, this way of looking at me and at other people. And you dress however you want."

"What's wrong with the way I dress?"

His eyes glanced over the blue fur headband I wore. "I love the way you dress. I love the way that headband matches your eyes, but not your clothes."

"These are my Sunday hangout clothes," I said, pouting. "They're not supposed to look hot and put together like your freaking designer suits."

He held me against his chest, running his big hands up and down my back. "Just shut up for a minute, because I don't know what to do with you. I don't know what to do about what happened last night."

"It's okay with me," I said, my voice muffled against his chest. "Your sadistic stuff. I work for Goodluck, which means I'm masochistic already."

He didn't laugh at my hilarious joke. "You don't know anything about my sadistic stuff, Sparkles. We've had some intense sex, that's all."

"Well, what else do you like to do? What are you into?" I pushed away and looked up at him. "Let's share. Bondage, spanking, floggers?"

"Hush. Look at me."

I obeyed, trying to seem both sexy and submissive. "It turns me on when you order me around."

"Does it? What if I don't order? What if I just take, what if I just do?"

He took my arm and dragged me from the kitchen over to the couch. It happened so fast I didn't resist. Next thing I knew I was draped over his lap, my arms trapped behind me as he yanked down my shorts and panties. I did resist then, flinching and fighting his grip, forgetting about the submissive thing as he bared my ass cheeks. He shoved my face into the cushion and made a shushing sound. "Let me be in charge for a moment. Give yourself over to a sadist. See how it feels."

"What are you going to do?" I asked, turning my head.

"Whatever I want. Nothing fatal." He smacked my ass, then squeezed it. A hot burn rose to the surface. It stung a lot for just a hand. I squirmed as he eased my cheeks apart, exposing all of me. *All of me.* I was almost relieved to be spanked again, a glancing blow that caught the sensitive underside of my ass.

I tried to be still, to submit, but my whole body tensed. I shuddered as he caressed me instead, his palm blazing a warm, firm path up my spine to my nape. He gripped the back of my hair, holding my head when I tried to hide my face.

"You asked what I'm into," he said in a level, quiet voice. "I'm into tears and power trips. I'm into capriciously hurting you because it's unfair, and because you'll let me do it anyway. I'm into reducing you to a sex object, and sometimes sharing you with my friends. I'm into bruises and welts on a regular basis, marks you'll wear like a uniform because I want you to. But I'm mostly into tears, Juliet, and tormenting you."

I stared at the diffuse pattern of my couch's upholstery, doing my best to stave off panic. He was right. My BDSM experience hadn't prepared me for the deeply intense and ominous speech he'd just delivered. *Hurting. Sharing. Bruising.*

Tormenting.

"Say something," he murmured when the silence strung out.

I shifted my head the scant inch his grip would allow. "I just...have some questions."

"Ask them."

I was still bent over his lap, a weak, surrendered, edge play novice trying to process what he wanted, and why, and how it might make me feel if I kept playing along.

"Is there any caring?" I asked. "I mean, do you want to hurt your partners out of disdain? Spite?"

"No."

"You don't hate the women you hurt? You're not angry?"

He flipped me over and pushed me back against the armrest, his hand on my neck. My arms flailed out. I was getting anxious from being manipulated like a rag doll. His gaze roved over my face, then locked on my eyes.

"There's no anger or spite involved," he said. "I deeply appreciate every woman who lets me hurt her. I admire the courage, the sacrifice it takes. I revel in my partners' reactions." He leaned over me, braced on one arm. "But that doesn't mean that I'm soft, or that I want to communicate love. Dominating and hurting someone is a tactile, physiological thing for me, a physical function, a release."

Don't cry. If you cry, he'll walk. Maybe I should have let him walk, but I didn't want to. I wanted to understand. I was drawn to him as much as he was drawn to me. I wanted to see if we could work.

Maybe...maybe what he described would feel as hot as our rough, grasping work room sex. I needed release, not some serious relationship, while I got my life back together. In that way, we were a lot alike. Or was that just a rationalization, because he was hovering over me with a gargantuan erection I could make out through his pants?

"What are you thinking?" he asked.

"I'm thinking how to convince you to...to let me try. Do you think I would be strong enough to withstand the stuff you like to do?"

"My sadism? Yes, you're physically strong enough." His lips flattened into a line. "But emotionally... That's the part that worries me. I'm not a psychiatrist. I wouldn't know how to fix you if some part of you..." He touched my head, wrapped his fingers over my addled brain. "If some part of you here got messed up."

I looked away from him. "I know a lot of crazy people. They're not so bad."

"Juliet."

"I'll try not to be too emotional, okay?" I could feel myself blushing, because my ass still smarted, and I wanted him to fuck me right now. "Maybe I'll get excited by your kind of pain. Maybe I'll love it. I might be as masochistic as you are sadistic. I've never done any of the edgier stuff, so I have no way of knowing—"

"Look at me."

His sharp command took me aback, but his tone propelled me to obey. I lifted my chin as he pinned my arms down on either side of me. Our eyes met, and his held mine with the full force of his dominant authority. Maybe his stare was meant to scare me. It did.

"I want to explore my fantasies with you, Sparkles. I want it very much. I want to do all kinds of perverse, painful, lustful things to you, but it will be pure power exchange. That's it. I can't give you love and forever after. It wouldn't be a romance."

"You've said that four or five times now." I strained against his hands. "How stupid do you think I am? My last 'romance' ended up with me getting trashed and making your godforsaken acquaintance."

He lowered himself over me, his arm snaking around my waist. Our lips almost touched. His cock felt like an iron bar against my hip. "When we go sadist/masochist together," he said, "we're going to have to work on that sassy mouth."

When, not *if*.

His knee pressed between my legs, force and dominance, and I wondered if I actually was stupid. In my vulnerable position, I could feel how strong he was, could feel the leashed violence in his touch. He *enjoyed hurting women*. For whatever reason, I wanted him to hurt me and make me come again the frenzied way I'd come last night.

"So...where do we start?" I asked. "If we're going to try this?" He still hadn't let me go.

"We start with warnings."

"Oh."

"I'm into full control, Juliet. Encompassing control." He stroked fingers down my bare hip and thigh, down to the waistband of my shorts, emphasizing my nakedness, my exposure. I pressed my legs together, hiding the heat and wetness his words had caused. "Has your BDSM research ever led you into the realm of consensual non-consent?" he asked.

I squirmed under his touch. "Is that some kind of fantasy realm?"

"No, it's not a realm." He let go of me and tugged my panties and shorts back up with an irritated sound. "Sit up, right here beside me. This is important—negotiation point one. Consensual non-consent is a fetish, a sexual practice. It means that I set the boundaries in our sessions, and you won't have the option to opt out of anything I desire."

"What about safe words?"

"I don't do safe words." He dismissed the cornerstone of safe, sane, and consensual BDSM with a flick of his hand. "I need my scenes to feel real, like I'm one hundred percent in control. Consensual non-consent means that you give up the ability to say yes or no once we've started exchanging power in a scene."

"But I can stop you if I have to, right? I can leave anytime?" My voice strained to the high end.

He gave me a dry look. "I'm not in the business of committing felonies. You would, of course, be free to leave our power exchange relationship at any time. But as long as you were in it with me, I would maintain complete control of you by any means I desired."

By any means... That could encompass so many things.

"Of course, in the beginning, we'd go slow," he said, noticing my alarm. "We'd start with short sessions, and stay within limited boundaries until we built trust."

"Like training?"

"Like, you doing whatever I demanded physically and sexually, and seeing if you could deal with it. It's not all sex," he warned me. "It's other things too."

"Oh."

"And that's all our scenes would be, finite sessions of physical and sexual release. I'm telling you that because I don't want to be like your last Dom, who led you on and wasn't honest with you. I'm being brutally honest. I know how I am, and I can't offer you much outside of physical sensation and control."

His expression softened. One of his hands lingered in the air, then moved downward to cup my chin. "I know that isn't what you're looking for. That's why I've tried to stay away, but you keep drawing me back. I'd like to explore this tension between us. If you met someone else, someone who was interested in a more traditional relationship, you could end our association at any time."

Our association. That sounded clinical and sort of sad, but the other part, exploring this tension, sounded necessary to me. I was glad Fort was willing to usher me into this edgy new world. Hurting. Spanking. Bondage. Force. Non-consent. Maybe even anal. I imagined, with him, it would be all the things.

"Can we go to your club?" I asked. "That place you told me about?"

He shook his head. "Not for a while. The club's an entirely different conversation. Maybe once we have a few sessions under our belt."

A few sessions. There was something really hot about *sessions*—Fort and me, sadism and perversion and sex.

Forget the relationship drama, the craving for love. For now, this was what I wanted. At least, I was pretty sure it was what I wanted. Before he left my place, he had me unblock his number on my phone. He said he'd pick me up the following weekend for the first of our trust-building sessions at his Blackwell penthouse. He told me to be ready for anything.

He also told me that if I changed my mind or felt any misgivings about going forward, that I was to block his number on my phone for good.

CHAPTER ELEVEN: FORT

I spent the next week berating myself for my lack of control, my stupidity. The more I knew Juliet, the more I understood she was a dangerous bundle of feelings and complications.

Why resurrect my complicated cravings for her? That's what Dev had grumbled as he swilled free champagne at the art opening. "Why are you here, man? This is some stupid shit."

Maybe. Probably.

I'd let Juliet into my personal dungeon next Saturday and see how far she'd let me go.

Maybe we'd both be surprised.

Chapter Twelve: Juliet

Fort sent a car to pick me up on Saturday evening. He didn't come get me himself, and there was no dinner date beforehand, because this wasn't about forging a relationship. This was about exchanging power and sharing physical pleasure, full stop. He'd been clear about that, and being fetched by a uniformed driver made it clearer.

It felt sexy and dangerous to be ushered into the black sedan, but it also felt weird, like I was playing a role that didn't fit me, at least not yet. I pressed my legs together in the back seat, arranging my skirt just above my knees so the bows at the top of my over-the-knee socks would show. He hadn't told me to wear socks with bows, but I knew he'd appreciate them. I already had a sense of what he liked.

There was a folded note card beside me on the seat with a bold, swirling 'S' on the front. 'S' for *St. Clair*. 'S' for *session*. I picked it up and opened it, scanning his message with dread and lust roiling in my stomach. *Good evening, Sparkles. I hope you're as excited to see me as I am to see you.*

It wasn't signed, but it didn't have to be. All of this was his doing. All these arrangements and processes were under his control. Fort St. Clair, playboy and sadist. Juliet Pope, possible masochist in search of more orgasms, because it was sometimes okay to do questionable, irresponsible things because a man really turned you on, and because you felt like trying something new.

After a smooth, silent trip, the driver pulled up at the Blackwell. As soon as I left the vehicle, a doorman emerged from the lobby and greeted me by name.

"Good evening, Ms. Pope. I'll show you to the elevator and key you up to Mr. St. Clair's floor."

Mr. St. Clair's *floor*? Fuck, he had a whole damn floor? And how did this doorman know my name? I was used to the clutter and informality of the Black Wall—my building was more art school dormitory than Manhattan real estate.

When the elevator opened, I was at Fort's front door. I remembered this from the morning after my drunken meltdown, remembered him leading me onto the elevator and down to his car. That had been almost six months ago now. I swallowed and mashed my lips together, and tugged at my hair. I'd left it down, since I figured he'd take it down anyway.

Before I could knock, the door swung open. Fort ran his eyes over my fitted burgundy dress, then down to my matching over-the-knee socks. He smiled.

"I've been waiting for you."

I bit my lip, trying not to blush as I entered his apartment. It was as spotless and elegant as I remembered.

"Are you nervous?" He put his hands on my shoulders and squeezed them. "You shouldn't be. I'm an experienced sadist."

"Oh, Lord."

"Come here. Have a drink with me."

I looked up at the high ceilings, then out at the city's lights as he led me to his kitchen. "Isn't it bad to do...uh...what we're going to do while under the influence?"

"Yes. It's also bad to play without a safe word. But in this case, you're in my hands and you're going to be absolutely fine, even if you have a few sips of wine to ease your nerves beforehand."

He popped the cork of an expensive-looking bottle on his counter and poured half a glass of red wine for each of us while I took in his effortless magnificence. Black sweater, dark jeans that molded perfectly to his physique. His sweater's cuffs were pushed up his forearms, revealing tanned skin with a smattering of dark brown hair.

"Here you go."

I took the crystal glass from his hand. His eyes went wide when I almost drained the thing.

"I don't like the taste of wine," I explained. "But I know it's good for me to down some from time to time."

He didn't quite laugh. It was more of an exasperated smile.

"Do you feel up to a session now? Want a little more liquid courage before we start?" He lifted the bottle but I shook my head. He recorked it and stowed it in the refrigerator. "I didn't even ask how your week went," he said over his shoulder. "How've you been, Jewels?"

I've been a wreck, I thought silently, putting my glass on his marble counter. "I spent most of last week thinking about you."

Damn it. Why had I said that out loud, after all his anti-romantic ravings? Probably because his jeans were incredible, and his sweater fit just right. I couldn't read any annoyance—or pleasure—in his expression. He straightened and looked at me, pressed his lips together and managed a small smile that had my nipples tightening. How had I ended up here, with this perverted, sadistic, disgustingly handsome man? *Because you got shitfaced at Underworld and stumbled around until he rescued you*, I reminded myself.

That was months ago, a chance, accidental meeting. I was here on purpose now.

"I'm excited to scene with you, Juliet," he said, moving closer, right into my personal space. A finger went under my chin, lifting my face to his. "But first, I want to be clear about three things."

"You don't want a relationship," I said. "That's the first thing."

The finger moved from my chin to my lips. "Shh. That's already been established. These are things specific to playing right now."

"Oh."

"First thing: You're going to be safe. No irreparable damage will happen to you, even if it feels that way at certain moments."

I nodded, wondering how numerous—and arduous—those moments might be.

"Second thing: We're clear that this is a serious deal, not some slap-and-tickle game." His gaze held oceans of warnings. "I need you with me, one hundred percent. I need you compliant and engaged the entire time, until I let you know the scene is over."

"Yes. Agreed. I mean, I'm going to try."

"And you'll tough it out when things get hard? Because they're going to get hard." He shut his eyes when a strangled laugh escaped me. "You know what I mean. Get your mind out of the gutter. We're not going there just yet."

I tried to look appropriately serious. "I remember—it's not all about sex."

"No. Sex is part of it. There's more though, which I'll show you. Okay, final rule, Sparkles. You can close your eyes, stare at the wall, whatever you want, but when I tell you to look at me, you need to look at me. Do you understand?"

I nodded, cowed by the gravity in his gaze.

"Answer *Yes, Sir*," he said. "While I'm in charge, you show respect, and you obey."

"Yes, Sir." My pussy clenched as his stare lengthened, and my thoughts spun off into lurid fantasies fueled by too many re-readings of *The Story of O*. His firm, warm grasp on my neck brought me back to reality. He kissed me, a hard kiss that tasted of fine wine, then took my hand and led me from the soaring-windowed living room into the central hallway. We passed the guest room where I'd stayed, and a room with closed double doors that must have been his bedroom.

"In here," he said, as he reached the last door. I expected more towering windows and pristine white decor, but instead found myself in a cozy, richly furnished home office in warm wood tones. It was more of a library, since the walls were lined with floor-to-ceiling bookshelves, each one filled with books and random curios of high-quality design. A large, rectangular desk dominated the center of the room, containing only a laptop, a stack of two books, and a gleaming model of three identical pendulums in contrasting earth tones.

The room was Fort: luxurious, elegant, and sexy as hell. Was this where he'd torment me? I imagined myself in the throes of agonized passion, thrashing around on top of his desk. I'd have to watch out for those pendulums...

I drifted toward them, dying to set them in motion. They weren't the click-clack balls that other people kept on their desks, the Newton's

Cradle with five hanging globes that whacked into each other with a tinny sound. These pendulums were conical, suspended from a burnished frame by long, slim wires.

"Can I touch them?" I asked. The frame was so beautiful, I wasn't sure if it was an office toy or fine art.

"You can touch them if you can explain the difference between kinetic and potential energy."

He chuckled at my expression and went to sit behind the desk. He looked perfect there, a relaxed, suave jewelry tycoon's son in his old-world library of loveliness. What was I doing here? I was so far out of my league, for both sex and pain.

"I don't know the difference between any kinds of energy," I said, clasping my hands in front of me. "I must have missed that day of class."

He reached to touch one of the pendulums, his large finger stroking the polished surface. Upon closer inspection, I realized the one he touched was smooth, dark wood, while the others were silver and brass.

"Kinetic energy is energy possessed by an object in motion," he said. "Like the hands of a watch, or the car you arrived in." He flicked the silver pendulum, the one in the middle, sending it back and forth on its filament wire. His fingers moved back toward the wood pendulum.

"Potential energy is energy an object possesses because of its position relative to some other object." This time, his hand lingered just beside it. "That energy doesn't exist until it's set in motion. Of course, all objects don't have the same potential energy." He flicked the wood pendulum but it didn't move as far, or with the sweeping acceleration of its shiny silver neighbor.

"That's very scientific," I said, watching the pendulums swing back and forth. At his gestured invitation, I sent the brass one flying. It went higher and faster than the silver or wood, but that was probably because I flicked it too hard. "I guess you have to know about physics and motion to design watches," I said.

"It helps," he replied in one of his lazy understatements.

I sent all the pendulums going again, trying to make them line up so they moved forward and back in unison. It didn't work, so I stopped them and tried again, but they weren't even close.

"Do you know the unit of measurement for energy?" he asked.

I thought a moment. "Watts? Kilowatts?"

"No. That's power."

"E equals MC squared?" It was the only other science-y thing I could recall.

Another chuckle. "You're getting closer. But no. Energy is measured in Joules."

"Jewels?"

"Not gems, Juliet. J-o-u-l-e-s." He set all three pendulums in motion, nearly in perfect tandem. "Considering the energy you put out, Joules would be an appropriate nickname for you."

Not just handsome, but devastatingly charming. I tried to hide my growing infatuation, since that wasn't part of the plan. "Goodluck says I should change my name to Starcomet."

He nodded and stood. "I can see that. But I prefer Sparkles. I think that fits you best of all." The pendulums started to slow, sending their arcs out of rhythm. I stared at them because I couldn't find the courage to stare at him.

"What about your nickname?" I said.

"I already have one. Fort."

I think that fits you best of all. He was like a fort: tall, strong, impregnable. Relatively safe.

"Are you ready?" he asked.

"Yes." I nodded. "Definitely, yes."

"*Yes, Sir.* When we're exchanging power, I prefer to be addressed as Sir."

"Oh, okay. Yes, Sir."

"You know that I'm going to hurt you badly?" he said, and it had the tone of a final warning. "I won't harm or maim you. But what we do tonight will feel awful to you, and I won't stop when I see tears."

Tears. Our first real session, and he intended to make me cry. He couldn't wait to make me cry. I could see it in his eyes and hear it in his rough voice, that he desired my tears with lustful intensity. I was potential energy, waiting to be acted upon by an opposing force, by this beautiful, dark-haired sadist. Whenever someone called me Jules after today, I'd think of Joules and remember this talk.

"What will make you stop?" I asked in a quiet voice. "If tears won't work, or safe words, how will you know if you have to stop our scene?"

"I'll know," he said. "Your body will tell me more reliably than any safe word could."

The pendulums came to a stop as he took my elbow. With a gentle nudge, he turned me toward a door in the back. I'd thought it was a closet, but when he opened it, it led into another, equally sized room. Instead of bookshelves, there were dark wood racks and cabinets that held an array of metal and leather gear. I was standing in a Dominant's torture chamber, located just through the nondescript door behind his desk.

I took a breath, studying my surroundings. Fort's dungeon was an expansive room composed of polished siding and black furniture, some of it with gilt shading. Real gold? The ceiling had thick, exposed beams embedded with large eyebolts every yard or so. A pair of leather cuffs dangled from chains near a high, small window that was just big enough to suggest open sky and freedom to a bound victim. The lights were low and stayed low, impeding my attempts to study the implements on the wall.

Aside from the pair of hanging cuffs, there was also a large spanking bench with padded leather upholstery, a tall, sturdy whipping post, and a butterfly-shaped, black resin chair with hardware that suggested all kinds of scary possibilities. In the far corner, a giant, solid wood 'X' displayed more chains and cuffs. I knew what it was for, knew it was called a St. Andrew's Cross. I pictured myself strapped to it, flailing in pain. I turned to him, trying to hide how scared and squirmy that made me feel.

"No cage?" I asked.

He gave me a look. "Not my thing. I can't get at you if you're in a cage. Anyway, you'd break your wings on the bars."

I didn't know whether to take that as a compliment or an insult, and I didn't feel brave enough to ask what he meant. He ran a hand over the front of his jeans. I could see he was already growing hard, and I was definitely wet.

"I'd like you to undress now." His voice was firm and low, inviting no discussion. "Place your clothes on the bench by the door, next to the sink."

I suddenly felt shy, but I pretended I was as experienced as the edgy submissives he played with at his private sadists' club. I took off my dress, and the pretty burgundy velvet bra underneath. I took off my over-the-knee socks next, leaving my legs feeling shaky and cold. I paused at my matching panties, long enough for him to murmur, "Everything," and then the panties came off too. He wanted nakedness. He wanted everything.

When I was naked to the skin, I faced him with my arms at my sides, trying to look natural. I was at peace with my body, with my wobbly thighs, my full hips. I had a smallish waist, which I liked, and nice, natural breasts. My nipples were rock hard.

Fort watched me a moment, then took off his sweater so he was bared to the waist. I gawked at him, half delighted, half aghast. Unfair, to compete with that. Broad chest, tempting ladder of hair-dusted muscles disappearing down into the waistband of his jeans...

"Let's get you tied down," he said, taking my arm and leading me to the post in the back left corner of the room. He thumped it a few times while I watched. "This is solid. It'll give you something to lean into."

I nodded, since I couldn't manage to utter a syllable. I turned toward it, but he stopped me and arranged me facing away from it.

"This way first. Raise your arms."

I stretched them up high, eager to please, but he pulled them lower, fastening them into cuffs at the top of the post. The cuffs felt very...inescapable. Even though they were leather, they felt rigid as metal against my skin. I stared at his chest as he tightened them with a ratcheting clasp that went *click click click*. As trapped as I felt, I could tell it was the kind of cuff that could release quickly if it had to. *You're going to be safe. Nothing irreparable will happen to you.*

I clung to his reassuring words as he tugged on the cuffs' tether to be sure I was secure. His eyes met mine, then skimmed past me, focusing on the far wall, where a rack held dozens of straps, paddles, crops, floggers, cuffs, chains, bars, clamps, canes...

"If you belong to a private BDSM club, why do you keep so much furniture and gear at your place?" I asked.

He crossed to the wall. "Because I want to."

He considered his selection of hurty things carefully, while I pressed my legs together and shifted on my toes. I was so aroused thinking about what would come, and the fact that I'd have no choice. I felt naked and vulnerable, and he seemed three times as powerful since he'd taken off his sweater. Without it, he was a wild thing, a wall of muscles. My clit was so swollen I could feel each throb of desire.

"Will I get to come by the end of this session?" I asked.

"Probably not," he said, turning back to me. "We already know I can make you come. We're trying to figure out other things. Now, no more conversation. Don't speak anymore unless I ask you a question."

I closed my mouth and watched him take a pair of silver, rubber-tipped nipple clamps from the rack. He tested each on his fingertip as he returned to me.

"I'm going to run some experiments on you," he said. "Learn your reactions to different things."

"Oh, okay. Yes, Sir."

"I wasn't asking for permission."

Oh my God. He cupped my right breast, ran his thumb over the nipple. Then he leaned and sucked my nipple into his mouth, worrying it between his teeth. My arms moved reflexively to push his head away. When I couldn't move my arms more than an inch, I arched against the polished post behind me. He placed a hand on my back before he moved to the other nipple, so when he sucked it, bringing aching pain to the tip, I couldn't do anything to get away.

"Oww," I whined through my teeth. It hurt more than I wanted. It hurt until it wasn't pleasurable. He drew back and looked at me, and pinched the nipple he'd just sucked, rolling it back and forth between his fingertips. When it was tender and sore and horribly sensitive to the touch, he lifted the first clamp and arranged it over my nipple. When he was satisfied with the placement, he let it fall closed.

I thought the clamp couldn't hurt as much as his tugging and biting, but it did, because the pressure was constant. While I gasped for breath, he attached the other clamp, letting the silver chain fall down against my skin. I felt cold, hot, shivery, scared. I pulled at the cuffs, desperate to slap the clamps off me to ease the pinching pain. The only result was a faint rattle and sore arms.

"It's okay," he said. "I know it hurts." He tugged each clamp to be sure it was secure, then moved back to the wall and picked up a short, thin, braided leather whip.

"Are you..." I almost choked. It was one of the most wicked-looking implements on the wall. "Are you going to start me out with *that*?"

"Hush."

He whacked it against his palm. The flicky sound almost made me wet myself. I thought he'd start out with a fur-lined paddle or something. Actually, I didn't see anything fur-lined on his dungeon walls.

"That looks like it might really hurt," I said, staring at the whip in his hands.

He stood in front of me, close enough that we almost touched. "Do you remember when I told you not to speak anymore?"

I nodded.

"You can make sounds," he said. "You can beg or swear or sob once we get started, but we're not making any more conversation. I've told you several times now to be quiet. I can't gag you during your first session, so you need to control the random comments, because they pull both of us out of the scene."

He reached out and I flinched, needlessly. The whip was in his other hand. His palm moved up and down my stomach, across tense muscles. He tugged at the nipple clamps, pulling my chest forward and renewing the pinching torment. "Don't cringe away. You're mine to hurt. You wanted this."

"I know, but it's so painful."

I didn't say anything else. I wasn't supposed to keep chattering, so I bit my lip to keep the words inside. He lifted the chain and smacked the underside of one breast with the whip.

"Oh my God, no." The screech burst out of me as a hot line of pain seared across my skin. That didn't deter him. No, he flicked me again, this time right across my tender nipple. It was fleeting contact, but it hurt like hell. I couldn't turn away because his hand was still against my stomach, but I tried, pressing my forehead into his shoulder.

He flicked my other breast, and the flash of pain stole my breath. Each time he flicked me, I gasped and jerked, yanking on the cuffs above my head. I wanted to ask how long he'd do this, but I knew it wasn't allowed. He flicked each breast at least a dozen times, tugging the clamps in between. By the end, my chest felt hot and swollen to twice its normal size. My nipples ached in a numb tempo, and the skin around them throbbed with fire.

Through all of this, his expression didn't change much, except to look mildly pleased.

"Time for these to come off," he said, tugging the clamps a final time. Somehow, I knew it would hurt for them to come off, just as it hurt for them to go on. He opened each one, removing them and inspecting my nipples while I endured the agony of returning sensation. His fingertips nudged each nipple, testing my response. I gritted my teeth. There was no blood, no injury, although I felt maimed. He finished with a hard pinch to each breast, followed by a series of stinging slaps.

"Ow, ow, *oww*..." I protested in a whisper.

"Turn around," he said, ignoring my complaints.

When I didn't react, he put his hands on my shoulders and turned me. I hunched against the post, resting my forehead against the wood, but he made me straighten by pulling back my hips.

"Posture's important," he said. "You can flinch and cower all you want once the pain starts, but while you're waiting, I want your shoulders up and your ass out. You want this, don't you?"

I sucked air through my teeth. He spanked my ass, then grabbed a handful of my hair. "The correct answer is 'Yes, Sir.'"

"Yes, Sir," I hurried to say, because my ass felt like it had a target on it. I watched over my shoulder as he went to the wall and returned with a leather strap, a striated bamboo spoon that was big enough to work as a paddle, and a slim wooden dowel. I prayed he'd start with the dowel; it looked relatively harmless. Instead, he set the dowel and wooden spoon on a nearby table—in my line of vision—and stood behind me with the strap.

I started shaking, really shaking. The strap looked huge, even in his massive hands. It was thick, black, and rectangular, designed with a sturdy handle.

"Posture," he said, when I started cringing.

I stood as straight as I could, making a soft, pleading noise. He held the strap doubled over in one hand and used his other hand to spank me a few times.

"Ow, ow," I said, mostly to myself. It was so hard to stand straight and still as he whacked me, his palm and fingers stinging me up and down my ass cheeks.

"This is a warm-up," he said. "I'm getting you ready to take a little more pain."

A little more pain? There was already quite a bit of pain. My breasts felt hot and sore, and any lingering arousal had been chased away by the sight of the strap and the "warm-up" spanking that hurt like hell.

I couldn't see him, but I could feel his presence. I wondered what he thought of my submissiveness so far. I wondered if I looked pretty to him, if my ass looked round and spankable. His hand left my hip, and my round, spankable ass had its first taste of the strap.

Ouch. I made a strangled sound. It felt heavy and intense, but not unbearable. The next stroke, though, was harder. I could feel the strap lifting my cheeks, glancing over my tender skin. Still, I could take this.

Well, I tried to take it. By the fifth stroke, my posture was bullshit and my legs could barely hold me up. If not for his firm hand on my shoulder, I would have jerked around and begged to be left alone. Instead, I sniveled into the post in front of me. "Ow! Please, ouch, God!" Seven strokes. Eight.

He put the strap down and I breathed out, sagging in my bonds. The whole strapping had taken what, less than five minutes? I was exhausted.

"I don't know if I can take anymore," I said.

He touched my neck and nuzzled his cheek against me. "I'm pretty sure you can. You're doing great, Juliet. I know it's hard to be hurt, really hurt, but that's what these implements are meant for. If I didn't hurt you, it wouldn't be much fun."

Fun? He had the bamboo spoon now. He started tapping my ass, delivering a steady tattoo of sharp, zinging smacks. I'd been scared of the strap, but holy hell, this felt so much worse. I bounced on my toes, then hopped. I pulled at the cuffs, desperate to reach back and stop him.

"Please, please. Stop!"

He had to be bruising me. The pain mounted, *smack smack smack smack smack*. I tried to twist away and he grabbed my neck. I felt the spoon trace down my thigh while his erection taunted me through his jeans. Torturing me—that's what aroused him. That's why he was so hard.

Aside from the massive cock against my bare, sore ass, I could tell he was turned on from his breathing. He used the spoon to nudge my legs apart, rubbing it over my clit. I pressed back into his chest, shocked at the hard squeeze of arousal, but he interrupted my pleasure by smacking my pussy with the stinging implement.

"No," I moaned.

"Oh, yes." Pure pleasure for him. His voice was low and rough. His cock felt huge enough to bust out of his jeans.

He stroked my clit again. Hit me again. I pressed my legs together, trying to stop him, but then he smacked the front of my mons and ordered, "Open."

I sobbed and opened, wriggling as he slid the devilish tool between my pussy lips. The smooth edge made my hips jerk each time it contacted my overstimulated clit. Then *whack*, and hot pain suffused my pussy. *Whack, whack, whack.* I jerked, arched, and sobbed, trying to climb him by bracing on his legs.

We were tangled together, bound victim, unbound force with two capable hands to grasp and punish me. Next time he stroked my clit, I ground back against him. I wasn't sure if I wanted sex or if I wanted mercy. His arm tightened around my shoulders. I started to cry.

"Does it hurt?" he asked.

Of course it hurt, but I knew he had to hear it. He wanted to hear me sob and beg, and it was so easy to give him that.

"Don't anymore," I shrieked. "Please!" My voice crackled with tears. "It stings so bad. Please don't—*oww!*"

He held my thigh to one side and whacked my clit, not once, but three times in succession as I bawled for him to stop.

"You want me to stop?" he asked. I couldn't answer because his arm was around my neck again, stealing my breath. I heard the bamboo spoon hit the floor, felt his hand against my ass undoing his jeans. My pussy was as wet as my tearful eyes. I felt the head of his cock at my pussy's entrance and then he was surging inside me, driving to the hilt. He growled like an animal, emitting a grunt for each of my sobs.

I danced on my toes once again, this time trying to process the fullness of his possession on top of everything else. He let go of my neck, pinched my sore nipples, then replaced his headlock with a hand beneath my chin. My clit throbbed every time he pushed my head up. I wanted to hide against the post but he wouldn't let me. I wanted to cower but he was in control, his other hand clamping over my pussy and clit. He pinched and worked my clit, pressing fingers against the sensitive nub to the point of pain. I bucked my hips, trying to escape his rough caresses, but he only fucked me harder and faster.

At some point my crying became whimpering, and my hips jerked forward as I worked my clit against his rough fingers. My feet hurt from hopping around, and my spine ached from arching and bending. He fucked me so hard he lifted me off the ground with each stroke, rattling the tether above me. When he grasped my neck and opened his teeth against my ear, my body came.

I say *my body* because the orgasm happened on its own, out of my control and out of my intention, and that made me cry hardest of all. It was the most conflicted, most powerful climax I'd ever had, an animalistic release. It was as if sex and arousal had exploded inside me, creating an orgiastic firework display, hot, shooting sparks driving me wild.

He must have come at the same time, while I was too out of it to notice. I felt him slump over me, his muscles going slack. His hand relaxed on my neck, then tightened again. My nipples and pussy still throbbed. My ass still hurt. I had tears in my hair and in my mouth, and my nose was running. When he pulled out of me, I tried to gather my sanity but my breath was still coming in short, panting bursts.

He held me against him, stroking my waist. "Are you okay? Look at me."

I turned my head. His eyes were narrowed, and very intense.

"Are you okay?" he repeated. "Hold my gaze, Juliet. Answer me."

"Yes, Sir," I managed to say. My voice sounded high and thin. "I'm just having all these feelings."

"Breathe." He tilted my head up, brushed away some tears, but they were replaced by others. "Deep breaths. Be still for a moment."

"I c-came after all."

"I know. Sometimes that happens."

His hands moved down my body to stroke my thighs, massaging them, holding them open so I couldn't try to squeeze out another orgasm, which I desperately wanted to do.

"Are we finished?" I asked. "Was that the end of our session?"

"Almost. I know your arms are hurting. Here." He reached above me and released my hands from the cuffs. As soon as I was free, I had two impulses. One was to shove him aside so I could run away screaming. The other was to throw myself into his arms, and that was what I did. He held me, stroking my back. His pants were still open, his zipper cold amidst all the heat between us. He was so warm and solid, but he was still a *Sir*. He maintained a reserve, a steeliness that I'd seen many times, but never this way. After hugging and comforting me for a moment, he turned me back to face the post.

"Put your arms around it," he said. "You're allowed to flatten against it for support, if you'd like." He paused. "You probably should."

I did as he instructed, nestling the solid post between my punished breasts, pressing my pussy to the wood so he couldn't hurt it anymore. While I watched over my shoulder, he did up his pants, shoving his cock inside, then picked up the thin dowel. I was glad he'd saved the flimsy, light implement for last, when my strength was pretty much gone.

"Put your feet together," he prompted me. "Ass out. No matter what, you're not to move. You're not to let go of that post until I tell you. Do you understand?"

"Yes, Sir."

"I'm going to give you three things to think about for next time." He paused. "If you want a next time. That's going to be up to you."

Did I want a next time? I hurt. I ached. My eyes burned from crying. But the sparks from my firecracker orgasm lingered, and I was still wet. His cum leaked out of me, trailing down the insides of my thighs.

"First thing..." I heard a whistle in the air, and then the impact. My legs buckled as a searing line of fire assailed my trembling ass cheeks.

"Oh my God," I yelled. "Don't!"

"First thing. Your body is mine once you hand it over. It's mine to hurt and mine to fuck. Without your surrender, we have nothing."

Nothing. No pain, no sex, no business together. This was his sexuality, and he needed everything or nothing. Oh shit, this was so intense. I wanted to beg him, plead with him not to hit me with the dowel again, but I knew he would, at least two more times.

"Posture," he murmured, and I reached down inside myself and mustered the strength to straighten my knees and my spine. My arms curved around the post, clenching with a trembling grip.

"Second thing." This stroke landed in a whistling burn across my ass, just above the still-throbbing first one. I'd been so stupid, so wrong. The thin dowel wasn't the easiest implement. It was the hardest, which was why he'd saved it for last. It was fucking satanic, straight out of hell. "I want you to remember that the only reason your tight little asshole wasn't punished tonight is because this was your first time. You can expect it next time. Make sure you're ready."

I coughed, almost choked. I'd never had anal, but I'd expected a kinky motherfucker like him to at least introduce a butt plug or two. But punishment? I squeezed my cheeks together, trying to protect that vulnerable orifice. *Next time.* When I clenched, it made the two dowel welts throb harder. *Do you want a next time? Could you survive a next time?*

"Last thing," he said in his scary Dom voice.

I couldn't take it. I turned to face him, to protect my ass.

"Turn around," he said.

"Please!"

My distress didn't move him in the slightest. Gave him a sadistic thrill, maybe, but didn't evoke pity. "Turn around," he said quietly, "or you'll leave this dungeon with ten lines instead of three."

This was why people had safe words, to escape moments like this, moments they couldn't bear.

But I could bear it. Not having a safe word meant I had to bear it, even if I didn't like it. He guided me around, making me grasp the pole again. All the yummy, orgasmic sensation in my pussy had fled by now, replaced with trembling terror. He waited, and I knew what he was waiting for. I squeezed my eyes shut, leaking tears, and stuck out my ass.

Thwack.

Ah, God. Breathe, breathe, breathe. I gasped and sucked in a sob. This stroke landed at the bottom, just where I sat. My buttocks clenched and unclenched, trying to process the pain. I felt his palm against my heated skin, tracing, then pinching.

"Last thing," he said, turning me around and taking me once again in his arms. "I learned a lot about you today." He nudged my face upward, searching my eyes. "Maybe it's all an act, or maybe it's pure force of will, but I think you have some masochist in you. I was hoping you would."

Chapter Thirteen: Fort

Her beautiful ass, with three perfectly spaced stripes across it...

I took a deep breath, reveling in her tears, noticing tiny silver flecks in her eyes that I hadn't seen before. I wanted to drink her in so I could remember everything.

Her cries, her shudders, her strength.

Her surrender.

And God, the way she clung to me now. I didn't want to let go of her. I didn't, not for a long time.

This wasn't a good thing. It was very, very bad.

Chapter Fourteen: Juliet

He held me in his dark dungeon until the tremors left my body, until my tears had dried on my cheeks. The exquisite bliss of my climax eventually faded away, but my ass and breasts still throbbed each time I shifted against him. When he released me, I started over toward my clothes. "Do I..." My voice hitched. "Do I leave now?"

"No. Sit down and wait for me." He shook his head as I skittered toward the bench by the door. "Don't get dressed yet. Sit right where you are, there on the floor. It's clean, I promise."

I sank to my knees, unwilling to put any pressure on my punished ass. I wanted to get dressed again now that everything was over, but he didn't want me dressed, and he was the Dominant in this game.

He moved around the dungeon, cleaning and replacing the equipment he'd used with me. Now that our session was over, now that I'd calmed a little bit, I was able to take a closer look at the dark, sleek surroundings, his furnishings and fetish gear. When I'd entered this place, I hadn't understood how much real sadism hurt. I'd fantasized about "scening," imagined orgasmic thrills and tantalizing flicks of a whip.

So, reality...actual whips hurt like hell. Spoons hurt worse, and thin wooden dowels were horrific.

I watched Fort's face, trying to figure out if our scene had gone well, or if I was a disaster. He'd said I had "some masochist" in me, but he'd said it in such a controlled way that I wasn't sure how to take it. He didn't look upset or angry, but he didn't look relaxed either, the way people were supposed to look after they'd done something enjoyable. If he enjoyed doling out pain, he ought to have been ecstatic.

Or maybe the pain he gave me was nothing. Maybe it wasn't enough to excite him. I didn't know.

He came to me when he was done and held out a hand. "Let's go clean up," he said. "When you're finished in the guest room shower, come out to the living room and we'll talk."

The guest room shower? Why not his shower? Why wouldn't we shower together after what had just happened? He needed space. That seemed the most likely scenario.

He walked me to the guest room, showed me all the toiletries, soap and towels, and provided a fluffy spa robe for me to put on afterward. I looked like hell, with tears and makeup smeared across my face. And my ass... *Oh God.*

I would have felt better if he'd showered with me, but he didn't. He wouldn't. As I stood under the water in my lonely shower, I thought that I needed more feedback and communication than this. I needed more connection, but he wasn't into connection. He was into *physical* and *sexual*, as he'd told me very clearly.

Damn.

I fondled my tender breasts, trying to wash away the pain without causing more. I inspected them as he had, and found nothing more than tiny, light bruises. My nipples looked completely untouched. My ass was another story, and my clit still felt swollen and sensitive to the touch. I couldn't see the redness and probable bruising between my legs, but I could see what he'd done to my ass—mottled marks in an irregular pattern, probably left over from the strap, and three parallel welts from the way he'd finished me off.

I ran my fingers over those welts, twisting to look down at them, at least the ones I could see. The one under my ass cheeks wasn't visible, but it hurt the most. I knew I'd feel it every time I sat down, at least until it healed. The idea of that triggered a new, spreading heat in my pussy and clit. My inside walls clenched, and I pressed on one of the welts just to make it hurt.

I think you have some masochist in you.

He was right, I was a masochist. The things he'd done to me were awful and painful, but I orgasmed even harder than I'd orgasmed last week in the gallery work room. I belonged to this edgier BDSM world, but I didn't understand it yet, or at least I didn't understand where I fit in. Could I keep things physical and sexy the way he preferred? Or would the extreme pain and pleasure trigger extreme emotions, a need to be connected to my Dom?

Fort and I needed to talk. I stepped out of his guest room shower and dried off, shielding my nude body with his sumptuous guest room towel. Who designed bathrooms with glass walls? I put on his robe, a white terrycloth dream sized for a man. I fluffed my damp hair and put on a little lipstick, and decided, after scowling at myself in the mirror, that I shouldn't spend the night. Two could play at this game of keeping a distance, of not falling in love. If I left tonight, he'd see that I could be his masochistic plaything and still live my own life.

I proceeded to the living room determined to keep things short, to sit with him for a moment and tell him how much I had to think about, and thank him for his time. No, not thank him for his time, this hadn't been an office interview. But I'd just breeze in and let him know I had to get going, that I was having brunch with Goodluck in the morning...

"Juliet." As soon as I entered, he ushered me toward the sofa. Instead of a robe like mine, he was in a tee and sweat pants, his head a mess of wet, curly hair. The wine and glasses from earlier had been moved to the coffee table. Mine had been refilled. "Please, sit down."

"I can't stay that long," I started.

"Come sit down. Let's cuddle a minute." He patted the cushion beside him. Okay, I could deal with some cuddle time.

I crossed to the couch and sat, and sucked air through my teeth. My ass hurt like freaking hell. He gave me a sympathetic look and pulled me close to him, and handed me the wine. I wasn't sure if he remembered what I'd said earlier, that I really didn't like it. He probably did. Making me continue to drink it was a form of sadism, but part of me needed it, so I drank.

"Is this expensive wine?" I asked, looking up at him.

He scratched one of his eyebrows. "I guess. I don't generally drink cheap wine."

"I don't even know why I asked that. I think I'm a little in awe of you now. And really scared of you."

He made some weird kind of twitch with his lips, like he wanted to smile but wouldn't. He was still the Dominant during this aftercare cuddle, and I still felt submissive, wrapped in his fluffy robe, in his arms.

"So, did I do okay tonight?" I asked. "Did I pass the test?"

"It wasn't a test." He took a sip of wine and put his glass down. "It was an exploration, so I could figure out what really hurts you and what feels good to you."

So he could more efficiently cause future pain. Of course that's what he'd been doing.

"It all hurt really badly," I said. "Nothing felt good."

"You came. Didn't that feel good?"

A flush bloomed on my cheeks. "I don't know how that happened. I felt so frantic, so hot and throbby, and then..."

He stroked a hand through my hair. "And then the pain turned into something else. It happens that way for some people. The adrenaline and arousal outpaces the negative sensation."

"I don't know. Even now, I can't explain how I felt or why I orgasmed. I just kind of went wild."

He nodded. "You take pain very beautifully. Was there any point where you felt...I don't know. Transported? Heightened by the pain?"

"You mean subspace?"

"That's one word for it."

"It was just pain the whole time," I admitted. "Even when I orgasmed...even then my body was hurting, and I felt scared and crazy, but I came anyway. How does that work?"

"I don't know, but I feel the same way about giving you pain. It shouldn't feel good, but it does." He ran a fingertip up and down my forearm, beneath the softness of the robe. "I think we should have another session and see what else we discover, if you feel up to it."

I nodded, but I also took a huge sip of wine. Then I said *Yes, Sir,* because he was looking at me like I should.

"It won't be any easier than this session, Sparkles. It will probably be harder."

I put down my wine, grimacing. I could tell it was good quality, but it still tasted strange in my mouth. "What's the alternative to another session?" I asked. "Never seeing each other again?"

I took his silence to mean that yes, we would never hang out again. Well, I wanted to hang out. I wasn't ready to separate my path from Fort St. Clair's. I wanted to see where this BDSM adventure would end up.

"I'd like to do another session," I said. "Sir."

He smiled, pulling me into his lap and hugging me against him. I buried my face in his neck. This was as much of a safe word as I got: *Another session, yes or no?* But it made me feel a little more secure about moving forward.

"So...when?" I asked when he released me.

He got that distant look again, the one I couldn't read. "We should wait a week before we meet up again. Process things. You should see how you feel after a couple days have passed."

"And let my ass heal a little?"

"Your ass will be fine." He lifted me, flipped me over, and draped me over his lap. I flailed for a second, but then I went still and let him manhandle me. He pushed up the back of the robe and traced fingers along the edge of my panties; he pressed one of the welts, as I had done in the shower. The same burst of arousal bloomed between my legs. "These marks will be gone by next week," he said. "I'll make more to replace them."

His voice was deep, rough, and matter-of-fact. The bloom became a burn.

"Do you want to go home," he asked, "or would you prefer to sleep here tonight?"

"I think I should probably go." It would have been nice to sleep in his arms, but I needed to be independent and strong, and not fall into another ill-advised "relationship" that wasn't really a relationship.

I went back to the guest room to dress, hiding my new marks under socks, undergarments, and my burgundy dress. When I returned to the living room, he said the car was waiting for me downstairs. I didn't expect him to kiss me now that I was leaving, but he did. It was a probing, demanding kiss, the kind where he grasped my face between his hands. It encapsulated a lot of what we'd done tonight: his controlled force, my straining acquiescence.

"I'll see you in a week," he said, releasing me. "If anything changes, let me know immediately."

"Yes, Sir," I answered, and the kinky title didn't seem so strange anymore.

* * * * *

I fidgeted through my brunch-and-business meeting with Goodluck. I wore my softest, most slovenly clothes, but they weren't soft enough to cushion my sore skin. I tried my best to keep my boss's attention as I went over the numbers from last weekend's art sales, but he was flighty as ever, and my mind was somewhere else. Every time I moved, I felt the welts on my ass. My breasts were sensitive against my bra, and my muscles ached, over-exercised by flinching and tensing in Fort's dungeon.

Of course, I couldn't explain this to Goodluck or any of my friends. I didn't want to confess that my darkest BDSM fantasies now seemed not so dark, compared to the stuff my new Dom was into. When Goodluck asked why I kept shivering in the middle of a sentence, I had to lie and tell him I was coming down with something.

"Coming down with something?" He scoffed. "You haven't been sick in all the years I've known you."

"There's always a first time." *Yes, like my first time in a sadist's dungeon last night...* "I'm just…not feeling like myself this morning. I don't know if I'm getting sick or if it's something else."

He paled. "Have you been eating spinach? They say it makes you stronger, but even the organic kind is full of toxins."

"Where did you hear that?"

"I didn't have to hear it, I can see it on the wilted, stunted leaves. It's criminal, all the poisons and pesticides blanketing our green world. Don't eat spinach, Starcomet. Don't eat any vegetables unless you grow them on your own."

"That sounds like a lot of work." I eyed his plate of waffles, biscuits, and sausage gravy. It wasn't fair that he was thin as a rail. I gestured to my bowl of fruit salad. "Are things like strawberries and melon okay to eat?"

"You'd better hope so." He gave me a mournful look. "Take care of your body, Starcomet. You need it to make your beautiful journey through the cosmos of expression—"

"I'll be fine, Goodluck."

"Why do you keep fidgeting and rubbing your eyes? They're red, by the way. Did you get enough sleep? All our bodies need hours and hours to dream."

I was lost if he started talking about dreams, so I blurted out, "Here's the thing, Goodluck. I met someone. A guy. A man, and we hung out last night. I was out late, that's why my eyes are red."

"You met someone?" He looked astonished.

"I do occasionally interact with people who aren't you. I know it's shocking."

He shook his head. "I didn't mean that. It's just...after Keith... Well, are you dating this person? Because your last relationship didn't end well."

"He's nothing like Keith."

"Thank God. So he's not a corporate scarecrow with a dead, desiccated soul?"

"He's a little bit corporate," I admitted. "But he does other things, too. He came to your gallery opening."

"Oh! Then I approve. How do you think he feels about eagles?"

"He loves eagles." I ate a possibly toxic blueberry, then a grape. "You remember that advertising campaign for Sinclair watches? The ads that your photos appeared in? He was also involved with that."

"Listen, Powerstar." He reached across the table for my hands, pushing my fruit salad out of the way. "I care about you very much. I don't want you to be hurt again. You're a sensitive soul, like me, and we have to be very careful when choosing our lovers. Tonight, before you go to bed, perhaps you should meditate for a few minutes."

"Oh, that's a good idea."

He let go of one hand to gesture toward the ether. "Think about who you are and what you want, and what this new relationship means for your soul. Then I want you to refocus your attention on me, because you work for me and I really need you to keep the business side going. If you start to slack, my agent will start to slack, the gallery owners will slack, they'll all start to slack."

"That went from comforting to scolding very quickly, boss."

He rubbed his temple. "I know. Please don't make me scold you again. I'm not good at it. Punishment has no place in artistic expression."

My eyes flew to his. Did he know something about Fort and me? Were my bruises showing? No, he was just spouting more kooky stuff.

"You know what else has no place in artistic expression?" he added. "Complicated relationships that drain your spirit and energy."

"Still scolding," I said. "Haven't you ever fallen for someone?"

"No. Art is my mistress. And my photographs, well..." He took my hands again, squeezed them. Hard. "They're my lifeblood. I need you to keep all of it rolling. All my balls flying in the air."

Oh God, why did he have to mention his balls? I smothered a laugh.

"If you're worried this new guy is going to steal me away from you and your art, you can stop now," I said, gently extricating my hands. "He's dead set against romance and falling in love, and right now, I am too."

"Ah. Thank God." His pinched, pale expression relaxed into a smile. "I'm so happy to hear that."

"Really, you're happy?" I scowled at him. "I thought you were all about the spirit of love. I thought you wanted me to be happy."

"I do. I want you to be a happy Boundless Art business manager. I'm not so concerned about the rest."

Ugh, so rude. I could have gotten another job. I probably should have gotten a different job years ago, but there was something about Goodluck's rabid self-interest that reassured me. I knew he didn't have the ability to be devious or two-faced. Maybe his sincerity was what drew people to his art.

It occurred to me that Fort was a lot like Goodluck, in that he told me the truth. He'd told me the truth at the Ivy, even though it made me storm out on him. He told me the truth in the back room at the gallery, with his words and his body. He told me the truth when we embarked on our perverted interactions. No relationships. No drama. He laid it all out there, right at the beginning.

And if I felt a little too much for Fort already, well...

It was okay to fall for someone, to harbor a secret crush. It was okay to find new interests.

Even if those new interests cause you to get hurt? Both physically and emotionally?

I was meeting with Fort again in a week, but I still hadn't processed everything I felt. Well, except that I wanted another session, and I hoped it would be even more transformative than the first.

Chapter Fifteen: Fort

I thought of Juliet often, but it was good to wait a week between our sado-masochistic sessions. It gave her body time to heal, and gave me time to step back and recuperate from the way she aroused me. It allowed me to focus on work, to hold meetings and send emails, and accomplish what I needed to do. It also gave me time to plan for Juliet's future sessions.

The only thing it didn't allow me to do was keep up with my friends and partners at The Gallery. Why had I chosen Saturday nights for our sessions, considering it was the only night of the week that The Gallery was open?

Because Juliet's different. She's exciting, and you needed a change from the status quo.

I texted my budding masochist Friday night after I finished dinner.

Good evening, Sparkles. Just checking in. Will I see you tomorrow?

It was the first communication between us since I'd kissed her goodbye and walked her to my door last Saturday night.

Hi. Yes, she typed a few minutes later. *I'm planning to come. Will you send a car around at the same time?*

Yes, I typed, and that was really all I needed to say, but I kept going, picturing her texting with me while propped against her pillows. *Has your ass healed?* I asked.

She sent two blushing emojis. *I've looked at it every day. The welts are mostly faded, shadows now. I'm good as new. Almost.*

Almost?

I still feel the marks a little, like ghosts.

A pause, then I typed, *Haunted by a sadist.*

Something like that.

I pictured her looking over her shoulder with her back to the mirror, inspecting the marks I'd put on her. Was she disappointed when they started to fade? I leaned back on my couch, putting my feet up.

Are you ready to go further this time? You seemed to enjoy yourself last time.

I did. A pause. *Are you going to try to get me into subspace?*

I'm going to try to break you. Agonize you. Make you lose your mind.

Why? You'll be stuck with a crazy submissive.

I laughed at her literal reasoning. So Juliet. Her hair was probably down. She was probably twisting it around her fingers when she wasn't typing to me. Or maybe her fingers were between her legs. Maybe she had on some of those socks...

You'll be bound, I typed after a moment. ***So even if you go crazy, you won't be able to do much damage. I'll probably fuck you extra hard to drive that point home.***

Oh God. That sounds intense. What are you saving for session three?

I'll figure that out. I started to type something, then stopped, then typed it anyway. ***Maybe we could go to The Gallery, if that still interests you.***

The Gallery? Your private club?

Yet. I corrected the typo. ***Yes.***

Why wouldn't it interest me?

I didn't answer for a long time, because I didn't know how she'd react to what I was about to say.

If we go to The Gallery, I typed, ***you aren't only mine. You're submissive to every Dominant there.***

Three dots blinked, then went away. Her reply finally came through. ***How many Dominants are there?***

I let out the breath I'd been holding. If she was curious, then she wasn't repulsed by the idea.

15-20 on a busy night, I answered. ***Sometimes just 4-5. But the number doesn't matter. What matters is the submission. The Gallery is a place of total female submission.***

More than your dungeon? I'm just trying to understand.

She was so sensitive about everything, so thoughtful. I wished I hadn't brought up The Gallery when we weren't face to face.

You won't understand until you go, I typed. *But we're getting ahead of ourselves. Get some rest, and before you turn in tonight, take a good long look at your ass in the mirror.*

Why?

So you'll remember how it looked before I got a hold of it and fucked it all to hell.

Wow, she typed. Three dots flashed and disappeared again, this time twice in a row. *Do you mean literally fucking my ass, or figuratively fucking it up with punishment, or what?* she finally added.

All of the above. I brushed a hand over the front of my pants, quieting my cock. *I'm going to let you go now. See you tomorrow, Sparkles. Sweet dreams.*

I could have asked for a nude photo, maybe a photo of her sexy, sock-clad knees. I could have enticed her to stroke her tits or pussy on camera, but I would have gone crazy when I couldn't touch her myself. I lay back against the couch and thought about how I'd hurt her tomorrow, how I'd make her come. I wondered if she was an anal virgin. I hoped she was, for sadistic reasons. I hoped she was terrified about what was going to happen when I saw her tomorrow.
But not so terrified that she wouldn't come to the session.
I couldn't wait for her to show up.

Chapter Sixteen:
Juliet

I stood outside Fort's door a full five minutes before I found the courage to knock. I waited with my fists clenched, checking in with myself. *Are you sure about this? You can leave now. He'd never know.* But once I left, that was it. Everything was over.

I'd prepared myself for tonight, both mentally and physically. I'd showered, shaved, primped, and donned a black dress and vampy underwear that made me feel wild and sexy. Everything would be okay. I trusted Fort. He hadn't shown any carelessness or lack of control during our previous session, and he'd given me no reason to suspect he'd lose control now. He was the epitome of control. But I was the epitome of uncontrolled emotions and loaded expectations—

Holy shit, Jules. Just knock on the door.

I knocked with as much confidence as I could summon. He answered the door in a coffee-colored sweater and another pair of alarmingly sexy jeans.

"Juliet." His voice rumbled seductively, making my stomach flip as he welcomed me in. He wasn't trying to seduce me, he was just being Fort St. Clair in all his glory: confident, assured, built to torment and fuck. I glanced at his crotch, then stared, like my gaze was caught in a tractor beam. When I looked back at his face, he wore a cocky grin.

"Back for more punishment?" he asked.

"Yes, Sir."

"Good girl. Sit down with me first. Another little drink so you won't be nervous..."

I was about to open my mouth and pass on more red wine when he held up a pink, sparkling spritzer drink. "It sparkles like you," he said. "And it's only mildly alcoholic."

"Like me," I said, smiling in appreciation as I sat on his couch. I liked the lowbrow wine cooler better than last week's expensive merlot, which made me feel cheap and slutty, but it was a kind gesture on his part.

"That's a great dress," he said, settling next to me. He moved the hem up my leg, running a fingertip over my upper thigh. "But where are the socks?"

I took a big sip of my drink. "I thought you might be getting tired of them."

"I'll never, ever be tired of them," he said with a half-smile. "Wear them next time."

"Yes, Sir." I drank too fast and got some spritzer bubbles in my nose. "I suspected you had a sock fetish."

"I've developed an intense sock fetish where you're concerned. But I have a little black dress fetish, too." His caressing fingertips left my thigh. His voice turned lower and huskier. "Are you excited, Juliet?"

"Yes, Sir." I held my glass in my lap, twisting it between my fingers. "Excited and nervous."

"That's perfect. Whenever you're ready—"

"Are you excited?" I asked.

He tilted his head back and leveled me with his direct hazel stare. "If I wasn't, you wouldn't be here." He took my glass and put it on the table, then cupped my head and kissed me, his typical hard, rough, blatantly possessive kiss. When he pulled away, it was to take my elbow in an unforgiving grip. "Let's get started. I've been fantasizing about the best ways to hurt you all week."

When he led me to his library this time, I took less notice of my surroundings. The suspended pendulums that had fascinated me so much the previous week now suggested the shape of butt plugs.

I suppressed the urge to repeat that I was nervous. He probably understood that from the tension in my arm. We entered his dark, otherworldly dungeon and the tension turned to shakes. I took deep breaths to center myself. I wanted this. I'd looked forward to the terror all week.

"Take off your clothes," he said.

I complied, trying to be sultry in spite of my trembling. I hoped he appreciated my pretty black lingerie, but he said nothing as I undid the bra's clasp and then peeled down my panties, lying all of it on the low bench just inside the door.

"Come here," he said when I was done.

I went to him, slouching gratefully into his arms when he opened them.

"Same as last week," he murmured against my ear. "I'm going to hurt you. I'm going to make you very uncomfortable tonight, but you're going to be safe. Do you trust me?"

"Yes, Sir."

He drew me back and I looked into his eyes, into sadism and mayhem, but also warmth. Something inside me melted. I felt bonded to him and his uncomfortable perversions in a deep way. He returned my gaze, going very still for a moment before he grasped my neck and yanked me toward him for a kiss. He forced his lips and tongue against mine, demanding submission to his will. *Yes*, I said in my mind. *Yes, Sir. Yes, Sir. Yes, Fort, I'm one hundred percent in.*

By the end of his savage kiss, my anxieties were gone. My sweaty palms had dried, and when he led me toward a black resin butterfly chair and pressed on my shoulders, I went to my knees with no resistance at all.

"I'm going to get some things ready," he said. "I want you to kneel there and think about surrender, about accepting whatever I choose to do to you. You belong to me for the next hour."

"Yes, Sir."

I felt like a very sexual being, his object, waiting for him on my knees. I only half-watched him making preparations, because it was too much for me to take it all in. I noted that he got a paddle and whip and set them by the spanking bench, and that he got clamps and a riding crop to set by the butterfly chair. Then he went to a chest of drawers and took out a medium-length dildo that graduated in thickness from the narrow tip to the wider root, which ended in a metal connector. He carried this to the chair and screwed it onto a bolt on the seat, testing it afterward to be sure it was secure.

I swallowed hard. I practically felt the blood drain from my face as he turned back to me.

"How experienced are you with anal sex?" he asked.

"Not experienced," I answered, my mouth dry. "At all."

"That's okay. After today, you will be."

He took a condom from the same dark chest of drawers, unrolling it over the dildo, all the way to the base. After that, he applied a layer of clear lubricant to the condom, so the whole thing shone with slickness. Next he brought the tube of lubricant over to me.

"Lean forward," he said. "Forehead on the floor, ass in the air."

I hesitated a moment, because once this all started, it wasn't stopping. He put a hand on my shoulder, a reminder he was in charge, and that made it easier to fold my body forward and lift my hips. I was rewarded with some sharp spanks to my backside, followed by a couple of hard squeezes. I gasped and tried to stay still as he parted my ass cheeks. I heard the squelch of the tube and felt cold liquid drip onto my asshole. Then, holy shit, I felt his finger spreading the lube around my hole. I made a small, panicked sound as one finger delved inside, pressing the slickness deeper.

"The important thing to remember," he said as he worked, "is that you need to stay open to whatever I shove into your ass. No matter how bad and uncomfortable it feels, you have to take it. Do you understand me?"

"Yes, Sir."

"Good girl. Stay here a moment. Don't lift your head. Keep that ass in the air."

My knees trembled as he left me. I heard him cross the room, heard water running in the sink. He was still fully dressed, and I was naked, so naked and vulnerable. When he returned he made me stand, then oriented me in front of the chair and held my panicked gaze.

"We'll go slow," he said. "But the shaft goes up your ass."

He had me spread my legs so I was straddling the narrow part of the chair, then ordered me to pull my cheeks apart and lower myself onto the shaft. I didn't know how I could be so wet when I was dying of humiliation and fear. I squatted down until the tip of the shaft poked my ass. It was narrow enough to slide in a couple of inches. He waited as I paused, acclimating myself to the novel sensation of having a dildo up my butt.

"I'll let you go at your own pace," he said, "but I expect you to completely seat yourself on the shaft. Take your time. You can do it."

Oh God, that was easy for him to say. I inched backward, feeling the shaft slide deeper. It hadn't hurt at first, but as I sunk lower, I felt my ass stretch to accommodate the added width.

"It's starting to hurt," I said through my teeth.

"It's not going to feel comfortable, but it's not that thick." His tone was firm and immovable. "You can take it, even if it hurts."

I pressed down again, feeling my hole stretch around the dildo even as it ached at the invasion. At last my ass cheeks rested against the chair's base, and I was fully impaled. I could feel the shaft deep inside me, holding me trapped in a way cuffs couldn't.

I still got cuffed, though. He spread my legs over the chair's "wings" and secured each thigh with a strap around the top of my knee. My wrists were buckled into cuffs at the sides of the chair. I was bound tight, my tensing ass impaled, my breasts and pussy exposed to his meditative gaze.

"Now..." He picked up the nipple clamps. "Let's see what we can do to make you squirm."

I eyed the clamps, already flinching. Sitting still on the shaft was bad enough. Once he made me start squirming... I steeled myself as he pinched my nipples, preparing them to be clamped.

"I'm using more severe clamps than last time," he said, "since this will be a more severe session. The good thing is that you're too bound to fight when the pain comes."

I gave a whine of fear as he opened the first clamp, which was indeed larger and heavier than the previous pair he'd used. He closed it on my nipple and my whole body curled in a wave of white-hot agony. My hips surged upward, the dildo sliding in my ass as I bucked up and down.

"That was just one," he said as I gasped. "Don't be a baby. You came here of your own free will, Sparkles. Suck it up."

He applied the other clamp and my ass contracted again on the dildo impaling me. He gave the clamps' connecting chain a tug, making me squeal at the added pinch of pressure, then left it to dangle between my breasts.

I wanted to beg him to stop, but I also didn't want him to stop, because even though it hurt, it excited me. I took deep breaths, trying to process the torturous nipple clamps as my ass squeezed at the pain. So much for being an anal virgin. I already felt like I was being fucked there. A butt plug, at least, had a narrowed neck at the end, before the flange. This dildo-chair arrangement kept me open as wide as the dildo's base, all the time.

Like being fucked. Because he's probably going to fuck you there by the end of this hour.

I couldn't think about that now, because I knew the girth of his cock was more than the size of the dildo. I studied his face, trying to guess what was going on in his sadistic brain. He picked up the crop, a long, braided handle tipped by a wicked-looking leather slapper. "This won't leave any lasting marks," he said, running it up my inner thigh. "So don't worry about that."

He started flicking my inner thighs with the slapper. It didn't hurt an excruciating amount, but it hurt enough to make me jump, and yes, squirm. As I pressed back from the pain, I felt the shaft slide deeper in my ass. When I threw my head back, gritting my teeth, the crop attacked my breasts. I shifted from side to side, trying to evade the stinging blows, but my arms were bound and each jerk made the clamps bite harder.

"This is awful," I cried. "It really hurts."

"Poor baby." He smiled as he said this, enjoying my distress. He returned to my thighs, flicking them hard, repeatedly, not hard enough to leave bruises but hard enough for a searing heat to build between my legs. My thighs turned pink, then scarlet as the torture continued.

"Ow, ow, owww." I barely felt the shaft anymore, the pain in my thighs was so much greater, but the smallest shift increased the clamps' pressure and made my nipples scream. I tried to pull my legs together, but the straps over my knees prevented me from moving them more than an inch or two.

"No," he said, tapping the crop beneath my chin. "Look at me. Legs stay open, exposing yourself to me. You're mine."

"Yes, Sir," I replied with tears in my eyes. "But it hurts."

"I don't care. Let me see your pussy."

I obeyed, arching my hips as far forward as the straps would allow. He paused to slide his fingers through my pussy lips. I was *so wet*. I must have been soaking his chair, my juices as shiny as the lube he'd put on the shaft.

"Ah, you want this," he said, sounding satisfied. "You love to be hurt."

I shook my head, grimacing through tears, but my body obviously loved it on some level. He shoved two rough fingers inside my pussy, plunging them in and out as I bobbed on the shaft in my ass. Just like that, I was about to climax. He must have known because he shook his head with a wicked gleam in his eyes.

"No, you're not allowed to come yet. I'm not done with you."

He took his fingers away, stood, and replaced his caressing digits with a prod of the crop against my slit. "What are we learning about Juliet today?" he asked. "That she's an anal slut? That she likes anal better than getting fucked in her cunt?"

I shook my head. I didn't think that was true, but he only laughed, then he flicked my pussy three times with the crop. Left, right, middle. With each flick, I tossed on the impaling dildo, trying to escape the punishment. Then he crossed to my other side and grasped my neck with one hand, making me hold still. More force, more dominance, and then agonizing slaps of fire on my pussy. He swung the crop hard, catching my pussy lips and my clit, making them burn. When I tried to twist away, he held my neck harder, running his hand across my throat.

"Take it," he said in a low, encouraging voice.

Whack. Whack. Oww, oh my God, I can't. Whack. Whack. Whack.

My legs shook and strained against their straps. My breasts quaked as my whole core jerked. When he finally stopped torturing my pussy, my body collapsed. He didn't let go of my neck until he kissed me, catching my gasp of relief in his mouth. One of my tears spilled over and he caught it with his tongue, licking it toward my temple. As I whimpered, he kissed my cheekbone and my ear, running fingers through my hair.

"Yes, cry, my horny little victim. If only you didn't enjoy this so much. You don't know what to feel, do you?"

I gazed at him through wet, wary eyes. He was right. I didn't know how to feel. I didn't know if I loved this or hated it, or both.

He drew away, laid the crop aside, and took off the nipple clamps. My whole body fell limp, to the point where the clamps' removal hardly registered, at least until the blood rushed into the newly freed tips and set them on fire.

"Open your mouth," he said. "And your eyes."

I looked up to find him straddling my bound body, his cock jutting from his pants.

"Open wider," he said, giving my cheek a quick slap and taking my chin in his hands. "I need to come, Juliet, because you're so fucking sexy. I need to come now so I can last longer when I'm fucking your ass."

"Oh." I wasn't all there. Was this subspace? I opened my mouth and swallowed against the pressure as he eased his cock between my lips. I couldn't take all of him, and I made begging hums of protest as he pressed beyond my comfort zone. A cough, a gag. A hand on my shoulder and his answering laugh.

"You can do it," he said. "Relax and accept it. This is what's happening to you right now. You don't have a choice."

Just as he'd filled my ass to an uncomfortable degree, he filled my mouth and throat, and I was forced to blink through my discomfort, crying tears of strain. In and out, deeper each time, never varying his rhythm except to give a little extra jab whenever I gagged.

"Suck me deeper, that's right." He grasped my hair, pushing my head against the back of the chair with each thrust. "I'm going to come so fucking hard, right in the back of your throat."

He was definitely going to come in the back of my throat, since he'd shoved in as far as my physiology would allow, and seemed to prefer hanging out there. I struggled now and again, bouncing on the dildo in my ass as tears streamed from my eyes.

The awful clamps were gone but my ass was still impaled and stretched, and now my mouth was too. I smelled his male scent, tasted pre-cum on the back of my tongue. I'd given plenty of blowjobs as a sub, given my Doms leisurely, fawning attention, but in this case it was all his doing, pure force, my throat being taken at his pace. My hands strained at my sides, but I had no way to stop him from plundering my mouth, no control, no way to protect myself. I had no way to plead with him to give me a rest and let me breathe.

When he finished, shooting ropes of cum down my throat, I gagged hard and swallowed, barely registering his satisfied growl. He pulled back, fisting his cock, and stared down at my tear-and-snot riddled face with a feral expression. He came back to himself a moment later, transformed to the controlled man I trusted. He got a towel and wiped my face with excessive care after fucking it so soundly, and held a glass of cool water to my lips.

"Take a minute," he said when I finished drinking. "Then we'll move on to part two."

Part two? I'd barely survived the first part. My pussy smarted with erotic longing, my clit aching for any contact besides the stinging bite of the crop. My ass clenched intermittently on the shaft, reminding me that I was no longer a virgin in any way, not by a long shot.

While I rested, Fort cleaned the crop and returned it to the wall, and placed the clamps back in the drawer he'd taken them from. Only then did he come to the chair and undo my cuffs and straps, and help me rise. I gingerly lifted my hips from the slippery shaft, glad he was giving me his arm to balance on.

"Over here," he said, leading me to the padded spanking bench on the other side of the space. It was actually two parallel benches, one low and the other higher. I bent over the high one as soon as he applied pressure to my shoulders. The bench was sturdy, providing support for my stomach and hips.

"Now spread your legs. A little wider." His fingers circled my ankles, buckling them into cuffs bolted to the floor. I rested my hands on the lower bench in front of me, testing my legs. I couldn't move them one millimeter, couldn't close them. My ass felt empty and sore. My pussy throbbed, still hurting from the crop, and yet bizarrely ripe for more sensation.

Fort walked around the front of me, taking each wrist and stretching it as far along the lower bench as it would go. He ratcheted the cuffs into place, so when he finished I was spread eagled, bent at the waist. A quick check confirmed what I already suspected—that my hands couldn't move with any more freedom than my feet.

I looked up at him, getting a chill from the satisfied, assessing glance he returned. What now? He'd put his cock away after he came in my mouth, so I knew I wasn't getting fucked yet. He picked up the long, thin, rectangular paddle he'd selected earlier, and I squeezed my eyes shut.

"Time for some paddling," he said. "Just remember to breathe when the pain feels like too much."

Oh, breathing. That would solve everything. I yanked at my bonds, squirming in a short protest before his hand touched my back.

"Be still." His voice reverberated in my pussy, as did his warning: "You can't get away."

I heard his arm rise in the quiet of the room, over the frantic huffing of my breath. The paddle connected with a crack, and I jumped, but didn't shriek or scream. The first three licks were painful but bearable. The paddle was light enough for him to hit me with a pretty good windup, and it imparted an agonizing sting, but nothing fiery like the dowel he'd used on me at the end of our last session. He stopped between each lick and squeezed my ass, tempering the sting with rough pinches. Checking for redness? I trembled and tried to squeeze my legs shut, to no avail.

The lighter strokes were a warm-up, of course. I realized that as soon as the actual paddling started, as soon as he drew back the implement and hit me full force. I let out a wail, my whole body tensing and jerking. Another blow, and another, right on top of each other, blazing across both my burning cheeks. I thrashed in the cuffs, my wails breaking into sobs.

No matter how hard I pulled my arms, no matter how hard I tried to kick, I couldn't escape his rapid, brutal paddling. The onslaught probably only lasted a minute, but by the end I was breathless from screaming and begging him to stop.

"I can't...I can't..." My voice broke. "I can't take that. It was too much."

"I decide if it's too much, remember?" His hand brushed over my cheeks, a light, ticklish touch after the horrible paddling. "You only have to take it. You don't have any choice."

I'll be damned if his words didn't heat up my pussy almost as much as my clenching, sizzling ass. The bench pressed against my pelvis, stimulating my clit, and I started to grind against it, mostly to get the pain to dissipate faster. He whacked me with the paddle, eliciting another scream.

"Keep those hips still. When I want you to come, you little maso-slut, I'll make you come. I choose when, not you. I always get to choose, and if you're a bad girl, you won't get to come at all."

You little maso-slut. He didn't say it in a mean way, but I still started bawling. The idea that he might not let me come... "How much longer?" I pleaded. "How much more will you hurt me?"

"As much as I think you need to be hurt. Now shut your mouth. The only words you need to say during our sessions are 'Yes, Sir.' Understood?"

I sniffled and sobbed, and squealed when the paddle connected again.

"Understood?" he prompted in a more dangerous voice.

"Yes, Sir!"

I knew this was part of the game. I knew we were playing, I knew we were both turned on, but I was also going a little bit out of my mind. When he picked up the whip, I cried harder, cried like a literal baby. He held the whip in front of my face and grabbed a handful of my hair with the other hand.

"We're almost done," he said in a low, soothing voice, even as he wrenched my hair until I whimpered. "I know you're hurting, but you'll be fine. Sink down into the pain. Let it rule you for a while."

He meant, *Let* me *rule you for a while*, and I wanted that, but I didn't know how much more I could take. I couldn't think about what had come before, or what might come after. When he stepped behind me with the whip, I could only thrash helplessly and whine like a trapped animal.

"I haven't even started yet," he chided, tapping my ass. This whip was a little sturdier than the one he'd used on me last time. I wondered if it would hurt more or less than the dowel, and how many welts I'd be looking at in the mirror tomorrow.

"Please," I begged, the quavering word leaking from my throat. "Please don't."

"Such good manners," he said, "but I think I will." He brought the whip down across the middle of my ass cheeks. I tensed up as I had with the paddle, flailing, going up on my toes, trying to survive the burn. He whipped another fiery line, and another. I'd hoped he'd stop at three like the dowel, but it wasn't to be.

"I want your ass cheeks to be nice and raw before I shove my cock between them." *Whack!* "It'll hurt more that way. Anal's only good if it hurts a little, or in your case, a lot." *Whack!* "You know why it's going to

hurt a lot, baby? Because your asshole's so tiny, and my cock is so big."
Whack!

I hated the way I was crying, the way I was losing my shit, but the whip hurt *so bad*, and unlike the dowel, he crossed strokes over other strokes, compounding the stinging. My ass felt like a tic-tac-toe board of pain, and he was still playing. Begging wouldn't stop him, and I didn't have a safe word, but I was glad, because I would have used it a million times already and I wouldn't have been able to reach this crazy, maddening place where my pussy was as alive as the whip against my flesh.

That didn't stop me from begging "Please, please stop" over and over until he finally lowered his arm. My ass was wrecked. I cried out when he grasped my cheeks and smacked them. "Am I bleeding?"

"No, Sparkles, you're not." Not an ounce of pity or tenderness, just pure sadistic sarcasm. He left me to sob for a few minutes, my tears falling onto the lower bench as he crossed the room. When he returned, I heard a cap opening, and felt the cold drip of more lube on my ass.

"It's time for you to get fucked in your asshole," he said, jamming a finger inside me. "You want that, don't you? A woman your age should have had tons of anal by now. You should let men fuck all your holes. That's what they're there for, aren't they?"

"Yes, Sir," I bawled.

He took my hips and held them hard. "Don't try to pull away. Don't clench or squeeze to impede me. Let me in the way you're supposed to. It's high time you learned how this feels."

I clenched my hands into fists as he pressed the head of his cock against my ass. I'd hoped it might still be a little stretched from my time in the butterfly chair, but it felt like I was being pried open all over again, only this time, he was so much thicker.

"Oww, owww!" I jerked away on pure instinct, and was punished with a yank of my hair. He twisted his fingers in my curls and leaned over me, pushing his cock a little deeper. My ass ached with dull, stretching fire.

"Let it happen," he said, as gentle as his cock was brutal. "This is what happens to masochistic sluts like you. You like this. You want it. You deserve all this pain, don't you?"

When I didn't answer, he squeezed my hair until I squealed, "Yes, Sir." His cock slid in me another couple of inches, and I tensed, praying for him to stop before he split me open. It wasn't hurting as badly as when he started, but I still didn't think I could take any more inside me. The impalement I felt in the chair was nothing. This was a hard, thick shaft of Fort's flesh pulsing inside me, sliding through lubrication that eased the way even when I didn't want any more inside. I clutched at the bench as he drove the rest of the way in, until I felt his balls dangling against my pussy lips.

"That's more like it." His low, feral voice communicated sexual pride. He let go of my hair and bumped his hips against my punished ass cheeks, holding my waist so I couldn't jerk to the side. "This is submission, Juliet. Hurting and straining to get away, except that you can't, and you like that." His fingers crept up my sides and around my breasts to torture my nipples as he withdrew his cock and thrust in again. He started a rhythm, in, out, in, out, moving along sensitive walls with so much girth I could feel the crown of his cock sliding past my entrance, along with the pulse of his veins.

"Do you like this?" he asked. "Do you like getting your ass fucked?"

I said no, because I needed it to remain a struggle. I needed to not like it, even though it was feeling hotter by the second. I squirmed, trying to get away. He chuckled and withdrew from me, leaving me empty and scared. Going back for the whip?

Instead he returned with another bottle of lubricant, this one runnier and thinner. He squeezed some into his hand and sluiced his fingers through my dripping pussy folds to my clit. The burn started at once, a hot, nagging sting that felt the same as getting hot sauce on your tongue.

"It's a form of ginger oil," he said. "Specifically cooked up for submissives with cocks in their ass, to show that things could always be worse."

I wiggled against the tingling, and clenched as it intensified, but nothing helped, and he wasn't done. He went to the chest of drawers and returned with a wooden clip a couple of inches in length. He coated it with the oil and held it up to my face. "Sometimes this goes on bad girls' tongues, but tonight it's going on your clit."

"You can't," I said. The wood was sturdy, and the spring looked hardcore. He was going to break me when the burning oil already had me bucking in agony. "Please don't."

"*Please don't,*" he mimicked in a high voice. "Be a good girl, Sparkles. Let it all work. You'll be coming like a banshee three minutes from now."

I shook my head as he crossed behind me and yanked up my hips to get at my pussy. He pinched the fold of skin protecting my clit, tugged it back and applied the wooden torture device to my sensitized flesh. The pain was immediate and unbearable. I tried to jiggle it off, bouncing on my toes, but it held on tight.

"I can't. I can't!"

He came around to look at my face, his eyes hazy with perverse satisfaction. I stared at this man, so beautiful, so deviant, with his gaze fixed on mine. I blinked and cried, and gritted my teeth as my pussy tingled and ached. I wanted him inside me more than anything in the world. I *needed* him inside me. I needed him to finish this, to take me wherever it was he could take me. Our eyes held, then he let out a soft breath.

"You can come whenever you like now," he said, "but only while my cock's in your ass."

After those words, he stepped behind me and positioned his cock against my asshole again. This time he slid steadily in, not leaving time for me to accustom myself to the invasion, but my body had knowledge it hadn't had before, knowledge about relaxing and floating along with the stretch and ache. It felt as tight and scary as before, but now I wanted it because it felt right. It felt right to be fucked there. It felt right to be hurt.

After a couple minutes of steady, firm thrusting, I found myself pressing my ass back against his cock rather than trying to shrink from it. I found my legs bracing rather than trembling, and my fingers spread wide in pleasure rather than clenched in a fist. The clip on my clit still hurt like hell—he jogged it with his balls each time he buried himself inside me—but it was a hurt that made my body soar.

I felt stretched in every way, stretched over the bench, stretched around his cock, stretched in my arms and legs as I tried to withstand his assault. My scalp smarted where he'd pulled my hair, and my pussy was still on fire, but an orgasm started to build inside me, firmly centered around his cock.

Each inch inside made my pleasure flare, and each pang as he withdrew fanned the need higher. I felt things happening all over my body, but what I felt the most, and what finally tipped me into climax, was his hard, thick cock deep inside me, taking me where no one else had ever gone. Taking me without care, as if it was his right, his Dominant prerogative. No gentleness, no allowance for my needs or sensibilities. It drove me wild with perverse sexual energy.

And then everything let go.

I'd been crying for what seemed like an hour, yet I cried some more through the intense orgasm as it spread through my ass and pelvis, and up to my sore nipples and breasts. The orgasm I had in our last session had been my strongest to date, yet this one put it to shame. I flailed over the bench, squeezing my ass around his cock as the waves overtook me, zinging sensation screaming along every nerve and vein.

He'd told me I could only come with his cock in my ass, but as I lay there shuddering I thought to myself, *how did I ever come any other way?*

And that scared me. I dropped my head between my arms, going limp as he rode my ass a couple more minutes and banged a growling climax against my tic-tac-toe emblazoned cheeks. As my orgasm's pleasure ebbed away, the clip on my clit hurt more than ever, but the burn in my pussy had finally calmed down. I must have washed all his evil, stinging oil away with my pussy juices when I came.

After he pulled away, he gave the clit clip one last, ruthless flick before removing it. I let out a sigh I hadn't realized I was holding. When he reached to undo my arms, I looked up at him, anguished. "Not yet," I said. "Please. I can't. Not yet." I only meant that I was still stuck in our scene, that I didn't feel safe enough to be released yet. His expression darkened with concern.

"Are you okay?" He wiped my tearful eyes. "Too much? Too far?"

"No." My tears increased, not dungeon-sex tears, but confused, overemotional tears. "It wasn't too much. I loved it." I tried to pull myself together, but I couldn't. "I loved what we just did," I said in a higher voice. "What does that mean?"

"It means you shouldn't be upset, because I enjoyed it too." His voice was kinder now, the way it hadn't been before. He ran a hand up and down my back, steady, warm pressure. "Let me know when you're ready for me to let you go."

He meant the physical bonds, but I was thinking of emotional bonds. They were forming despite my best efforts, and I couldn't seem to keep them in check. He waited ten minutes for me, stroking his hand along my spine and between my shoulders until I calmed and came back to wherever I'd been before I left. He took me to the guest room shower and stayed with me this time, cleaning me up when I was too spooked to touch my skin.

"I left a few marks," he said, turning me around to inspect my ass. "Good ones. But nowhere they'll show."

I wasn't even sure I cared about that. What if the world saw the marks?

But I couldn't let them show. People would judge. My work associates and friends, and Goodluck...

"I think you should stay here tonight," he said as we dried off after our shower. "In fact, you'd better stay in my room. You might need me, or I might want to fuck you again in the middle of the night."

I couldn't imagine more sex with Fort. At the same time, I couldn't imagine not having more sex with Fort, night and day, 24/7. I was still somewhat dazed, so I agreed to sleep in his bed. I didn't even put my clothes back on.

It didn't seem right to have any barriers between us after what had just gone on.

Chapter Seventeen: Fort

Beautiful, exhausted Jewels. I snuck from under the covers after she fell asleep, and drifted around my house for a while, pacing off nervous energy. Was it a mistake to let her sleep over, in my bed, no less? I felt I didn't have a choice. She'd bought in to my perversions so bravely, accepting all the shit I did to her. Not just accepting it, but letting herself like it. I loved watching her come.

But I also loved watching her cry.

She wasn't like the women who frequented The Gallery, who drenched themselves in tears as they chased their own perverted fantasies. Juliet cried from real pain, and persisted through that pain to her pleasure on the other side, and I never would have known she had that ability if I hadn't kept coming back to her. Maybe that was why I kept coming back, why things had progressed so quickly once I gave in to my urges. She was sleeping in my fucking bed. What the hell?

I went into the dungeon to put everything away and collect her clothes. Had I done too much to her too fast? I'd been careful. She'd complained that her ass hurt when she slid beneath my sheets, but I knew I hadn't done any lasting damage to her body when I'd de-virginized her asshole.

I walked down the hall and spread her clothes out on my guest bed. Without thinking, I laid them on the side where I'd handcuffed her the night we met.

Don't get melodramatic about this one, Forsyth. Don't fall in love with her just because she's good at taking pain, just because she's beautiful when she cries those real tears. The love thing has never worked for you before.

I blew out the breath I was holding and returned to my bedroom, sliding in beside Juliet. I rested a hand on her ass, and it was still there in the morning, unconsciously tracing the whip welts I'd made. I came awake surprised that she was there. Her side of the bed was a shambles of rumpled sheets and overturned pillows, which became even more rumpled when she executed a huge stretch.

"Ow," she said. "My ass hurts."

"That's what happens to bad girls," I said, bringing her awake with a slap to her sore bottom. "Want to go to my dungeon again? A morning session this time?"

She scooted away. "Please, not yet."

"I'm joking. Are you ready to get up?"

"Sure, I'll... I'll just..." She looked around like I expected her to dress and exit.

"Your robe's still in the guest bathroom," I said. "There's no hurry. I'll make you some tea."

"You have tea?"

"Now I do." I stood, angling away from her so she wouldn't see my rigid morning wood. My body wanted to ravish her, but my mind knew a cuddly morning fuck would send too confusing a message. "Meet me in the kitchen, Sparkles."

It wasn't a big deal to pick up some tea to make for her with my coffeemaker. The machine was designed to do both. While I made coffee and tea and waited for her, I set out some other things on the counter, breakfast rolls and cold cuts, and a few different types of olives. I fucking loved olives. What was taking her so long? She must have been investigating her new marks in the mirror.

"There you are," I said when she finally appeared. Yeah, she was blushing.

"Good morning." She brushed a hand through her hair. "*Late* morning. What time is it?"

"Eleven o'clock. You missed church."

She laughed at my joke and slid onto the bar stool next to me. I enjoyed watching her little gasp of pain as she settled on her sore hindquarters. I'd paddled her hard for a beginner, and whipped her over top of it, eighteen neat stripes. I'd been hoping for twenty, but since I didn't allow my partners to use safe words, I had to err on the side of caution. For her, eighteen had been enough.

I pushed over a steaming cup of tea. "It's your basic Earl Grey. I hope that's all right."

"It's wonderful, thank you," she said.

"Milk or sugar?"

"Both, Sir, please." The *Sir* fell out of her mouth so easily, bringing a jolt of lust to my cock and balls. I felt very "Sir" this morning, because she was so tousled and sedate. I wondered if I'd disturbed her sleep last night, tracing my fingers over her whip marks.

"What do you have planned for today?" I asked.

"Well, since I already missed church..." She wrinkled her nose. "Just kidding. I usually spend my Sundays hanging out and catching up on email. Sometimes my boss and I go out for brunch."

"Did I make you miss that?" My words sounded gruffer than I meant them to. "Have something to eat."

We both fed ourselves for a moment, sloppy Sunday-morning noshing with fingers, interspersed with sips of coffee and tea. Meanwhile, all the things I'd done to her the night before banged around in my head. The black chair, the paddle, the clit clip and ginger oil while she was tied down over the spanking bench...

"Are you all right?" she asked. "You seem restless."

"I'm fine. How are you this morning, Sparkles?"

She shifted on her sore butt. "I'm okay." Then everything else spilled out of her like a gushing river. "I mean, I feel okay, but also a little scared of you, and I feel... I feel changed. It's like, last night, you turned me into a different person, which was really crazy, but it's also amazing that you can do that. Did you mean to do that? I mean, was that what you wanted?"

I blinked at her. "What kind of person did I turn you into?"

"A sexually voracious person."

"I think you were that before."

She shook her head. "I wasn't. Not...in that way."

I wasn't sure I believed that, but I could understand that she felt insecure now, in the light of day.

"Was I okay last night?" she asked. "I mean, do you think I'm good at this stuff? Compared, you know, to the other women you do this with, at your club? What's it called again?"

"The Gallery. You should remember that, since you work for an artist."

"Yeah, that's true."

I studied her a moment, rubbing my forehead. "Here's what I wanted out of last night: to make you cry, and to feel sexual pleasure. Both of those things happened as far as I could see, so from my perspective, it was a great session."

"Oh." A little of the anxiety left her expression.

"Do you want to meet again?" I asked, slicing an olive and sticking it in my mouth with a piece of bread.

She stared at me. "Yes. Of course. Why wouldn't I?"

I chewed and swallowed. "Think about what I did to you. I strapped you down with a dildo in your rectum. I punished your pussy for the pure thrill of seeing you scream. I called you a slut and tore up your ass so bad that you almost passed out."

"I didn't almost pass out."

"Your whole body was shaking."

"Yeah," she said. "Because it hurt like hell. You should see what it feels like."

"I know what it feels like. There's nothing I do to you that I haven't tried on myself first."

"Even the chair?" she asked, raising her eyebrows.

I raised my brows in response. "You think a pervert like me's never had something up his ass? If you prefer to play without safe words, you have to know how things feel."

"I respect that," she said. "I guess there's more to being a sadist than recklessly hurting people."

"Recklessly hurting people isn't the objective." I looked into her eyes, so blue, so utterly lacking in guile. "So I didn't go too far last night?" I pressed. For some reason, I needed to hear her say it.

129

Instead she asked, "How did you find out that you liked to hurt people? You know, sexually?"

"You're changing the subject."

"Please tell me," she said in a begging voice. "I like what we do together, I really, really do, but I'm curious how you got into it. How you discovered it was what you liked."

I took a sip of my rapidly cooling coffee and put it down with a grimace. "It wasn't a discovery, so much. I fantasized from a young age about hurting the pretty girls I liked, and making them cry. Not that I wasn't taught to respect women," I said, moving toward my coffeemaker. "I knew the difference between reality and fantasy, but my fantasies..."

I stared down at the counter, remembering torrid afternoons stroking myself, mulling depraved scenarios that were worse than any available porn. "I used to daydream about the feeling of a woman struggling under me, trying to escape. It started when I was very young, when I didn't realize those urges were sexual. I thought something was wrong with my soul. My parents never hit me, never emotionally or sexually abused me, but these fantasies of force and dominance excited me from my earliest years. Not just force and dominance, but hurting a beautiful woman to the point of tears. God, I was so afraid to let it show." I laughed, watching my coffeemaker as a fresh cup hissed out. "I thought I was a psychopath. Imagine my relief the first time I stumbled onto an S&M site and realized I wasn't the only one, not by a long shot."

"I bet you went crazy when you were finally able to fulfill those fantasies."

"To an extent. I started learning and exploring, mostly online at first, and at clubs like Underworld. Eventually I connected with a woman who was willing to let me experiment, and experienced enough to show me the ropes."

"Do you still keep in touch with her?" she asked.

I snorted. "No. She was only doing me a favor. She thought I was a jerk."

"I don't think you're a jerk," she said, popping an olive into her mouth. "I'm glad I met you, and I'm glad you're showing me all this stuff. I feel like we're just on the edge of things." Her lips curved in a smile. "You know, potential energy."

I thought of the pendulums in my office, thought of all the world's energy measured in Joules. I wasn't sure it would add up to the way she affected me last night.

Meanwhile, I stared at my hands and thought of all the energy they represented, all the questionable things they could do. I'd shoved my fingers in her tender, virgin asshole. I'd whipped her and called her a maso-slut.

I'd also made her come so fucking hard.

"If you want to keep going, we can certainly go deeper in our explorations," I said after a heavy silence. "Do these Saturday sessions work well, or would you prefer some other day of the week?"

She shrugged. "I'm flexible. My evenings are free, except when Goodluck has an art opening."

"Why don't you come over tomorrow evening for dinner, so I can tell you more about The Gallery?" I heard the words even as I resisted saying them. "I think you'd enjoy going there." *And other people would enjoy you, too.* For the first time in a long time, the idea didn't make me hot.

"Dinner sounds wonderful." She ate the last olive on my plate. "But are you sure they'll let me into The Gallery? Considering I've only recently migrated over from the slap-and-tickle world?"

"If I vouch for you, they'll let you in."

She scooted to the edge of her chair, then winced as she was reminded of last night's activities. "So, we could go tonight if we wanted? Or tomorrow night?"

"No." I put on my stern Dom face. "We can't go to The Gallery until we've had a long talk about what goes on there, and made some preparations. There's a uniform you have to be fitted for—"

"A uniform? What kind of uniform?"

"A sexy uniform. And we couldn't go tomorrow, anyway. The Gallery's only open on Saturday nights."

"Oh." She drank the last of her tea, then looked at me with a confused expression. "But you spent the last two Saturday nights with me."

"Indeed. I think I mentioned before that I find your over-the-knee socks both fascinating and irresistible. The fact that you have a decent pain tolerance makes it even better."

"Decent? Just decent?" She pushed her plate away and pretended to storm off, but I caught her wrist and pulled her into my arms. Her scent and sweetness enveloped me as I grasped her hair and pressed a kiss to her neck. She breathed out against my skin, then nipped my earlobe between her teeth.

"Sparkles," I murmured, going instantly hard. "You say you're afraid of me, but I don't think you are."

"No, I am, but I like being afraid."

My fingers curled around her shoulders, delving under the robe. I felt her body tense as I kissed up the line of her neck and opened my teeth against her jaw. She melted when I grasped her around the waist. I was strong enough to break her in half, but I didn't want to. Her gorgeous surrender was enough.

"Potential and kinetic energy," she said, pressing her breasts against my chest. "Can we have sex again?"

I gathered the robe up above her waist so I could squeeze her ass. She yelped, squirming. I grew harder still, but I said, "No. Maybe tomorrow night." I wanted sex, but I didn't trust myself to fuck her at this moment. I released her with a sharp crack to her bottom. "Go put your clothes on, and then you need to be on your way."

* * * * *

I had to get her to The Gallery, so I could have my fill of her without these one-on-one moments that were so fraught with her careless emotions. She insisted she was afraid of me, but I was afraid of her too, afraid she'd misunderstand my capacity for relationships and make me break her heart. Breaking a heart like hers would be like felling a California Redwood. You'd have to be a real asshole to damage something so beautiful and rare.

I didn't want to be that asshole.

At the same time, I couldn't really picture her at The Gallery. It was a place for people who loved themselves more than they loved each other, for people who expressed their emotions through whip marks and screams. Not that the Dominants and submissives at The Gallery didn't care for each other—they just cared more about getting off. Maybe she'd hate it.

Well, if she hated it, she wouldn't have to go back.

I finally got my emotional little maso out of my apartment so I could regroup, and shake off the tension she brought to my life. I sat on my sofa and leaned back, opening my fly. My dick was a marvel of rigidity. I had it bad for her, which was okay. Passion was fun. I'd eventually get over my lusty obsession and everything would be okay.

I worked my hand up and down my length, taking my time to celebrate how delectable she was, how fine and full of complex colors. Plum. Cherry. Burgundy. Ivory. Aqua blue.

I pumped harder, remembering her sobs, the copiousness of her tears. During last night's scene, her curvaceous body had tensed and trembled with unique grace. Oh, and the way her legs strained when I cuffed her over the spanking bench and pushed into her virgin ass...

I came with a grunt, spewing cum over my hand and stomach. My phone rang just after, flashing Devin's number. I hauled myself off the couch and cleaned myself up before calling him back.

"Fort!" he said. "Am I interrupting?"

"No."

"I'm heading to Munich tomorrow. Want to tag along for an overnight? We'll have just enough time for an adventure at the Persian Kitty."

"Can't. I'm meeting with someone tomorrow night."

"Meeting with who?"

I heard voices and a loudspeaker in the background. Dev was doubtless striding through some foreign airport or train station, wheeling his luggage behind him. "You haven't been to The Gallery in weeks now," he said. "Don't tell me you're still fucking around with that quirky art manager person?"

"Quirky art manager person?"

"Saying she's quirky is nicer than saying she's weird. You said she was weird."

"I said she was unconventional." I leaned on the counter, guarding my words. "And yes, that's who I'm meeting."

"She's bad news, man. She's a glitter sub. How far could things go?"

"She's not a glitter sub. She's a masochist, Dev, the real deal. We've done a few sessions, and she gets off on it."

"But...?" I could hear his impatience over the phone. "I hear a but in there."

"It's just...she's not like the masochists I'm used to. When I hurt her...when she looks at me..." *When she looks at me, her gaze pierces a little too deep.*

Devin laughed. "If you don't like how she looks at you, blindfold the girl. You're in charge, man. Cover her eyes."

"I can't. I need to be able to read her. Blindfolds are prohibited at The Gallery for that reason."

"Oh, God. You're not thinking of bringing her to The Gallery?"

"Why shouldn't I?"

He snorted. "There's a big difference between sado-fucking a chick at your apartment and taking her to The Gallery. A world of difference. Not to mention the preparation, the paperwork and testing..."

"We're kind of...fluid bonded already."

This time his snort was more like a growl. "Shit. I'm hanging up. I'm done. No, wait. One last thought. Every time we talk about this girl, you say *she's this, she's that, I just don't know.* Don't bring her to The Gallery unless you know she can take it. None of us want the drama, Fort."

"I'm as invested in The Gallery as you," I replied, keeping my temper in check by thinking of Juliet and her tear-filled gaze. "I don't want drama, either. I'll prepare her beforehand, so don't worry your pretty head about it." I ignored his muffled curse and decided against a third cup of coffee. "Enjoy the Persian Kitty, Dev, and fly safe."

Chapter Eighteen: Juliet

I knocked on Fort's door at eight o'clock, and felt my usual jolt of attraction when he opened it.

"How many pairs of those socks do you own?" he asked, raking me from head to toe.

"This is the last pair you haven't seen," I said, doing a shimmy in my pale blue sheath dress. My socks were blue with silver bows. "I'll have to start shopping for some more."

"Mmm. Maybe I'll shop for some too." He pulled me into his apartment and planted a kiss on my lips. The lights were brighter than usual, or maybe it was darker outside. When he released me, his arm lingered on my back. "This is the time I usually ply you with alcohol, but I cooked food this time."

"Yay, dinner."

"It's nothing special. Come sit down."

He led me to his dining room, a formal set up with padded, upholstered chairs, a glittering chandelier, and, of course, a huge window-wall looking out on the world's most spectacular view. There was a simple salad on the large, rectangular table, and a platter of baked fish in lemon sauce and capers. My mouth watered from the smell. He went to the kitchen and returned with a plate of roasted asparagus that looked magical.

"These are all my favorite foods," I said. "How did you know?"

"It's all about the asparagus. Fish and capers are a given."

"The Mediterranean diet." I slid into the chair he held out for me. It felt cushy and soft, at odds with his penthouse's color scheme of bronze and gray. "How much does all this cost?" I murmured.

"What do you mean?" he asked, pouring me a glass of water from a crystal pitcher.

"Sorry. I'm being rude. It's just...the penthouse, the furnishings, the view..." He didn't answer as he sat beside me at the head of the table. "I mean, I live in a refurbished shipping container."

"Very hip of you."

I put my napkin in my lap as Fort prepared a plate for me. It all felt very date-y and romantic, but I knew it wasn't a date. There was a paper on the other side of him. I couldn't read it, but I could see that it contained paragraphs and lists. "So, tell me about The Gallery," I said. "Please. I'm so curious that I've been making up crazy ideas in my head."

"The Gallery isn't crazy or dangerous." He paused as I moaned over my first bite of fish. "Enjoying that?"

"God. Yes. Go on." I took a sip of water and ate some of the vegetables, seasoned perfectly with olive oil and salt. My plate was half gone before he even started talking.

"So, the first thing you have to understand about The Gallery is that it's a very classy place. It's not some hole-in-the-wall sex dive with cum-stained windows and sticky floors."

I was glad to hear that. Although I never knew there were sex clubs with cum-stained windows and sticky floors. Disgusting. "So, you're saying it's well maintained?"

"Yes, and everyone watches out for everyone else, so the rules are always followed."

"Safety rules?"

He paused a moment. "Yes, safety rules. Although people do things at The Gallery that probably wouldn't be allowed in a lot of BDSM clubs." He touched my hand when I stopped chewing. "I'm describing this badly. Nothing illegal happens there. No underage porn. No animals. No drugs. It's a self-policing community in a beautiful setting. It's at the top of the Bridgeport building, in a refurbished clock tower. I guarantee you've never seen anything like it."

"There's a view?"

"No, but there's a giant clock. It doesn't work anymore." He grimaced. "Yes, it kills me, but I haven't been able to find the parts to fix it, and people who are there aren't watching the time. It's a very timeless place."

"It sounds amazing. Do you have pictures?"

"No pictures allowed. Cameras and phones are checked at the door." I watched as he took a bite of fish. "Privacy and discretion are taken seriously there, so..." He waved his fork at me. "Nothing I'm telling you can be told to anyone else. You've been let in on the secret, now you have to keep it. Do you understand?"

His voice made me squirm on my still-sore ass cheeks. "Yes, Sir." I picked at one of the silver bows on my knee. "I have a question, though. If it's so private and secret, how does anybody find it? How did you learn about it?"

"Through Devin. Well, through Devin's friend, Milo. He was one of the early members, and had a lot of input in the design. Ever heard of Fierro violins?"

I smashed a caper and swirled it in the lemon sauce. "You and your wealthy social circle." Everyone had heard of Fierro violins. They were the next best thing to a Stradivarius, with a similar cost. "I thought Fierro violins came from Italy?"

"They do, and Milo's family is ten times richer than mine," said Fort with a shrug. "But he spends a lot of time in New York, and he's a pretty cool guy."

"A sadist?"

He took his last bite of fish and put down his fork. "Every man at The Gallery is a sadist, Juliet. And every woman goes there to submit to a power greater than herself."

"Do you and your friends have a financial stake in this club?"

"Somewhat. The membership fees are pretty expensive. I also have a psychological stake in the club, because I know my needs will be met there. All kinks and urges are accepted. There are no limits, no safe words, no societal restrictions. Here's the thing about The Gallery." He pushed his plate away and leaned closer to me. I stopped chewing and swallowed. "It's a place where you leave the real you at the door."

"The real me?" I swallowed again, harder this time. "Like...Juliet?"

"Yes. Juliet is left at the door. Fort is left at the door. Inside The Gallery, you belong to your Dominant and every other Dominant currently in that space. And when it's over..." He watched me, pursing his lips. "When it's over, you walk away and go back to real life."

"Wait." I studied him, trying to read his expression. "Go back to what you just said. You belong to your Dominant and every other Dominant...?"

"Yes. Like a painting in a gallery. Everyone can look at you and admire you. Everyone can interact with you. You're there for the visitors to enjoy."

There for the visitors to enjoy. I tried to wrap my head around this statement. "So when women are there, they're like...group property? Anyone can sleep with them?"

"Sex isn't really the focus. I told you that before. It's not about sex. It's about power. It's about owning and partaking in all the beautiful things."

"The beautiful women, you mean."

"The beautiful submissives," he countered. "Who are there of their own free will, because consensually non-consensual dominance and submission is their kink."

"Consensually non-consensual dominance and submission?" That was a mouthful.

"We talked about this before. You consent to give up consent for the duration of your interactions." A touch of impatience crept into his voice. "Are you shocked?"

"I don't know." My mind was racing over his words. "I mean, I know you and I trust you, but I won't know any of the other people there. At least, I hope I won't. I feel okay doing scenes with you without a safe word, but—"

"There won't be anyone there you can't trust."

"How do I know that?"

"Because I'm telling you that, and you trust me, yes?"

I stared down at the mess I'd made of my plate. "I trust you. But..." *But that's because I'm attracted to you. I'm turned on by you. I let you hurt me because you get me hot.* "What if I don't want to do a scene with someone else, and they want to do a scene with me?"

He didn't answer for long moment, just looked at me with his deep hazel eyes. His dark brows registered subtle tension, but not as much tension as I felt inside. "It's not a love thing," he finally answered. "It's not a romantic date, to go to The Gallery. It's a physical thing. If you're turned on by sadism and dominance, every man there will know how to tap into that desire. Every man there will be able to excite you."

"So you just...what? Take me to The Gallery and offer me to all your friends?"

He leaned back in his chair. "Are you getting upset, Sparkles?"

"No, I'm trying to understand how it works. Do you put all the submissives up on auction blocks? Stand them along the wall until they're chosen?"

A smile teased the corners of his lips. "Would you enjoy that? Being auctioned off? Put on display?"

I pictured a room full of men like Fort, dominant, sexually voracious men who were rich and powerful enough to join a club to get what they wanted, access to a horde of submissive females all the time. The idea turned me on to a surprising degree, but it frightened me too. I wasn't exactly a seasoned masochist, and I wasn't a petite beauty like the woman Devin had brought to Goodluck's show. "I'm not sure I'd like that," I admitted. "What if no one wanted me?"

His eyes took on a cynical cast. "Really? Are we fishing for compliments?"

"No. Seriously." I held out my glass for more water. "It's a possibility."

"It's not a possibility," he said, ignoring my outstretched glass. "But for the record, here's how things generally go. A submissive comes with her sponsor—her Dominant or Master—and that's who she spends the bulk of her time with. If a scene develops and draws other people in, it's a good thing. More pain, more pleasure. More fun."

He pushed back his chair and gestured me over to him, taking me in his arms. "The Gallery can transform you if you go into it with an open mind. What you can't do is walk into the club with the idea that you exclusively belong to anyone. You and I aren't exclusive, right?" He said it kindly, gazing into my eyes. "We've been clear about that from the start.

Our thing is about physical and mental connection, and experiencing sexual thrills that 99.9 percent of the population is too afraid to think about. Going to The Gallery is doing that same thing, only adding other like-minded people."

"When you put it like that..."

He squeezed me as I shifted on my toes. "What are you thinking? Yes? No? Not your thing?"

"I don't know if it's my thing. It might be. Like scening with you...I didn't know I liked it until I did it."

"Let me show you the fine print." He reached for the paper I'd noticed earlier, sliding it in front of us while his arm tightened to pull me into his lap. "Any submissive who plays at The Gallery has to read and agree to these five rules, and sign at the bottom. They want every participant to be on the same page."

"I'd have to sign this now?" I asked, turning back to him.

"No. At the door. You're supposed to read and sign it every time you come."

"Sounds very legal."

He laughed. "It's quasi legal. It's more a good faith agreement that you won't cause shit if you don't enjoy yourself as much as you hoped."

I looked down at the paper, scanning the bulleted list while he finally refilled my water. *Number one: All submissives must be accompanied by a sponsor who will manage their conduct and care. No unsponsored submissives will be admitted.* I did a mental eye roll at that one. God forbid some poor woman wandered in there unprepared.

Number two: Any submissive brought into The Gallery shall be considered communal property and shared in any way her sponsor desires. I was glad now he'd warned me about that one in advance, or I would have choked on it. I took a deep drink of water, imagining a faceless stranger forcing me to his will. It turned me on more than I thought. My face flamed despite my best intentions as I moved on to number three.

The Gallery is a no-safe-word zone. The submissive's limits will be determined by her sponsor.

The last part captured my attention, made me feel a little better about the whole sharing thing. "Ok, so your sponsor basically stays in charge of you. Like, even if some other Dom wanted to interact with me, you'd be there to make sure they don't stab me in the neck."

"Of course." His gaze roved over my throat, then his tongue blazed the same path. "I'd never let anyone stab you in the neck. Your neck is too perfect to ruin."

He caressed my breasts, stoking the fire that burned hotter with each perverse "rule" I read. I peered down at the fourth line. *All submissives must strictly adhere to The Gallery's dress code.*

"What's the dress code?" I asked.

"What you might expect," he said. "Fetish lingerie. Don't worry, it's nothing extreme." His hand traced the curve of my waist, then slid back up to my breasts, pinching my sensitive and very hard nipples. "We use a private costumer. If you decide you want to go, I'll give you the address so you can get measured and fitted. They'll send me the bill."

"How will they know—"

"I'll arrange everything. You'd just show up."

My hips moved as he fingered my nipples, then pinched, resurrecting the lingering soreness from our last session. "You're really turning me on right now," I said.

"Keep reading. One last thing." He read it instead, lowering his voice for emphasis. *"Any submissive not agreeing to these terms may not be admitted to The Gallery. Any resistance or refusal of these rules is cause for immediate expulsion from the premises."*

"So if I decide in the middle to disobey some guy or put on some other outfit, I'm out of there. If I yell out a safe word—"

"Then I'll punish you for being a brat," he said, giving the side of my leg a spank. "Joking aside, if you disagree with any of these rules, don't agree to attend as my submissive. That's the point of spelling things out like this. The Gallery only works if everyone plays along."

His erection grew thicker and more insistent against my ass cheeks. "I think maybe I could do this Gallery thing if you're there to keep me safe."

"I'd keep you safe." His breath feathered the back of my hair. "And I'd hurt you while we were there. But you seem to enjoy that well enough."

Goosebumps rose along my arms and neck as bite followed breath. His teeth closed on my nape, making me shiver. I reached back to caress his bulging cock through his jeans, then searched for the button.

"No," he said. "Naughty girl. You don't take. I give."

He spread my legs and shoved hard fingers against my pussy. I was so wet, so soaked. I was sure he could feel it through my panties. He made a guttural lust noise that proved me correct. I wanted him. I wanted The Gallery. I wanted whatever he wanted, even if it was perverse and unnatural.

He pushed me onto my knees and undid his jeans. While I took him in my mouth, he unzipped my dress and pushed it down over my shoulders. My breasts were in his hands, then my nipples were pinched and tormented, driving me on. It wasn't fun giving him blowjobs. It was an exercise in lack of control, in submitting to greedy dominance. When he shoved his hips forward, I took his cock as deep as I could, and still my nipples were punished. When I whined in protest, his only answer was a satisfied growl.

I gagged and he chuckled, a low, sadistic rumble. "It's okay, Sparkles. That'll happen a lot. Get used to it." He pulled out of my throat and made me stand, then bent me over, facing the table, so my hands were braced on its edge. My soaked panties were yanked down, my skirt flipped up to bare my welted backside. "This beautiful ass," he said, parting my cheeks. "And these gorgeous marks." He traced along the lingering welts and bruises, then spanked me, making me jump.

"Jesus, I need to spank your ass," he said, moving me again, manipulating me until I was bent over his lap in the dining room chair. I looked up, looked out his window at the city's lights as he ran his fingers over my quivering butt. An old-fashioned over-the-knee spanking. How quaint. How naughty and patriarchal. I had a ten-second reprieve before the first blows fell.

Ow. Ow. Ow. Oh God, it wasn't quaint at all. It stung like hell.

"That—really—hurts," I gasped, between jerking and flailing.

He tightened his arm around my waist and continued his assault. I struggled, finding it hard to breathe through the overload of sensation. His hands were huge and the spanks were hard and resonant, one after the other. "My ass still hurts from before. Please!"

"It's good to have a hurting ass. It makes everything better for you, Juliet. I know."

"Oh God!"

"I know from this." He paused, his fingers probing my drenched, hot cleft. "Are you ready to be fucked?"

"Yes. Please!"

I was hauled about again by his huge, firm fingers, and deposited astride his lap with my dress bunched at my waist. He pulled at his fly and a moment later he slipped inside me, shoving his hips upward to fill me to the hilt. "How's that?" he asked. "Feel better?"

"Yes, Sir. It feels wonderful."

"Even with your sore ass?" He added a smack on each side for emphasis. It smarted like heck but also felt so good—I'd gotten to the point where I didn't question why. I rode Fort's cock, my pleasure heightened by the throbbing scarlet handprints on my ass. I tried not to think about how connected I felt to him, how perfect it felt to be fed by him, held by him, hurt by him in this room above the city, and brought to a climax that blurred my eyes.

* * * * *

I had to get up early on Wednesday to make the appointment for my Gallery fitting. I couldn't believe they had their own costumer. The woman was soft spoken on the phone, agreeing to meet me at her Soho studio. When I got there and rang the bell, she ushered me inside with a smile.

"What a pleasure to meet you," she said. "You're Juliet Pope?"

A flush rose in my cheeks. I thought this might all be conducted by pseudonym. "Yes, I am."

"Don't worry," she said, noticing my unease. "I promise I'm discreet about who I outfit—that's why they trust me to do this. And I've been to The Gallery many times. My name's Michelle, and I work in the Metropolitan Ballet's costume department. So you're going to visit The Gallery for the first time?"

"I guess. When the costume's ready."

She smiled. "I'll have it for you in less than a week. There's not much to it. Have you seen the design?"

"My Dominant told me it was fetish-y, but I haven't seen a picture or anything."

She crossed the small, crowded space to her work desk and returned with a fashion sketch. I scanned the black outline of the lingerie with alarm. "That's very skimpy."

"It's skimpy, yes, but it'll look lovely on your figure."

"This figure?" I gestured to my round hips and mediocre chest.

"It's designed to accentuate the female anatomy."

I studied the lines of the fabric that composed the bra...if it could be called a bra. "Is that lingerie, or a harness?"

"It's a peek-a-boo bra, made of mesh and lace. It exposes the nipples."

I understood why that might be necessary. I pictured my clamped, erect nipples poking out from the sexy black bra and blew out a breath. My blush still hadn't gone away. This woman was outfitting me to be a sex toy for rich Dominants. But if she'd been to The Gallery, it wasn't like she could judge me, or expose me as a freak.

"If you'd just get undressed," she said. "Down to your panties, if you don't mind."

I did as she requested, placing my jacket, jeans, and t-shirt over her desk chair. She led me to a platform near the shaded window, clutching a worn notebook in her hand. I studied her soft, pale brown hair as she knelt to measure my inseam and hips. Something in her posture suggested submission, even now.

"Old school," I said as she wrote down my numbers. "That notebook."

"Oh, there are years of submissives' measurements in here." She tweaked one edge of the book. "Sometimes I look through them for fun, I suppose to see how many shapes and sizes we come in. Some of us are larger, like me. Pleasingly plump, I like to say." She put the measuring tape around my waist and laughed. "Some of us are more svelte. Goodness, I won't be jealous. My Master loves my shape."

I didn't think Michelle was that "plump," just a healthy, middle-aged woman, nor did I find myself at all svelte. "How long have you been going to The Gallery?" I asked.

"For years now. Master and I are getting older, so we don't go as often as we did. But when I go, it's like being home again."

"Are you and your Master married?"

I wasn't sure why I asked. It wasn't any of my business, but she answered with another laugh. "Oh no, we're only compatible as power exchange partners. We're both married to other people who are kind enough to share us. My husband is a mild, sweet man. He can't give me what I need as far as pain, but I love him to pieces."

I had so many questions, all of them unforgivably nosy. "Can I ask you something?"

"Here come some cold hands," she said, as she prepared to measure around my chest. My nipples tightened but she ignored that. "And you can ask me anything, Juliet. I'll answer as well as I can."

"What's it like to be there?"

She collected her measuring tape, rolling it around a finger. "I can't really answer that for you. The Gallery is a different experience for everyone who goes, for every Master and slave, Dominant and submissive. For some, it's a frantic trial, just as they want it to be. For others, the pain and lack of control is a meditative exercise. Others want to be humiliated or treated like an animal. What you see isn't necessarily what's going on between people." She measured my torso, then my neck. "It's noisy there, with voices, screams, and commands, but there's a lot going on inside people as well. Some participants are stoic and don't make a peep."

I wondered what would go on inside me. I wondered if I'd be noisy or silent, frantic or meditative.

"Are you worried about going?" Michelle asked.

"A little. I'm new to the whole consensual-non-consent thing. I'm worried I won't be good at it."

"Your Master wouldn't have invited you if you weren't 'good at it.'" She put air quotes around my words. "Lack of confidence is an all-too-common submissive trait."

"He's not my Master, just someone who's teaching me about sadism and masochism. I mean, he's a sadist, so I guess I'm a masochist."

She gave me a strange look. "You guess? You're either a masochist, or you aren't."

"I am," I said, feeling naked under her gaze. "And my Dom is great. He makes me hurt in really awesome ways. He makes me crazy, in a way no other guy ever has."

"All of that sounds familiar." Her concerned look turned to a smile. "I can tell you'll do fine by the way your eyes glaze over when you talk about him."

"His name is Fort St. Clair," I blurted out. "Do you know him?"

She leaned to write more measurements in her book. "I know of him," she said, not looking at me. "He's very handsome, and good at what he does, judging by the women he plays wi..." Her voice trailed off. My face must have given away my jealousy of those unknown women. Now she looked pensive again. "You have feelings for him? Mr. St. Clair?"

"No," I lied. "Well, sometimes. It's just the intensity of the whole thing. We're not romantically involved."

"You can get dressed now. I have all the measurements I need."

She took her notebook to her desk, turning away to give me privacy while I put on my clothes. "Wait until you see how gorgeous The Gallery is," she said. "So gothic and elegant, and the grand rotunda above, dark with shadows. Pure fantasy made real."

* * * * *

Four days later, a nondescript package from Michelle's address was delivered to my doorstep via courier. I signed for it, then hurried inside to check out my "uniform." The black lingerie was folded into crisp, white tissue, each piece as slight and soft as down as I pulled it out.

For starters, there was the cut-out bra and a skimpy garter belt, both embellished with delicate beads and lace. Three pairs of black stockings, with instructions on where to buy more, and curled in a loop at the bottom, a thin, silver-toned leather collar with a tiny, decorative lock. I had to get a magnifying glass to see the small words inscribed on the body of the lock: *Property of The Gallery*.

I tried on everything, as Michelle's note prompted. *I hope it fits*, she wrote.

God, it fit so well I could barely look at myself. The boning in the bra pushed up my smallish breasts, making them look spectacularly lush. The cups' openings framed the pale, sensitive skin surrounding my pointed nipples, as if offering them to whoever looked at me. The garter belt was cut to frame my pussy lips in the same way the bra highlighted my nipples. There were no panties. The stockings came to mid-thigh, cinched by heavy-duty clips decorated with the same tiny beads as the rest of the lingerie. Understated black stiletto pumps kept me on my toes, literally, making me look even more like a sex bomb.

The stark, black lines around my breasts and hips suggested a harness, even though the uniform wasn't a harness. It bound me, displayed me. I buckled on the collar last, and I was glad the outfit didn't have any panties. My pussy would have caught them on fire, I was so turned on.

I texted Fort that I had my uniform, that I was ready to go to The Gallery whenever he was. He told me to take a picture for him, but then he texted a moment later and said I shouldn't.

Why? I wrote.

Because I want to see it the first time on Saturday. I'll pick you up at 10:30. Make sure you have everything you need.

Everything I need?

Uniform. Collar. Dots blinked. A pause. **Bravery.** Another pause. **Are you still sure you want to go?**

I definitely want to go, I texted, staring at the boldly sexualized woman in the mirror. **I'm ready for it now.**

Chapter Nineteen:
Fort

I went shopping for Juliet on Tuesday, not for socks, although I might have bought some if I knew where to find them.

No, I went shopping for the perfect coat, since she couldn't ride up the Bridgeport's elevator in lingerie. I found a beautifully tailored designer trench, black, lined with butter-soft silk. I had it delivered to her apartment with a note. *Wear this over your uniform. There are no changing rooms there.*

Then I tried to focus on work, on spring retail numbers and meetings, but my thoughts kept returning to Juliet and the fetishized lingerie she'd wear to The Gallery on Saturday beneath my accompanying coat. Was it too soon to take her there? Was she enough of a hedonist to understand why it turned all of us on?

Shit, if she wasn't, things would get awkward. It could mean the end of us, which would be okay, I guess. Disappointing. Maybe I should have waited.

Too late now.

I knocked on her door Saturday night with equal parts anticipation and anxiety. She answered in her new black coat, letting me into her apartment with a shy smile on her lips. Her hair was done up in a pile of curls. I stared at her neck, at her slim collar, a collar with the level of quality someone like her deserved.

"Hello," she said, cinching the coat's belt tighter at her waist. She looked me up and down. "No leather vest and chaps?"

I brushed a hand over my dark suit, starched white shirt, and striped blue tie. "We have a dress code, too," I explained. "Have to keep things classy."

"You look nice."

I brushed my unruly hair back from my forehead and studied her next, touching the arm of her coat. "It fits you perfectly. Are you wearing your uniform under there?"

"Yes." Her sweet voice rasped, suddenly gone dry. "Yes, Sir."

"Show me."

She looked terrified to reveal what she had on underneath, which was silly, because I'd seen the uniform hundreds of times. Of course, I'd never seen it on her. She undid the belt and opened the coat slowly, like a timid, adorable flasher.

I let her see all the lurid approval in my gaze. Jesus, she was voluptuously beautiful, the dark angles emphasizing all her feminine curves. I'd seen the uniform hundreds of times, but not like this, on my blue-eyed, wild-haired sparkler. Breasts, belly, hips, pussy, legs, all the lovely parts of her body on display. Black four-inch stilettos completed the ensemble.

"Do you like it?" she asked, when my silent perusal strung out. When I didn't answer, she started to close the coat, but I raised a hand to stop her.

"No, let me look a little more. I'm just trying to..." *Pull your shit together, Fort.* "You're beautiful," I said. "It suits you so perfectly."

"The only thing missing is the socks," she said, joking.

I reached for her, needing to touch her, needing to run my hands over the bared parts of her body. I pushed the coat back and let it drop, so her naked nipples and belly were pressed against my front. I held her with one arm and grasped her nape with the other, trapping her for my kiss. I fed her my hunger, my approval in a violent kiss. I had to restrain myself from pushing her back on the floor and mounting her.

No. That wasn't what tonight was about. I pulled back, distracting myself with the way she touched her lips. Her fingertips were so delicate. I traced my less-delicate fingertips along her silver leather collar to the dangling lock.

"Thank you for doing this with me." I tugged the lock to pull her close for another kiss. This one left me feeling a bit more sane. Definitely invigorated. I felt ready to introduce her to the pleasures of The Gallery. "I'm going to do everything I can to give you a good experience tonight," I said against her lips. "And I'm going to hurt you, baby, in all the best ways. Just trust me, and everything will be fine."

I pulled away and picked her coat up from the floor. I helped her put it on and wrapped her up tight, my little package, cinching the belt and straightening the collar to hide the other collar, the one that was just for me.

Well, for everyone at The Gallery, if things went all right.

"Will we be arriving late?" she asked.

"No. We'll arrive just in the thick of things. Scenes start around eleven, and midnight is the witching hour, when everyone gets down to business." I took her hand, squeezed it, and let it go. "It's best if we get into our roles now. It'll make things easier when we get there."

"Okay. Yes. Yes, Sir."

All week I'd been imagining ways to torment her, but now, with her in The Gallery's collar, none of those fantasies touched what I wanted to do. She avoided my gaze as I helped her into the car, perhaps because I looked at her like a predator. Like a sadist, but that was my role. She fulfilled her role too, biting her lips as she gazed out the window, a uniformed vessel for my passions and desires.

Chapter Twenty: Juliet

He was silent on the way, letting me stew in my nervous, submissive juices. I squirmed in the seat, trying not to drench the lining of the coat where I sat on it. I was already so wet. My nipples rubbed against the fabric, reminding me of my peek-a-boo bra the whole way there. The driver stopped outside the Bridgeport, and Fort came around to open my door. He took my elbow, leading me past the doorman, into the building, and over to a gleaming bank of elevators.

My eyes darted everywhere, taking in the lobby's regal decor. It was quiet. There were no other dark-suited men or trench-coated women arriving at the same time as us. I still burned with exhilarated shame.

Once we were in the elevator, he used a key to take us to the clock tower level. He didn't say anything, but he stood close to me, a steady, comforting presence at my side. My stockinged knees knocked together when the elevator stopped and the doors slid open. We exited into a lobby of sorts, far larger than I expected. The foyer rose two stories, decorated in the way he'd described, with carved wood molding and gilt etching. A young man stood at a mahogany podium beside a fire. He eyed me as Fort led me over.

"How old is he?" I whispered.

"Old enough. Hush."

Fort greeted him, calling him "Rene." Now that we were closer the man looked a little older, but still awfully young to be working the door of a sex club. His skin was perfect, his lips full and suggestively bee-stung. His manner was deferential, almost effeminate, but at the same time, he looked strong enough to throw out any unwanted visitors.

"I'll be happy to take your submissive's coat," he said. "And your jacket, Sir, if you'd like."

"Thank you."

Fort looked at me expectantly as he shrugged out of his suit jacket. I untied the coat's belt and unbuttoned the six buttons, taking far too long because of my shaking fingers. I was pretty sure from Rene's mannerisms and speech that he was gay, but he was still a man, a stranger I didn't know who was about to look at me in all my perverse sexual gear. I took a deep breath and lifted the coat away, handing it to him. Cool air rushed over my skin, hardening my already exposed nipples.

Rene inspected me with detached diligence, taking in the collar, bra, garter, stockings, and stilettos. This was as perverse as the rest of it, having this gay, beatific, muscle-bound man-child act as gatekeeper for their Gallery of sado-masochism. He wasn't looking at me to admire me; he was checking to be sure I was properly dressed in the prescribed uniform.

After that, he held out a page to Fort, containing the same list of rules he'd shown me at his apartment. Fort handed it to me, and Rene gave me a fountain pen so I could sign. His smooth, flawless twenty-year-old cheeks unsettled me, because I was sure mine were bright pink. I signed the non-legally-binding agreement and handed it back. Without a word, Rene moved to the adjacent ivory-gilt door and swung it open.

Fort caught and held my gaze, giving me strength when I wanted to turn tail and run. I wanted this, yes. I wanted him. I steeled myself and let him lead me up a set of stairs to The Gallery's inner chambers.

There were two open stories—a main floor, and an upper floor with stairs that rose to a rounded dome. An iron balcony looked down on the larger room we stood in, but it was currently unoccupied. Victorian sconces illuminated walls covered in dark gray wallpaper embossed with a vine and floral pattern. One whole side of the space was taken up by the inner workings of the clock tower's face, surrounded by frosted-glass

Roman numerals facing out to the city. At some point, the clock's huge hands had halted at seven forty-five.

I drew my gaze from the clock to check out all the other spaces of the dungeon. There were too many racks and benches to take in at once, far more than Fort had in his home dungeon. The floor was weathered, lacquered wood, and dark leather sofas and club chairs were scattered around the main floor, dividing it into sections. And in those various sections were men, all of them clothed, and women, all of them dressed like me.

No, all the men weren't clothed. Some of them had their cocks out, stuffed in their submissives' mouths or hands, or between their thighs. A couple of men were working over a hissing, squealing woman, whipping her as she flailed on a rack. In farther corners, women danced in agony, suspended by sturdy chains from the ceiling. I'd expected frenetic beatings, noise and commotion, but The Gallery's vibe was of elegant, picturesque pain.

"Forsyth St. Clair," said a deep voice.

Fort turned, and I turned with him, hiding myself, then remembering that I couldn't do that. I stood at his side, regarding the same blond man who'd accompanied Fort to Goodluck's art opening. He was dressed in a white shirt and dark dress pants like Fort, but with a lighter colored tie. It didn't make him look any less dangerous. When he noticed me, his eyes widened, then narrowed on Fort.

"Really?" he said, with an ironic tilt to his mouth.

"Juliet, do you remember Mr. Kincaid from the gallery opening?"

"Yes, Sir," I answered, keeping my attention on the man I'd come with.

Devin chuckled as I inched closer to Fort. "Come out, little sub. Let's see what we have here."

I glanced at Fort but he was looking at his smirking, muscular friend with an impenetrable expression. I took a step forward and tried not to look scared or ashamed while Devin ran his spooky-pale eyes over me.

"Isn't she a picture?" He didn't touch me, but he looked at every part of me. That's when I understood, really understood, what it meant to belong to every man there. "Enjoy your visit, Juliet," he said.

I felt Fort's hand at my back, guiding me away from Devin toward the far end of The Gallery. "Thank you," I murmured, and I didn't know if I was replying to Devin, or to Fort's possessive touch. "What was that about?" I asked, as soon as we were away from him.

"He doesn't think you should be here," Fort answered tightly. "It doesn't matter. Let's get you settled somewhere so I can get to work."

Get to work, the work of hurting me, and probably fucking me. Across the room, the sub who'd been squealing through her whipping was now enthusiastically thrusting her hips against one of her tormentors' cocks. The other man was rolling on a condom. There were sex noises everywhere, mixing with the pain noises in a heady soundtrack of lust.

Fort led me to a padded bench with an adjustable 'V' beneath it. He showed me where to place my legs against the 'V' so he could bind my thighs to it with leather straps. This part of the bench was adjustable, so the victim could be spanked with their legs together or pried open wide. He fixed my legs somewhere in the middle—wide enough to make me feel vulnerable, but not so wide that anyone who walked by could look up inside me.

The "uniform" I wore hid nothing, of course, not on me or any other woman there. It could hardly be called a garment, more like seductively placed bits of fabric and binding. When he bent me forward over the static part of the bench, my exposed nipples rested at either side of the narrow chest support. My torso wasn't bound, but my hands were cuffed to short chains at my sides so I could only move so far.

I looked back at Fort in his formal tie and starched shirt. His belt was opened, his erection bulging against the front of his pants. No words were needed for this scene, although a few soothing words would have been welcome. The situation was enough. The bench, the cuffs, the leg-spreading 'V,' even my skimpy costume. He pulled the belt from his pants with a whooshing sound and doubled it over as I strained to peer over my shoulder.

"Eyes to the front," he said.

I obeyed. A moment later, his belt thwacked against my ass, sounding louder and scarier than anything else in the room. I gave a strangled groan as the next blow fell, followed by another, then an entire volley of steady cracks. I didn't want to cry out, didn't want to bring attention to myself, but it was hard under his sustained assault.

The worst thing was that I knew this was only a warm-up, that he was only reddening my cheeks all over to prepare them for harder punishment. Something about the bench and the bondage made the belt feel way worse than it was.

I started to squirm, clenching my cheeks, tossing on the bench, but with my legs bound I couldn't go anywhere, and with my hands bound, I could do nothing to shield myself from the continued belting. My fists clenched and unclenched until he finally stopped. Only then did I take stock of my body, of my feelings. I was hot. Aroused. Not shocking, considering my recent sexual history. My nipples seemed to wait to be hurt by him. My ass throbbed as if chanting for *more, more, more...*

He rubbed my lower back, a fleeting, comforting touch to ground me, then walked across the room to a row of cabinets. He opened one that was ostensibly his. I thought of high school lockers, even though these cabinets were dark, polished wood. I saw lube and a medium-sized butt plug, and clenched my ass in reaction. There was nothing like the feeling of watching your Dominant walk toward you with something like that in his hands.

I tried to relax as he pressed the tip to my hole, but even with lube, the plug stretched me. His progress was slow but inexorable, opening me millimeter by millimeter. I couldn't stop the whine of discomfort as the widest part slid into my hole. When the plug was finally in, he eased it free again, adding more lube, fucking the plug in and out of my asshole so I couldn't get too comfortable with the invasion.

"How does it feel to get fucked with this plug?" he asked.

"It feels bad, Sir," I said hoarsely.

"It's not even close to the size of my cock. When I fuck your ass later, it's going to hurt a lot more."

What could I say to that? I moaned and raised my head to look around the room, saw some men watching me, some other subs checking me out even in the midst of their sadistic scenes. *You're in The Gallery. You are submissive flesh on display for the pleasure of these wealthy, perverted men.* The wealthy, perverted man behind me withdrew the plug until the broadest part was clenched within my sphincter, and held it there.

"Do you want me to stop?" he asked, rocking the plug a tiny amount. "Should we try something else?"

"I don't know." The "something else" would undoubtedly feel just as bad, or worse, than what he was doing to me now. With a chuckle, he slid the plug home again, allowing my tight ring some respite as it closed around the narrower base.

"Are you still tied down tight?" he asked me. "Your arms and legs are okay?"

"Yes, Sir."

"Let's make a few marks on your ass before we move to another area. A rattan cane should do the trick. It'll feel similar to the dowel I used on you. Perhaps a little more painful."

I turned to look at him with dread. The dowel had been utter hell, so I wasn't sure I could handle something more painful. He took a cane from a rack on the wall and I started shaking, squeezing on the hard toy buried between my ass cheeks. "I don't know... Sir... I don't know if I can..."

"You can. I wouldn't do it to you if you couldn't take it. There's nothing worse than a whiny little maso who says *I can't, I can't*." He moved his arm, and brought the cane down—*thwack*—across the middle of my cheeks.

And despite what he'd just said to me, I yelled "I can't!" twice more in my most piteous, desperate voice. The cane's sting roared along my nerve endings, lighting them on fire. He paused and rubbed the single welt.

"You can, Juliet," he said. "Really, you don't have any choice. I won't give you more than you can bear."

But one stroke already seemed more than I could bear. The second stroke was as awful as the first, a harrowing impact followed by a bloom of fiery torment. I tried to kick my legs but they were bound, tried to free my hands but the cuffs wouldn't even let me bend my arms. I squealed and held myself taut as another stroke fell. On the fourth stroke, I started begging, sobbing, blubbering words that made no sense. "Please, please, I can't, it hurts, I want you to, I want you to stop..."

"I know it hurts," he said, rubbing my ass. "That's why you're here, to be hurt."

I sensed more than heard another person approach our scene space. Hands smoothed over my clenching, twitching ass, and I could tell they weren't Fort's hands. When I turned, I saw Devin standing to the side of me, his thick, flaccid cock lolling from the fly of his pants.

"Those are some beautiful lines," he said to Fort.

"Thank you."

"She's tougher than I thought. Maybe she is Gallery material."

Devin's unwelcome fingers traced over the freshest cane welt, making it throb anew, but Fort did nothing to arrest his friend's careless groping. No, my Dominant was sharing me, letting other men touch me. I knew it was part of the deal for this place, but it didn't make it any easier for me to get used to. I wondered if it was a rule he put up with, or if sharing his partners was something he preferred.

"Look at this ass," Devin said, squeezing my cheeks, then spanking them hard enough to make me gasp. "I haven't seen an ass this round and perfect in ages." Devin's grasping fingers parted my ass cheeks, pausing, holding them open. Pure, devastating humiliation. A thumb brushed over my sodden, swollen clit, too forcefully to feel good. "Horny little thing," he said. His lewd chuckle attenuated to a growl. "Let me take her ass, Fort."

"No. She's plugged right now."

"I'll take it out."

His finger left my clit and twisted the plug in my ass, at the same time he thumbed my sensitive welts. The pain these men dealt was unending, yet so capricious on their part. The tears from Fort's caning spilled over again, harder than ever. I trembled in dread as Devin held my cheeks open and nudged at the plug.

"You want a big, fat cock in your ass, little maso?" he asked. "I'd probably split you open. Maybe you'd like that."

I shook my head and whimpered, unable to summon words. I felt Fort push Devin's hand away. "Why don't you fuck your own sub's ass instead of trolling the newbie?" he asked, a curt denial of his friend's request.

"None of my subs can act as distraught as this one. She's so...unconventional." Devin was in front of me then, kneeling down to look in my eyes even though he addressed Fort. He wasn't seeing me, just a bound sex object. "At least let me take her mouth while you're making her cry."

"Not today. Not right now."

Devin stared at me as I choked back a sob. "Ah, this is hard for you," he said in a soft voice. "Fort's really hurting you, isn't he? This isn't Underworld, dear, or some kinky art show. It's real fetish, real sadism."

"Can I continue?" asked Fort. "If you're done flirting with my sub?"

"By all means, continue. I'd like to watch."

Fort drew back the cane, painting my ass with another fiery line. I was crying too hard to summon a scream. Devin studied me, his lips curled in a faint smile.

"Do you want him to stop?" my blond tormentor asked. "Should I tell him to stop?"

I shook my head.

"Answer me properly. I know he's taught you that."

"No, Sir," I said, trying to hold my voice steady even as I waited for the next stroke to fall. "I don't want him to stop."

Devin rose to his feet, pumping his now-massive cock. "Have at her, man. She doesn't want you to stop."

The next stroke brought a scream from my throat. Pain. Evil. Fire. Devin had left, gone to stick that cock somewhere, but I still felt the squirming, uneasy threat of his exposed erection on top of the blistering pain on my ass. Fort gave me two final strokes, spacing them out so I had time to beg and whimper in between.

"Rest a moment," he said when that was finished.

I went limp, letting my body align to the curved bench, letting it hold me now that my muscles had turned to a quivering mess of overstimulation. My ass smarted, red hot with pain, and the butt plug reminded me there was more to come. When he unbound me and helped me stand, I reached to soothe my ass, but he wouldn't let me. When he offered his arms, I fell into them, burying my face against his chest. His hands roved over me, tracing my uniform's stark lines, pinching my nipples.

"I'd ask if you're having fun, but..." His voice trailed off, replaced with a low hum of satisfaction. "Look at me."

I raised my eyes. His carnal regard made all the pain fade away, or at least relax into something more bearable. I stared, trying to imprint those deep hazel recesses on my soul. As suddenly as he asked for me to look at him, he turned away, leading me toward the opposite side of The Gallery. He relieved me of the thick plug in my ass, then led me toward a high, wide, iron bondage arch cemented into the floor.

There were a variety of other racks and bondage points in this section of The Gallery. Ten or so feet away, a woman writhed on a web-like chain structure as her Dominant tortured her with a crop. Just across from us, in my direct line of sight, another submissive was cuffed on her hands and knees on an adjustable platform, being fucked with rough authority by a tall, brown-haired man. His bangs fell over intensely dark eyes as he gripped his sub's hips, driving into her. From the noises she made, it wasn't as painful as it looked.

"Raise your arms." From the sharp tone in Fort's voice, I wondered if it was the second time he'd asked me. Maybe he just wanted me to pay attention rather than looking around the room. Even so, I couldn't help glancing back at the fucking couple. The Dom yanked her head back, his fists wrapped in her hair, ropy muscles working below his rolled-up sleeves as her ragged screams carried to the somber walls.

"Does that look fun?" Fort cuffed my hands above my head, to either side of the iron arch, giving me precious little room to move. "A nice, rough fucking? You'll get yours soon enough." He cuffed my ankles next, forcing my legs wide with a spreader bar. Once I was secure, he released me and drove a couple fingers through my pussy lips, then up inside me until I had to rise up on my toes.

"Please, Sir," I said. I wanted to ask for an orgasm, but I knew I wouldn't get it, not yet.

"Please what? Please hurt me some more?"

I flushed hot as he pumped his fingers in and out. I was so wet, you could hear it.

"You want some cock?" he said in a gravelly, somber voice. "You're so fucking wet." He removed his fingers and spread my juices across one cheek. "Too bad you're not getting any cock in your hot, juicy cunt, Sparkles. I hope you can come from having your asshole fucked. Otherwise, you won't find much release tonight."

Each nasty, profane word from his mouth made me hotter. He tilted up my chin when I avoided his gaze for shame at my own perversity.

"Tell me what you want, girl."

"For you to fuck me, Sir," I said. "For you to h-hurt me." He paused, and I added the rest of it. "To hurt me however you want."

"That's a good girl."

He crossed to his personal cabinet of torture devices and returned with a three-point set of solid metal clamps. After applying a severe clamp to each of my exposed nipples, he parted my soaked labia and knelt to apply the third to my throbbing clit. I never got used to the pain of being clamped, the way the sudden application took my breath away. And my poor clit... That clamp hurt worse than the ones on my nipples. I kicked my legs as if that might alleviate the pain, but it only made it worse as the heavy connecting chain swung from the motion.

He stood back to watch me struggle, a satisfied gleam in his eyes. I was sure my makeup was already smeared from my sobbing fit over the bench. The single tear that escaped and rolled down my cheek probably didn't worsen things much.

"I love the way you cry," he said. "I love the way you take this pain for me. Let's try something new."

He went to a rack of implements on the wall, a far more extensive and terrifying collection than he kept at home. After a moment, he selected a thick, leather, strappy thing with a split down the middle. "This is called a tawse," he said, returning to me. "It hurts as much as a cane if applied correctly, although the pain is different. Are you ready?"

"Yes, Sir," I said. My voice shook as much as my arms and legs. I could take a step backward or forward in my spread-eagled position, but that was all. He started out in front of me, flicking the front of one thigh, then the other. He barely tapped me, but the sting was full-bodied, making me jump. My nipples screamed as the clamps swung, and my clit... My clit was beyond help.

"I'm scared," I said. "Please, Sir..."

"Hush."

"What if it's too much?"

He took my chin in his hands, kissed my forehead, then held my gaze. "I keep telling you. Try to understand, Sparkles. I'll never give you too much."

"I...I trust you, Sir, but..." I cast a look around the busy dungeon, but the only sound I heard now was my frantic breath and his low voice.

"No buts." He tugged the clamps' chains where they intersected, causing a burst of pain. "Who's the submissive here, girl?"

"I am."

"And I'm your Dominant, right?"

"Yes, Sir," I said, cowed by the censure in his voice. "I trust you."

"I'm not going to damage you. I won't leave any marks that will be seen. I'm saving the real fun for your ass just before I fuck it. Understand?"

I swallowed hard. "Yes, Sir."

The next two blows came to my outer thighs. The tawse might look like a strap or belt, but its punishment felt worse than either of those things. After that, he landed a strike to my already sore ass cheeks, and I squealed in terror. That one would leave a mark.

"Ow. No. Please!" I squirmed, dancing on my toes, trying to keep my balance in the stilettos. I think I only gave him a more inviting target. He made a noise of approval and took up a stance behind me, just at the edge of my peripheral vision. My tawsing began in earnest, hard, excruciating spanks as I wailed and flailed, doing a convulsive dance in time to the blows. *Ow. Ah. Ahhhh.* It hurt so badly. I turned my head, trying to catch his gaze, trying to express that this was too much for me on top of the caning I'd endured earlier.

He stopped to give me a break, although it wasn't really a break, since he traced the outside of my nipples and made them throb worse.

"Breathe," he said. "You can do this. A few more."

"No, Sir, please!"

"Time to take the clamps off, Sparkles. How brave you're being." He kissed me, thrusting his tongue deep in my mouth as I whined against his lips. I wanted him to take them off, but I dreaded the returning sensation. My clit felt ready to explode as I pressed against the front of him, feeling the outline of his solid erection. He let go of me and removed each clamp, watching my face to enjoy every flinch, every tremble of my lips. When he unclamped my clit, he shoved his fingers back in my pussy.

"You're going to be bruised on your gorgeous ass, on your round, firm cheeks where no one can see. The cane and then the tawse, pretty girl. I'm almost done leaving my marks."

He slapped the evil tawse against my mons, a sharp crack that made me burst into fresh tears. He held one of my hips and moved around me to deliver more blows to my ass. By now the sensation had bypassed stinging and moved on to hot, awful agony. I couldn't get away from his punishment, but I couldn't take much more either. I jumped and shifted, throwing pleading looks over my shoulder, but he was focused on his task. One of my stockings came loose, sagging against my upper thigh. He stopped to reconnect it with deft fingers, then grasped my chin.

"Prepare yourself, Sparkles. I want your asshole, now. You're going to give it to me."

"Yes, Sir," I sobbed through my teeth.

He moved behind me, squeezing my forlorn butt. It hurt so much already that the pressure didn't make much difference. I watched as he walked to his cabinet to grab a bottle of lube. On the way back he unzipped himself, grabbing his hugely rigid cock, pumping it as if it could possibly get bigger. Like the other men around us, he didn't undress beyond the necessary amount to fuck me.

He lubed my ass quickly and efficiently, shoving in a finger or two to smooth the way as I moaned and went on my toes. His hands were rough on my hips as he positioned himself behind me.

"It hurts," I said.

"I haven't even started."

"My ass hurts from earlier. From the tawse." My clit ached too, the kind of ache that needed an orgasm to fix it. "Please..."

"*Please...*" he mimicked heartlessly. "Cute, but ultimately ineffective. Shut up and let me do what I want to you."

I felt the head of his cock press against my hole. I clenched, unable to help it. I received a slap to each welted cheek for my trouble.

"Can't you fuck my pussy?" I knew I sounded whiny, but I was approaching my pain threshold. "Please, Sir?"

"You're complaining a lot for someone who's supposed to be my submissive." He pressed his cock forward again, breaching my anal ring. I bit my lip, pushing back, doing my best to accept the painful pressure.

"That's better," he said, as he managed to ease in an inch or two. He waited with his fingers tucked in the waist of my garter belt, a merciful enough sadist to let me adjust before he drove all the way into me. "Do you know why I like fucking your ass more than your pussy?" His whisper made my asshole pulse around his cock's thick crown. "I like it because you struggle so beautifully. It hurts so much, doesn't it?"

"Yes, Sir," I cried.

"But you like it. Once I'm inside you—" He shoved another few inches, an unavoidable onslaught. No safe words. No control. "Once I'm inside you, you start shaking with arousal rather than fear, and that excites me. Push your ass back against me, naughty girl. You do the rest, because you're the one who needs this. Show me how deep you want me to go."

I shook my head as if to deny his words, but my body obeyed, my hips pressing back to draw his cock into my most tender, vulnerable orifice. When he was buried all the way inside me, he rocked back and forth, teasing me, creating uneasy friction even with the lube.

"Good girl. I'm all the way inside your ass now. You love it deep, don't you, baby? Deep and hard."

Now that I was well-lubed and stretched to the hilt, I got it deep and hard, and only his hands on my waist kept me from collapsing in my bonds. There was something about being taken so carnally, with such disregard for my comfort. Other couples still scened around us, but I didn't notice them or hear them anymore. My world was Fort's power and his cock ramming into me as I hung from the iron arch.

Then I felt an unfamiliar presence, someone in front of me. I opened my eyes to discover the Dom from earlier, the one who'd fucked his submissive on her hands and knees with such violent possession. His eyes were blacker than any I'd ever seen, his skin a warm olive-gold. As Fort plowed into me, the man flicked one of my exposed nipples.

"She needs clamps," he said, giving the nipple a twist.

Fort's voice rumbled from behind. "I just took them off her."

"Oh. Then this must hurt you." The Dom's lips widened in a debonair grin as he twisted the other one. I tried to shrink away, but Fort was still behind me, driving into my asshole. "Hello, sweet thing," the man said. His voice held a faint accent, one I couldn't place. "Don't mind me. Whenever someone new comes, we're all interested."

I felt Fort chuckle, felt his breath against my ear. "Juliet, meet Milo Fierro. Milo, yes, I'm sure her nipples hurt."

The man made a pleased noise. "May I?"

At Fort's grunt of assent, he toyed with my nipples some more, pinching, flicking, tugging them like they were toys. His toys. I blinked back tears, avoiding his gaze, but Milo didn't seem to like that. He pinched harder to regain my attention. "Why won't you look at me, lovely?"

I closed my eyes. "Because I belong to him."

He tapped my cheek, a light slap, shocking my eyes open. His black eyes had turned frighteningly stern.

"That's better, little submissive. You might be his, but you also belong to me, don't you? That's what The Gallery's about." He rubbed a hand over the front of his pants, calling my attention to his stiff, obvious erection. "The only reason I'm not in your pussy right now is because I wouldn't fit with his big dick plowing your ass."

"Don't scare her, Milo," Fort murmured. "Help me hurt her. She wants to come."

"Oh, it's like that?"

I leaned my head back into Fort's strength, sighing as his hand tightened around my neck. A keening sound rose in my throat, a sound of relief, a sound of pleasure. Yes, I wanted to come. I'd been tortured for an hour now, riled into a tangle of stimulated submission. Milo slid a hand around my upper back, preventing me from shrinking away as he opened his teeth on my nipples, alternately sucking and biting the already-sensitive tips.

"Oww. Ohhh." I made begging sounds, felt them vibrate against Fort's palm as it pressed to my throat.

"Don't touch her clit," Fort gasped. "She has to come from having her ass fucked, or not at all."

The man he called Milo looked in my eyes and laughed. His dark eyes danced with amusement because he knew I was so close I was about to explode. "All the best sluts learn to come from a cock up the ass. It feels better to us sadists, you know, to fuck you and hurt you at once. Some sadists only use their submissives' assholes for that reason."

He bent his head again, sucking my nipples hard enough to bring tears to my eyes. Fort's hand squeezed my throat tighter to match the rising pain Milo imparted. His cock pummeled my ass, and somehow, between his forceful fucking, my bound arms, my loss of control, and Milo's awful nipple torture, the orgasm that had been building inside me broke wide. I lost control, gasping, choking on pleasure, bouncing back against Fort's cock as tears squeezed from my tightly shut eyes.

Both my tormentors seemed amused as I twisted in my bonds. I surged forward against Milo, wishing I could rub my clit on something to increase my orgasm's intensity. Neither man would let me. Both of them held me as firmly as the cuffs at my wrists.

When I returned to my senses, I jerked my shoulders, trying to dislodge Milo from my nipples, trying to arrest his awful sucking, especially now that I'd come. All I wanted to do was to rest, to not be touched.

"You wish I'd stop now?" Milo spoke in a low taunt, his long hair brushing my cheek. "But your Dominant's pleasure is what matters here, and he's still fucking your ass. This pain I'm causing makes you squeeze on his cock in a delightful way. Listen to the sounds he makes. Do they please you?"

I shuddered, gritting my teeth. "Yes. Yes, Sir. But—"

"No buts. Whose pleasure matters, his or yours?"

"His, Sir."

His pleasure matters. You're the submissive, meant to serve. I felt submissive, letting Fort yank my hair and pummel my ass as Milo continued his tireless nipple torment. I could tell Milo was the type of Dominant who liked to teach lessons. I said a silent prayer of thanks that I wasn't one of his submissives, like that girl he'd fucked on her knees earlier.

Finally, when I was about to lose my mind, Fort buried himself inside me and stayed, humping my hips, climaxing forcefully as he squeezed my neck and pussy. Milo smiled and gave my nipples one last tweak. A faint, patronizing smile, and he was strolling away, letting me recollect my senses as Fort gasped behind me.

My orgasm had exhausted me, the finale to a long, strenuous evening. Maybe he could tell I was close to finished, because he released me gently, almost tenderly from my bonds, then collected me in his arms. We stood together a long time, then he wrapped me in a blanket and walked me to a nearby couch. There was already another couple on it, another blanket-wrapped submissive whispering with her Dom. All around us, scenes were winding up. I wondered if I looked as wrecked as the other women.

"So you survived," he said, cradling me in his lap. "I hope it was a good orgasm."

"It was." Even now, those were the only two words I could string together. He stroked my back, my arm, the bare expanse of my right thigh. After a few more minutes had passed, he roused me, making me sit up. "Look at me, Juliet."

I did, and the intensity of his eyes scared me. He seemed to be searching for my thoughts, like he might find them written on my face, amidst the tear streaks and smeared makeup.

"Was The Gallery anything like you thought?" he asked, cupping my chin to hold my attention.

"No, Sir." It wasn't. I never could have imagined the things I'd experienced today.

His eyes probed me, studying my expression. "Did you enjoy it?"

I touched my sore breasts and shifted on my still-throbbing ass. Had I enjoyed it? I'd come like hell, that was for sure. But at what price to my body? My psyche? My emotional life? One thing I'd discovered was that other sadists scared me. I only trusted Fort. I only felt comfortable with him, but I was afraid to admit that. This wasn't a relationship. He'd said it so many times.

"I feel great right now," I finally answered. *I feel great in your arms, in your embrace.* "But during our scene, things were pretty painful."

"Good pain or bad pain?" he pressed.

"I don't know. It was bad pain, but it turned me on. You felt how wet I was." I shook my head. "I don't know. I had a lot of feelings. Maybe I need to process for a while."

"Feelings happen in places like this," he said, letting me snuggle back against his chest. "It's okay to have feelings. Just tell me if you think there's anything I need to know. You know, things to do differently next time, or things you really weren't okay with. Consensual non-consent doesn't mean you have no input at all."

"I know."

"It's just that sadism and masochism works best for some people if there's an element of...desperation."

Desperation. That word fit my feelings perfectly. My fear was that I'd grow desperate for all the wrong things, things he had no intention of giving me, things like love, sincerity, and connection. I rested my face against his neck and tried not to think about that now. I just drifted, safe in the circle of his arms.

Chapter Twenty-One: Fort

When we left The Gallery, I took her home to my place, made her spend the night in my bed even though I recognized her need to "process," to be alone. This had been her first time at The Gallery, and I'd pushed her harder than I meant to, so I couldn't say goodbye at the door as I had with my previous subs.

Fuck.

She was nothing like any of my previous subs. From the moment we arrived at The Gallery, that was obvious, and every other Dom took notice. I'd barely been able to stomach sharing her, even though sharing was usually a big part of the fun for me. When she'd told Milo *I belong to him*, I could hardly handle it, except to fuck her harder, faster, deeper. I couldn't deal with such loyal, abject submission when I'd done so little to deserve it.

Now I couldn't sleep, but I couldn't make her leave. I had to have her near me, because I didn't want to sleep without her. I felt energized beyond physical capability, and sickened by my need to have her close.

I liked order and independence, and my thing with Juliet wasn't fucking orderly. It wasn't neat and predictable like watch gears working, clicking into place.

I gazed down at her exhausted face and thought how fragile and asymmetric her features were. From the moment I saw her, I thought she was beautiful, but I didn't realize all the other layers I'd discover beneath those jewel-blue eyes and tousled brown curls. Those damned over-the-knee socks.

She was too much for me and I knew it, but I couldn't let her go. At least not yet.

Chapter Twenty-Two: Juliet

I woke the next morning trapped by an octopus. No, it was only Fort, his arms and legs all over me, heavy with sleep. The sun was bright, blinding. How long had I slept? Was it afternoon already?

"What time is it?"

Fort opened his eyes and reached to tap his tablet, squinting at the display. "Eleven forty-five."

"Shit. Half the day gone already. Although your bed felt pretty good."

He sat up, looking as bleary as I felt. My bones and muscles were practically creaking. Also, my phone was dead.

"Can I borrow your charger?" I asked. "Sorry. If you need me out of your hair..."

"No, charge away. At least enough to make it home."

He took my phone and plugged it in beside his bed. I blinked sleep from my eyes, pulling the covers up, feeling weirdly naked in front of a guy who'd seen every part of my body the night before. Even his friends had seen every part of my body. Not only that, but I had nothing to wear home but fetish lingerie and a flasher coat.

"So..." He looked at me, equally uncomfortable with our morning after. "Have you processed at all?"

"The only processing I've done so far was sleeping," I admitted. "I was so wrung out last night, I barely remember going to bed."

He touched my arm, gave me an awkward kiss on the forehead. He was the one who'd insisted I sleep here, so I had little sympathy for his morning-after unease.

"Can I use your guest room shower?" I asked.

"Sure." He finally seemed to come awake. "I'll get you a t-shirt and some pants to put on. They might be a little big, but you probably don't want to put your Gallery clothes back on."

I made a face. "I'd rather not, until I get them cleaned. Actually, can you take something like that to the cleaners?"

Fort eased out of bed and crossed to his closet. "From what I understand, it's better to hand wash everything." He disappeared inside and came out with a shirt and sweatpants that were far too long for my frame. Well, I could roll up the pants. It was the thought that counted.

"I promise I'll get these back to you soon. Maybe next time we..." My voice died out. We hadn't officially discussed whether there would be a next time. Part of me wanted another adventure at The Gallery, but part of me felt like it would be dancing on the edge of a cliff. For a place that was supposed to be pleasure-without-strings, it gave me all the feelings.

"Okay, anyway..." I scooted off the bed, wincing at the residual soreness. Fort took my arm, stopping me before I could leave the room.

"Let me look at you." He turned me, brushing a hand over my bottom with a low whistle. "Someone did a number on you last night, Sparkles. Your ass is a mess."

"I'm pretty sure that someone was you." I smiled in answer to his undisguised delight. "Are you proud of yourself?"

"Yes, very. Don't pass out when you look in the mirror."

"I'll try not to."

Just like that, I really wanted to go to The Gallery again. I went into the bathroom—which I was starting to think of as "my" bathroom—and turned my ass to the mirror. God, it was something to behold. Lines and bruises, none of them overly garish, no broken skin, but still, it looked awful. I understood his satisfied expression now. There was something about the pleasure he took in his sadistic conquests, and of course, I found pleasure in them too.

I took a long shower, cleaned up, and put on the clothes he'd lent me. They looked silly on my shorter frame, but they were soft, which was a boon to my sore and sensitive skin. When I returned to his bedroom, he was dressed also. Jeans? Sigh, it would be days before I could tolerate jeans. He was putting my coat on a hanger, with my uniform pieces in a bag underneath.

"Hey, you should probably look at your phone," he said over his shoulder. "A buttload of messages came through as soon as your phone powered on. I didn't read them. Okay, I glanced at the last few. Your boss is a loon."

"Goodluck texted me?" He didn't do that very often. He preferred showing up at my apartment at all hours and banging on my door. But if he hadn't been able to find me...

I scrolled through to the beginning of the text storm, noting the liberal use of emojis and capital letters.

"Crap, he's been looking for me since last night." I'd set my phone to silent, and neglected to check my messages before I fell into Fort's bed. "Sometimes he just really wants to talk about things."

"He seemed to want to talk about candlelight," Fort said, looking over my shoulder.

I lit a candle. Please come see.

STARCOMET

COME SEE

After that he texted three flame emojis, and a dozen or so exclamation marks.

Pls answer SC. You have never seen anything like these dancing shadows.

The texts went on, two dozen or more about five minutes apart, talking about candles and scents, and how flames could be magic. He asked me repeatedly how he'd never noticed this magic before. Someone who didn't know him would assume Goodluck was high, but he never used drugs.

I scrolled down to the most recent ones.

Why aren't you answering me? I need to talk to you.

I'm going to do a show w/candles. Theme of candles, light on people's faces. OK?

OK??????

He followed that with alternating skull and fire emojis, three solid lines.

PLS ANSWER ME

YOU KNOW I AM YOUR BOSS

I just lit another candle. The flame is like a new spirit, calming me.

Sorry I was angry.

I AM STILL ANGRY WHERE ARE YOU

??????????????

DO YOU EVEN UNDERSTAND ABOUT THESE SHADOWS??? *What is in the shadows, Starcomet?* **WHAT?!**

Please come to me. I'm crying.

I sighed and texted him.

Sorry, boss. My phone died. On my way home, call you when I'm there.

"I have to go," I said to Fort. "I'm sorry to rush out."
"I'll drive you."
"You don't have to."

He held the hanger with the coat so I couldn't reach it. "I'll drive you. No arguments. We need to get you back to the Black Wall before Goodluck's head explodes."

It was easier to go in Fort's car than to wait for a driver or take the subway, even if our conversation during the ride was a little stilted. I knew he wanted to talk about The Gallery, what I'd thought of the whole experience, but it was too much to hash over while I still felt half asleep, so we talked about safer things. Small talk. When he pulled up to the Black Wall, I gathered my coat and uniform.

"Thanks for the ride," I said, turning to open the door.

"Juliet."

I turned back to him. He wanted to talk, but I was afraid of what I'd say. "I'm sorry, Fort. Please. I have to go. He's going to get crazier about this whole candle thing before he calms down."

"Okay. Call me later though, after you've...processed."

Did he want to hash over our experience at The Gallery for sexy thrills? I didn't think so. He was worried that I was hiding uncomfortable feelings, that I was upset.

"Everything's fine," I said, touching his hand on the gearshift. "Let's talk later."

I got out of the car and crossed to the stairwell, feeling silly in my sweatpants and stilettos. When I got up to my floor, I found Goodluck crouched beside my welcome mat, cupping his hand around a silver taper candle's flame.

"You're going to burn your fingers," I scolded. "Why don't you have a holder for that?"

He gave me an accusing look. "The holder is me. Where have you been? I asked you to call me."

"I know. I'm sorry." I shifted my coat to the other hand. "I was out late doing a...a thing."

"A thing? How late?" He stood, still cupping his candle. "It's almost one in the afternoon, in case you haven't noticed. You still have sleep all over your face."

I knew my eyes were puffier than normal from crying last night. "I'm sorry I didn't answer your texts. My phone died. Please, Goodluck. Chill out."

"Chill out?" he said, flinching as if I'd slapped his face. "I experienced things last night that you can't imagine. I needed to talk to you about it. How long have we worked together? You know that inspiration comes when it comes."

I rubbed my forehead, wondering how it had come to this. I was tottering on black stilettos in a chilly stairwell in someone else's clothes while an artist in meltdown-mode chewed me out.

"I'm sorry I wasn't here to listen," I said, even though I wasn't.

He frowned at me, his ocean-blue eyes filled with emotion. "You have to be here when I need you. I can't work like this."

"Look, I'm going to go in and change into some other clothes, and do something with my hair, and then we can talk, okay? I'll come upstairs and knock."

"Starcomet!"

"That's not my name," I said, struggling with the lock while trying not to drop my coat, or the bag with my uniform. "Don't catch me on fire. I'll come upstairs in ten minutes."

"Okay," he snapped, like I was the unreasonable one.

I had too much on my mind to deal with his crazy-artist tantrum right now. I went into my apartment and kicked the door shut behind me, juggling the coat as I threw down my keys. I dropped everything on a chair and took off the stilettos, and went into my bathroom, grabbing a pair of pajama pants on the way. I took off Fort's clothes and put on a bra—a real one, not a peek-a-boo one—then turned around to inspect my butt again in the mirror.

Holy hell, what a mess of bruises and marks. I gingerly prodded one of the bruises. It didn't hurt that much. The welts were what hurt. I pulled on a pair of thong underwear and turned back to the mirror, splashing water on my hair. I heard the door bang, heard Goodluck's voice as he entered my living room.

"I need you to call someone about candle modeling. Who was that girl we used last year—" His voice cut off with an ear-piercing shriek.

I'd left the bathroom door open, so he could see me as he skipped down the hall. I spun around, covering my ass.

"Goodluck! Get out of here."

He gaped at me. "Holy fucking shit!"

"I'm not dressed. Leave!"

But he didn't leave. He crowded with me into my bathroom, throwing his candle into the sink, where the flame hissed out. "What the fuck happened to you?" Goodluck had gone sheet white. "Holy tears of the goddess. What happened to your butt?"

"Nothing. It was..."

"Oh my God."

I grabbed Fort's shirt from the counter and yanked it over my head, its excessive length covering my ass, but Goodluck pushed it up again. He gawked. "You are so, so hurt."

"I'm not hurt. They look worse than they feel," I said, pushing his hands away and pulling on my pajama bottoms. "And they were consensual."

"Consensual with who? The Marquis de Sade?" He let out a soft breath, like my life choices were too awful for him to accept. "Your body is your temple, Juliet. It moves and sustains you. It makes art for the world. How can you hurt your beloved body this way?"

Juliet. He almost never used my given name, so he was using it now to send a message. We were about to have a tragedy, like my namesake. We were going to end up a couple of corpses by the time we were done.

I moved by him, out into the living room where I could have some space to breathe. I wasn't even sure last night was worth all this. Had The Gallery turned me on? Yes. Did I enjoy it as much as scening with Fort privately?

No. There was something missing, some intimacy or connection, which was probably why Fort liked The Gallery better.

"Are you listening to me?"

Goodluck's voice brought my head up. "What? What did you say?"

"We can go to the police. Whoever did this—"

"I wanted him to do this." My words rose over his shocked voice. "For some reason, my body likes to be hurt. I just discovered this. You always talk about discovery, about trying new things, about keeping your soul fresh. I enjoy the way it feels to...to be hurt. It's called being a masochist."

He looked more horrified, not less. "Your soul is crying right now. Your body is sick. Your mind is sick if you want that kind of hurt, those bruises, those welts. My God, they'll leave scars. It's him, isn't it?" He ran his hands through his wild hair. "That man from the ad campaign, the one you've been running around with, he's making you think you want this. I told you, he's worse than Keith. He's hurting you even worse."

I put my hands over my ears. "I don't want to talk about it. What Fort and I do is none of your business."

"The integrity of your body is my business. You are a human being who must be cared for. You're my friend."

He tried to take my hands away from my ears but I held them there harder. Soon we were struggling, pushing at each other like scrapping children. It would have been hilarious if it wasn't so sad.

"Get the fuck away from me," I yelled. "I know we've had a special, close working relationship. I know you care about me, but Jesus, I need some space right now. If you can't give me space when I ask for it, then I'll—"

"What?" he said, interrupting. "What'll you do, quit? Work for some other artist who's half as talented as me?"

I covered my eyes. I couldn't cry now. Goodluck went nuts when I cried. "I don't want to quit, but I can't be only yours," I told him. "You do this every time I date someone. You criticize and poke into my business. You want me to yourself, so you vilify them."

"Because they're all assholes," he yelled. There was no sign of the serene guru here, just a scary, disapproving boss. "It boils down to this, Juliet: you're either with me, or you're against me."

"This isn't a war!"

He spoke over me. "I need one hundred percent of you, or..."

Or I don't want you anymore. He didn't have to say it. I understood it in his hard, unsympathetic gaze.

"Well, thanks for sharing how you feel," I snapped. I felt judged and shamed. I felt punished all over again, but this time the pain didn't turn me on. "Maybe this comet is dying out. These things have a physical life."

"I can't talk to you right now." His voice cracked on the last two words. "I just...can't."

He left my apartment, slamming the door. I swallowed hard and started counting to distract myself so I wouldn't cry. *One, two, three, four, five, six, seven, eight, nine, ten, eleven, twelve, thirteen, fourteen, fifteen...* I counted to one hundred and still felt shitty. I tried to think about science, about Fort's pendulums swinging, about potential and kinetic energy. Relationships had that kind of energy. They were always changing.

But I'd worked for Goodluck for so long. I loved him. He loved me in his kooky way. Managing his art empire was the only job I'd ever known, and it made me feel like I was part of something special. Goodluck had been my world for years now, the only relationship in my life that ever worked. If we parted ways...

Ugh, I wanted to go back to Fort's penthouse and beg him to hold me. No, I couldn't do that. I went into my bathroom and picked up Goodluck's unevenly melted candle. I'd have to buy him a holder, maybe a nice glass candlestick as a goodwill gift. Maybe we could talk about things, negotiate some boundaries for our working relationship. I carried my phone around all day waiting for more messages from him, but none came.

* * * * *

I went out for groceries later in the afternoon, determined to cook dinner, but when I got home, I went straight to the couch and curled up under a blanket. I wasn't hungry anyway. I flipped on the TV, looking for a distraction. News? God, no. Home improvement shows? A little better. I watched them tear down the walls of an old Victorian, letting my mind drift. I had feelings to process, but watching TV felt easier. Later, when I felt stronger...

My phone rang, displaying Fort's name on the screen. A surge of excitement was followed by ambivalence. Was I angry with him? Yes, a little. My life wasn't spiraling out of control on its own.

I picked up the phone and greeted him in a reasonably steady voice. He cut right to the chase.

"Come over. Let's have dinner."

I pulled the blanket tighter around me. "I'm sorry, I'd rather not. I've had a long day."

A pause. "Would you like me to come over there?"

"I won't be good company."

"You can be any kind of company you want." His kind, deep voice was melting my resolve to spend the night sulking. "We didn't have time to talk about The Gallery this morning," he said. "And I think we should."

I hugged myself, pushing my head into the sofa cushion. "Then let's talk."

"I'd prefer to do it face to face."

"I don't know if that's a good idea." I got off the couch and headed to the kitchen. I needed some tea to relax me. "When you're near me, I can't express myself the right way."

Another pause. "Are you grouchy because you had to talk to your boss all day about candles?"

"No. He was too angry to talk to me, because..." I rammed the tea pod into my machine with a little more force than necessary. "Because I wasn't there for him when he needed me."

"Did you get in trouble?" he asked in a mocking tone. "Did Goodluck Weirdface yell at you?"

"Yes, he yelled at me. We had a big argument, which was really shitty."

When he spoke, it wasn't mocking anymore. "I'm sorry," he said. "It was my fault you weren't at home. I just thought...after last night...I wanted to keep you close to me, in case you felt post-traumatic stress, or some kind of drop from everything that went on."

I watched my tea spit into my cup, feeling my resolve melt a little more. He might be dead-set against love, but he cared about me. "The Gallery wasn't that traumatic, not really. It just..." *It just made me feel even closer to you. Every time you hurt me, I feel closer to you and I don't know what to do about that.*

"How's your ass looking today?" he asked.

"The same. Awful. I mean, I think it looks sexy, but Goodluck barged into my apartment while I was changing, and he saw the marks, and..."

"Oh no."

"Oh yes. He wasn't happy about it, and he guessed it was you that made them." I took my tea and phone and headed back to the couch, climbing under the blanket again. "It doesn't matter," I said when Fort didn't speak. "It's my personal life, my personal business. He won't come after you or anything. I told him it was consensual, that I liked it."

"What did he say to that?"

I sighed. "He said my soul was crying, and my body was sick."

"Surely he knows about kinky sex, about sado-masochism? There are enough elements of it in those photos he creates."

"Kinky elements?" I bit my lip, thinking. "In Goodluck's photos?"

"Hell, yes, in Goodluck's photos. Have you ever really looked at them? There's a reason they're so popular."

"I guess we all see what we want to see," I said, pulling my knees up. "You know what? You can come over if you want. Maybe it would be good for us to talk."

As if on cue, I heard a knock. "I'm in your stairwell. Let me in."

I put down my tea and went to the door. So much for slapping on a little makeup before he arrived. When I opened the door, his gaze was trained on me, taking me in with unsettling intensity.

"Evening, Sparkles," he said, brushing past me. I felt bedraggled in my yoga pants and t-shirt, while he smelled and looked wonderfully crisp. His light tan sweater showed off his body without hugging it, and his jeans clung to his crotch and thighs with the usual perfect fit.

"How did you get here so fast?" I asked.

"I was on my way to your place when I called."

He opened his arms and I accepted his hug, the one I'd desperately needed earlier, after my fight with my boss. Our hug turned into a grope, and then he lifted me so my legs were around his waist. His leonine eyes locked on mine. His cock hardened between my spread thighs, or maybe it had already been hard. I was definitely getting wet. He walked me over to the couch and dumped me onto it, crawling over me.

"I thought you wanted to talk," I said.

"I do want to talk. I also want to do this."

His hands wandered over my body, insinuating themselves under my t-shirt, pushing up my bralette and squeezing a nipple. "Are your tits still sore?"

"They've been sore all day." *And I thought of you, and now you're on top of me and...*

"Poor baby." He nuzzled me, his fingers tracing down to pull at my waistband. "I was hard on you last night. What did you hate the most?"

That was easy. "I hated when your friends talked to me. When they participated in our scenes."

"They knew you wouldn't like it. That's why they did it. They're sadists, like me." He tsked when I pushed against his chest, and held me down harder. "And you liked that you didn't like it. You liked how awful and scared they made you feel."

My hackles rose, even as my pussy throbbed. "That's not true."

"It is true. I was there, I saw the whole thing. I saw how you suffered to make me happy. God, you turn me on."

By now, my yoga pants were around my hips. A finger shoved inside my pussy, then his fly was open, his hard cock jutting against my bare skin. I closed my eyes and thought of The Gallery, of the men strutting around in their formal clothes with their hard cocks flagrantly displayed.

"Take these off," he growled, and I contorted my body to shed the stretchy pants while he finger fucked me some more. I spread my legs, my eyes still closed.

"Look at me," he said. He yanked his jeans down to his thighs and pushed inside me right there on my couch. I groaned as my bruised ass slid across the cushion, my body invaded by the power of his thrusts. I didn't want to like it, but I did. I opened my eyes and tried to stop myself from falling under his spell again, but it was hopeless. I was hooked on his force and intensity. I knew I'd go back to The Gallery and expose myself to more sadism because he drove me wild. His friends could touch and hurt me, but I'd still be wet for his cock.

"Come here. Come closer." He squeezed me against him, until we couldn't be any closer than we were right then. He was so big, so warm. I felt his teeth on my neck as he rode me, and his body was all the bondage I needed to climb toward orgasm. I was tired, my muscles strained from stress, but I loved the aches and pains as I moved for him.

"Yes, yes," I sighed.

"Did you need this all day, baby? Did you think about my cock fucking you all day?"

"Yes, Sir."

"Say it. *I thought about your cock all day.*"

He fucked me harder, making my voice shake as I cried out, "I thought about your cock all day."

But I'd thought about more than that. I'd thought about chains and cuffs, and a clock tower in the sky. I'd thought about the way he wouldn't let me leave his apartment afterward, and now...

Now he was deep inside me, holding me tight. We were so close we might have been the same body. Our hearts were mashed together, and my nipples slid against his chest hair, one more discomfort to thrill me.

"I'm going to come," I gasped. "I need to come. Please let me..."

"Come for me. Now." He tightened his fingers around my wrists as he spoke, stretching my arms high over my head. I fought to close my legs, to grip him harder, but he wouldn't let me. He denied me at every turn, but all it did was make me hotter. His legs spread mine wide as he rode me, one knee on the ground for leverage. His pelvis ground against my clit, his arms held me down, and I started to come.

I arched, letting out a stuttering breath, riding the pleasure while being ridden in return. His thrusts never stopped as I contracted on his length. He was so hard and deep inside me. My orgasm vibrated with intensity before it ebbed into a wrung-out bliss. I curled my fingers around his hands, feeling his grip slacken as his own climax arrived. He let go of one wrist and grabbed my ass instead, pressing my pelvis to his, drilling me with brutal force. It triggered another orgasm for me, my body caught up in passion and sensation. Our bodies hit a heightened note together, both of us straining through a gasping finale.

He came to rest, but his hands grew taut again. One held my ass, keeping me close, while the other slid around my fingers and closed tight.

"I can't move," I whispered.

"You're not allowed to move."

He was still inside me, his cock buried deep. When I squeezed on him, he groaned and pressed his lips to mine. His kiss was voracious, and I kissed him back, transported by our closeness.

"I never want to move," I said when he let me take a breath. "I wish we could stay like this forever."

His hazy gaze sharpened, fixing on mine. All the softness, the connection of the moment before disintegrated. I realized too late that there had been too much love in my voice, too much need and affection.

"I'm sorry," I said, which made his expression darken even more.

"What are you sorry for? Don't be sorry." He stroked my forehead, his voice pitched to distance, rather than the need I'd communicated. "Are you okay?" he asked after a moment.

I wasn't sure what he meant by "okay." Was my body okay after his forceful fucking? Was my mind okay? Was I okay with the aftermath of The Gallery? Maybe he meant all of that.

"I'm okay," I said, but it might have been a lie. "I feel a little tired, even though you were doing most of the work just now."

"I like working you over. And if you're tired, that's a good thing, because I'm sure you're ready for bed."

I sighed as he withdrew. "You can stay here if you like. If you're tired too."

He didn't look at me as he moved away, sitting back on his haunches. "Thanks for the invitation, but I have to go."

"Oh."

"I would stay, but I'm flying somewhere with Devin in the morning. I'll be gone until Friday."

"Where are you going?"

He hesitated just a moment too long. "Morocco." He caressed my cheek, then busied himself buttoning up his jeans. "You should get some rest, some quality sleep after those orgasms."

"Yes, Sir. I'll try."

He wasn't going to Morocco. I knew him well enough now to know when he told a lie. I'd royally fucked up with my *I wish we could stay like this forever*. He'd obviously only wanted to see me tonight to get his rocks off. I flushed, thinking about how excited I'd been when he called me, how thrilled I was that he *cared about me*. As usual, my understanding of my relationship with someone was way off. Pathetically off. Embarrassingly off.

I reached to collect my yoga pants and pull them on, wondering if this was it, if I would ever see him again.

"So, have fun on your trip," I said, trying to sound casual. "I bet it's beautiful in Morocco."

"Yeah, I've been a lot of times." He turned away, heading to my door, then turned back again. "Do you want to go to The Gallery with me next Saturday?"

"Oh. Sure, if you want to," I said.

It doesn't mean anything, I scolded myself silently. *It only means he wants to get off again.*

He gave me a quick kiss and strode to the door, ready to go. No tea, no cuddles, no insistence on my company tonight.

It didn't escape me that he'd allowed me to stay with him after the regimented, public experience of The Gallery, but after what had just happened between us—the comfortable intimacy we'd just experienced—he was anxious to leave. It was so easy for me to forget that he preferred distance to intimacy. Whenever we were face to face...

What we'd just done felt like love, but it wasn't love. From the way he kissed me on the forehead and retreated, it felt more like an impulsive mistake.

Chapter Twenty-Three: Fort

Dev, I need to go somewhere

??? Where?

Doesn't matter. Just somewhere that isn't here.

I'm flying to Geneva in the morning if u want to go.

OK

Why, what's going on

Nothing. Just need some air.

Chapter Twenty-Four: Juliet

I plodded through the next week like a zombie. It was the week of Valentine's Day, with love and roses everywhere, but for me, there was so little joy. Goodluck gave me the silent treatment and canceled two appearances, leaving me to clean up the mess.

I started to think seriously about quitting as his manager, maybe leaving the art world altogether. I could say goodbye to the weirdness and high-maintenance personalities, go back to school to learn something new, something practical like nursing or accounting.

Would I feel like quitting in a week? In a month? I'd never last a month if Goodluck didn't forgive me for abandoning him during his candlelight epiphany.

And all this drama was because of Fort, because of the angst and upheaval he brought to my life. Damn it, I was falling in love with him, and it wasn't only that Valentine's Day was in the air. I couldn't understand my deepening feelings for him, but I also couldn't deny them anymore. The way he looked at me whenever he saw me, the way he kissed me, the way he put his hands on me all the time, it read like love to my heart, but it wasn't love. At thirty-two, I was finally realizing that the men I gravitated toward were men who *couldn't love*.

All day Saturday, I thought I should cancel that night's foray to The Gallery. I picked up the phone, my finger hovering over Fort's name, but in the end I couldn't do it. I didn't want to give up the chance to see him, the chance to enter that fantasy world again, because once I ducked out of going to The Gallery, Fort would be lost to me.

So I tamped down my inconvenient and unreasonable emotions and pulled my wild hair back, smoothing it into a tight bun. I shaved and put on my revealing uniform, and applied new waterproof makeup that wouldn't run when I cried. I took my coat from the closet, pulled off the dry-cleaning plastic, and stared at the elegant black garment before wrapping myself in it. Juliet's invisibility cloak.

When Fort arrived, I felt a little better about my decision. The Gallery would be fun. We would be two adults having sexy fun together. He looked relaxed, all put together in his suit and tie. He kissed me, a quick, rough kiss before we headed downstairs. I felt less nervous than last time, now that I knew what to expect. The collar felt a little more natural around my neck, and the harness-like garter belt seemed to caress rather than confine me.

"I've been thinking about you all day," he said in the car, delving under my coat and rubbing his hand up and down my thigh.

"I've been thinking about you all week. How was Morocco?"

"Hot."

I still didn't believe he'd gone to Morocco, but his hand felt so good and firm against my bare skin that I didn't challenge him. He seemed tight-lipped. I guessed he was doing his Dominant thing, so I looked out the window and summoned my inner submissive. It was Saturday night in Manhattan. There were couples everywhere, laughing, holding hands, heading out for dinner or drinks. I wondered if any of them got off on pain the way we did.

"We don't have to go to The Gallery," he said, abruptly. "We could play at my house. We could...I don't know. Go see a movie."

A movie, like a normal romantic couple, so I could fall even deeper in love? "I'm not dressed for a movie. But I don't care. It's up to you."

He frowned. "We're on The Gallery guest list. We might as well go."

"Yes. I think every time I go, I'll get better at it."

I couldn't tell if he wanted me to go, or if he wanted me to plead out. I couldn't read him on a good night, and tonight he seemed especially closed off. Once we arrived at The Gallery, we were greeted by Rene and ushered into the echoing elegance of the clock tower, where the hiss and swish of punishments surrounded us, along with whispers and moans. As I looked around the room at busy hands and busy mouths, I realized how much trust mattered, and how much I'd come to trust Fort during our acquaintance.

No, it wasn't trust. It was love.

I didn't want anyone else to touch me, because I loved him. I didn't look around or preen like the other submissives, eager for any Dominant's attention. I only wanted one man's attention.

A groan of pleasure made me turn to the left. I saw Michelle, my costume fitter, on her knees, giving her Master an ardent blowjob. She was here for sex and fulfillment. What was I here for?

To spend time with him.

I realized then that I should have agreed to the movie. Hell, I should have broken things off with Fort a couple weeks ago.

"What are we going to do with you tonight?" he said. "Where can I take you next?"

"Somewhere awful," I replied, avoiding his gaze. "Somewhere painful."

I wanted to get away from the emotional part of me that kept rearing its ugly head. I wanted to be like Michelle, a willing, open vessel eager to be used. I hoped my "sponsor" would be able to get me there.

After another moment of scrutiny, Fort led me to an area near the middle of the main floor, to a padded beam lowered nearly to the ground. It was around four feet in length, with a threaded socket set into the center of the vinyl top. I had an idea what the socket was for, an idea that was confirmed when he opened a drawer to the right of the beam. It held an array of packaged dildos that graduated in size from average to ridiculously massive.

I'd asked for awful and painful, which must have been why he selected one of the larger ones. The solid, black shaft matched the black vinyl padding on top of the beam, creating a daunting vision as Fort screwed in the dildo. As much as the thing scared me—it had to be three inches or more in diameter—my pussy had grown more than slick enough to take it. In a few short weeks, he'd trained me to equate fear with lust, and pain with pleasure.

"Time to take a ride," he said, nudging me toward the beam. I eyed the tool that would soon impale me. I thought it must be made of silicone or rubber, until he had me straddle it and sink down. The dildo felt cool and smooth as stone, a hard, unyielding phallus wedged inside me. Even with my sensitive clit and dripping pussy, I felt uncomfortably full. The beam was low enough that my knees touched the ground, allowing me to squirm and twist. I could have stood up again to relieve myself of the intrusion, but I didn't dare.

He left me to accustom myself to the shaft. I rose gingerly up and down on it by squeezing my thighs as he crossed to get some nipple clamps from his cabinet of pain. I'd developed a love/hate relationship with those clamps. I shuddered in dread just to see them in his hands, but at the same time, I knew I'd almost come when he applied them. There was something about his face as he did it, the stern brows, the pursed lips, the gleam of sadism tempered with curiosity. *How much will this hurt her?*

How much do I love him?

I moaned as he approached. He made a shushing sound and held out the first clamp. "Hold up your tit for me, Sparkles. Offer it to me for punishment."

The cupless bra already framed my breasts for his pleasure, but I obeyed and pushed up first one breast, then the other, so he could clamp my nipples. We stared into each other's eyes as he did it, the tormenter and the tormentee. The biting pain quickened my breath and made my pussy clench on the shaft inside me. It was, of course, impossible for me to close my thighs.

"Arms up," he commanded. He cuffed my wrists to a chain hanging over my head, so I was on my knees, stuffed and clamped, trapped at his mercy. He stood in front of me then, one foot on either side of the beam, and tipped up my chin. He took down my hair, tossing the pins away, undoing my carefully crafted bun with a few careless passes of his fingers.

"That's better," he said, as I tossed my hair back from my eyes. His fly came down and his cock emerged, already thick and stiff. I wished I could touch him, welcome his cock to my lips, but he'd taken that power away from me. His hands fisted in my loose hair, drawing me forward as he ordered me to open my mouth.

I obeyed, straining when he barked, "Wider!" He shoved in deep, choking me. I gagged and stared up at him, trying to focus on pleasing him. At the same time, I had to deal with the painful clamps torturing my nipples, and the rigid shaft in my pussy. My body tensed, searching for balance as his thrusts threw me off kilter. My lungs ached, and my eyes teared up as I struggled for breath.

"Breathe through your nose," he said, tapping my hollowed-out cheek. Then he drove deep and squeezed my nostrils shut, laughing when I whipped my head back and forth. I only had the sick feeling of suffocation for a moment before he let go, but it was enough. Tears squeezed from my eyes as I choked against his cock.

"Okay, that was mean," he said. "Take a breath."

That was all he gave me, one short breath before he thrust in again. I tried to calm down and suck him properly, breathing through my nose, leaning into his assault. I still gagged with almost every thrust. He didn't cut off my breath again, though I waited in dread for him to do it. My eyes overflowed until my cheeks were drenched. By the time he came, my chest was covered in drool.

I swallowed his cum with a spasmodic gulp, and still opened my mouth for more. My mind didn't want more, no, but my body... He'd restrained me and hurt me, and had his way with me, and that made me want *more*.

He tousled my hair, looking down at me with a combination of exasperation and approval. "You're a mess, Juliet. You need more training on sucking a man's cock."

He left me to panic as I shifted on my knees and stared at the front end of the beam. What did he mean, more training? Was he going to invite some other man over here to fuck my mouth? I could hear male voices all around me, laughter and talking. All of them owned me, but I didn't want them to. I didn't belong here. Even if my body enjoyed this, my heart didn't belong here. I realized that now.

Fort returned—alone, thank God—and mopped my wet cheeks and chin with a damp towel. He cleaned the drool from my chest, making the clamps swing, making them hurt even more. When he took them off, I almost cried with relief.

"Oww," I whined as the blood rushed back to my nipples. I swung from my bonds, hoping he'd let me rise off the shaft. Instead, he used a pedal beside him to raise the beam inch by inch until the toes of my shoes could barely skim the floor. The higher he raised it, the more the pressure grew between my legs. He cuffed my ankles to the floor, not that I could have moved anywhere with the thick dildo inside me. If only I could have rubbed my clit on the beam's slick surface, but the dildo wouldn't let me move my hips at all.

My thoughts raced, my emotions in a whirl. When Fort was beside me, I felt ready for anything. When he held my gaze, I was so hot, so ready for release. All the boxes were checked. Restraint? Yes. Pain? Yes. Crying? Yes. Hard tools being jammed into my orifices? Yes.

"Please," I said, straining on the shaft within me. "Please...Sir..."

"I know." He watched me struggle to balance on the tips of my stilettos. "Do your arms hurt?"

"A little. Yes."

"Let's fix that."

"Fixing that" consisted of lowering them from above my head to my lower back, where he cinched them with an added strap around my waist. My arms felt less strained in this position, but I'd gone from less bondage to more bondage. My thighs trembled. I looked down at my silk stocking tops and the garter clips that held them. Even that was bondage.

If you don't care about sharing me with others, why do you bind me so hard in our scenes?

I wished I could ask him. Instead I stared at him, processing too many emotions.

"Stop that," he said. "Stop looking at me like your world's about to end. You want this."

Yes, I wanted this. I wanted him.

I wanted him to feel the same sense of connection I felt, but he didn't. He avoided my gaze, going to the wall for a slim leather whip. When he returned, he whacked it across the fronts of my thighs, and I whined at the sudden, biting pain.

"Don't be a baby," he said, when I stared down at the developing marks. "It hurts, but I'm not hitting you that hard."

"It hurts, though. It really hurts."

He answered that with another set of blows, two on the inside of each thigh as I bucked on the beam. Now the phallus was fucking me, because I couldn't stop hopping up and down. The chains holding my ankle cuffs rattled with each jump. My pussy was full and wet, and Fort was hurting me, and oh God, I wanted to come. I needed to come, but I couldn't unless he touched me.

Then the tip of the whip teased between my legs. I cried out and arched my back, needing more. *Let me come, let me come. If you won't love me, at least give me that.*

The pleasurable prod against my clit disappeared. "You're a masochist, aren't you, Juliet?"

His tone of voice indicated only one correct reply, which I gave him. "Yes, Sir, I'm a masochist."

"Then you'd probably prefer more pain."

He went back to swatting my inner thighs with the whip, quick, sharp bursts that drove me out of my mind. I tried to process the sting, tried to transform it into something that might let me come, but it didn't work. A moment later, he stopped. Prodded my clit again.

I moaned at the blissful sensation even as I knew the delicious, teasing contact wouldn't last. This was a game to him, a game to see how miserable he could make me, how hard he could make me cry. If he didn't want me to come, I couldn't come. I was his. I endured all this for him. I stared at him, going subspace-y, letting him see just how much pain I'd take for his pleasure. I understood now why consent wasn't necessary in scenes like ours. He could take anything from me, have anything, and I'd only give him more.

Instead of looking pleased, his lips twisted in frustration. "Jesus, I told you to stop that."

As quickly as I'd found subspace, he jerked it away from me. "Sir...I..."

"Stop looking at me like that, like you're doing this for me."

He took a step back. I was flabbergasted. I thought that was what submission was all about. I'd thought that was the purest, highest form of surrender. "What? I don't understand."

"Get your emotions out of it. You don't have to *understand*. You have to—" He swung an arm around the space, gesturing with the whip. "No one else looks at their Dominant like that. They're here for the pain, for the enjoyment."

"I— Sir— I am—"

"You have to be in it for yourself, not for me."

"But I— I want to do this for you." Tears rose in my eyes. "I come here for you."

"No, you come here for you."

"Partly, but also to please you. Because I—" I hesitated, but the words still came, the horrible, disastrous words. "Because I feel connected to you here, in a way I've never felt connected to anyone before. There's this depth to our scenes—"

"Jesus, there's no depth to anything, Juliet, except that dildo in your cunt. I mean, look at you."

His hard gaze raked over my slut costume and restraints while I stared at him, traumatized. His hazel eyes went storm-dark, then he dropped the whip and turned away. Tears blurred my vision as I watched him stride the length of the dungeon and walk out the door.

Oh God. He couldn't... He didn't...

He had. He'd left me. A minute went by. Two minutes. Three. I watched the door but he didn't return. I looked around, seeing blurs of Dominants, none of them my own. Where was he? Was this more sadism? A punishment?

The tears in my eyes spilled over, but I couldn't wipe them away. My hands were bound. My legs were bound. My body was under someone else's control, and that someone had left me.

"Jesus." It seemed an eternity before I heard the rough voice beside me. "What the fuck? Where's Fort?"

I screwed my eyes shut, ashamed, trying to find my voice to speak. "I—I don't know. He left a while ago. I don't know."

"He left? Open your eyes. Look at me."

I did, and hot tears flooded my cheeks. He put a hand on my back. "Get her a blanket," he said. Fingers worked at my wrists. "Fuck, fuck, fuck. What the ever-loving fuck?" His arms came around my sides, undoing the strap at my waist. My tears cleared enough to recognize Fort's friend Devin and the elfin submissive he'd brought to Goodluck's premiere.

Whispers rose and other noises in the dungeon faded away as people moved toward me, fencing me in. I wanted to hide but I couldn't move. Devin waved someone away. "No, I've got it. Give her some space."

He lowered the beam so my feet could reach the floor, then knelt and undid my ankle on one side, while his submissive undid the other.

While they worked, another man wrapped a blanket around my shoulders and talked to me, a steady stream of quiet, soothing phrases I barely heard. I was so humiliated, so defeated. Devin chafed my hands. "Juliet." He waited until my eyes fixed on him. "Juliet, do you remember me?"

I nodded, too mortified and wrung out to speak. From erotic heat and subspace to this cold abandonment...it was too much to take.

"I'm going to lift you off the beam, okay?" he said. "I'm going to go really slow. Are you still wet enough, or do you need lube?"

I shook my head, just because I was horrified by his question, but he took it as a yes, and his submissive went scurrying off at his signal. That was when I realized the dungeon was silent, that almost everyone who'd been playing had disappeared.

"Please take me off here," I said.

"I don't want to hurt you."

"Please." I almost said *Sir*. "Please help me. I want to go home. I need to go home."

He ignored my pleading, rubbing my back until his submissive returned. "Be gentle," he said, and she was touching me, smoothing lube around my pussy's opening. "I've sat here too," she said. "It's not always easy to get up."

I fixed my eyes on her sympathetic smile, using it as an anchor while she replaced the moisture that Fort's desertion had dissipated. When she seemed satisfied, Devin put an arm under my leg and another around my waist, his muscles straining to be gentle even as he lifted me as dead weight. "Okay?" he asked.

I wasn't okay. I was falling apart, even though he lifted me so slowly and carefully that I felt no pain at all. The pain was centered in my soul, in my heart, in the trust that Fort had smashed to pieces. That trust was all that had held our fragile relationship together, and now it was gone.

Again. I'd failed again. I'd trusted someone I shouldn't have trusted, and convinced myself that he felt more for me than he did. I felt furious, belittled. Maimed. Abandoned, but it was what I deserved for being stupid *again*. I tried to stand as soon as I was free of the huge phallus, but Devin held me tighter.

"Wait. Take a minute."

"I want to go home." I started crying again. I didn't want Devin to hold me, but I found myself pressing my head against his shoulder, seeking solace. He carried me to a nearby sofa and held me, wrapping the blanket tightly around my body. His submissive brought some water for me. After all this, I still didn't know her name, which seemed horribly sad.

"What happened, Juliet?" Fort's friend Milo, the Dom with the long hair, stood behind the couch, his eyes intent with concern. "Why did Fort leave you? Was he sick?"

"No, he was angry. He said..." I thought back, trying to remember what I'd babbled to him, what had been so bad that he had to walk away and leave me. Devin's submissive held out a tissue. "He said I was too emotional. Then...I don't remember... I guess I said something that upset him."

Devin scowled. "There's nothing you could have said that would excuse his behavior."

I knew his words were true, but I still felt a sick sense of blame, of shame for something I didn't understand. I wanted to hide myself. I wanted to hit something. I wanted to scream until The Gallery's glass clock face shattered.

Milo leaned closer to me. "What do you want to do?"

Hide. Hit. Scream. Shatter.

"Do you want to go see him?" he pressed. "Talk about what happened?"

I really started bawling, because these men were idiots. I never wanted to see Fort again, and he clearly wanted nothing more to do with me.

"He left me," I said, swiping at my tears. "I don't understand why." But I understood that all my relationships failed, so this should have been expected.

"It's against the rules for him to leave you," said Devin. "We should go to him. Discuss this. He needs to apologize to you."

"No." I struggled off Devin's lap. "I don't want to see him. I need to go home."

He exchanged a look with his submissive. "We'll take you home. Rachel, go and get her coat."

"Yes, Sir."

Rachel was her name. She had a name and I had a name, and all of this was just games. Horrible, dangerous games.

I turned to Devin as soon as she was gone. "Did Fort go to Morocco with you?"

"What?" His pale blue eyes narrowed. "Morocco?"

My hands curled into fists at my sides. "Fort said he went to Morocco with you."

"Yes. We've gone many times."

"This week! Did he go this week?"

Devin blinked at me. "Not this week. He tagged along on a trip to Geneva the last couple days. It wasn't that exciting, but—"

I put my head in my hands.

"Did he promise to take you to Morocco?" Devin asked. I couldn't reconcile his kind voice with the rude Dom who'd taunted me last week.

"No," I said, choking on the word. "He hasn't promised me anything. He never promised me anything."

Milo touched my back, but I stiffened. It wasn't that I didn't want comfort, I just didn't want it now. I didn't want it here, and I didn't want it from a man who'd scared me last week.

Rachel returned with my coat and I retreated to The Gallery's black and gold bathroom to stare at myself in the mirror. My waterproof makeup couldn't resist so many tears. I was a mess, both inside and out. I hid in a stall until Rachel came in after me, coaxing me out and down to Devin's car. They both insisted on walking me to my door, and Devin offered to have Rachel stay with me all night.

Rachel turned out to be pretty nice. Devin turned out to be a decent human too, but I needed to be alone to heal from the huge wrong turns I'd taken lately. I should have canceled The Gallery. I never should have gone in the first place.

I should have had a few less drinks that night Fort found me outside Underworld, so he wouldn't have noticed me at all.

Chapter Twenty-Five: Fort

Milo and Dev arrived just after one in the morning. I thought about refusing them entry, but the confrontation would come at some point, so why not now? I let them in, then went back to collapse on my couch. They took the chairs across from me, sitting up straight. This wasn't going to be a relaxed conversation.

Devin took the first shot. "Are you ready to explain, you fucking asshole?"

Both of them glowered at me. They were still dressed from The Gallery, fresh from the scene of my crime. I wondered if they'd go back to finish their Saturday night fun after reaming me out.

"I'm sorry," I said. "Is Juliet all right?"

"She was taken care of, but I wouldn't say she's all right." Milo's voice was sharp as a razor. "You left her bound and impaled on a raised beam. She wasn't in anyone's care for several minutes." His eyes darkened with incredulity. "You walked away and left her all alone."

"Yeah, because I couldn't stay with her. She was getting too weird and emotional. The way she looked at me..." I twisted my hands together. "You don't understand."

"No, I don't understand," said Dev. "Nobody does. Dominants don't do that to their subs, ever." If Devin's gaze was fire, it would have reduced me to ash. "Why did you leave her in the middle of The Gallery alone?"

I couldn't explain the intensity of feeling that had sent me running, or the depth of despair that followed. I had no excuses, just my fucked up inability to give Juliet the connection she wanted. The connection she needed. I dropped my head and rubbed my eyes. "I don't know. I don't fucking know."

Dev came at me, shoving my head up. "You don't know? Really? I was the one who had to clean up your selfish goddamn mess. I was the one who found Juliet looking around with that dazed, bereft expression, and I'm not going to forget it anytime soon. So fucking explain why you did it."

I shoved his hand away. "You know why I did it."

"Say it out loud, motherfucker. Because I'm not sure you know."

Milo stepped between us. "This isn't about Fort and his issues. It's about Juliet."

"That's where you're wrong," snapped Devin. "It's one hundred percent about Fort and his issues." He leaned toward me, his eyes narrowed. "What did she say? Something that touched you? Something that moved you? Did she tell you she was doing this for you, that she loved you?"

"It's none of your fucking business."

"You know how this works," said Devin. "You knew the danger, you knew she was a bad idea from the beginning. And you know the fucking rules: never, ever fuck with the vulnerable." He poked a finger into my chest. "And definitely don't storm out of a sex dungeon while they're bound, when they're supposed to be in your care."

He turned away on the word *care*, like he couldn't even look at me. I understood. I hadn't been able to look at myself either since I'd left. I couldn't tell either of them the truth, that I had fallen hard for her, that I maybe already loved her to the point of terror. They thought this was everyday playboy relationship-avoidance bullshit.

I wished that was all it was.

I hadn't ever felt this way about a woman, and no woman had ever loved me, I was sure of that. No woman had ever looked past the money and status to see the man, or try to understand him. No woman had ever kicked through my walls to the longing underneath, but Juliet had looked at me in that dungeon with startling emotion in her eyes, and the bricks started crumbling. She accepted my sadism and roughness, my childish self-protectiveness. She loved me anyway, her gaze encompassing her entire soul.

And I wasn't enough for that soul, no matter how much I loved her.

I couldn't explain any of this to my friends. In their eyes, I'd fucked up and acted like the asshole they knew me to be. I'd hurt the first woman who cared for me, the *real* me, destroyed her trust and abandoned her in the worst situation imaginable, when she couldn't protect herself or walk away. I'd punished her because she made me feel something real, something deep and overwhelming.

It was hateful behavior. I didn't deserve love.

I looked up as Devin slammed the door behind him. Milo was still there, his lips set in a thin line. "You're out, Fort. Six months. Next offense is permanent."

"I'm out of what?"

"Out of The Gallery. Don't come back until you have your shit together. Six months is the minimum, but you might want to take a year."

"A year? For one offense?" I needed The Gallery now. I needed to go there to numb the feelings Juliet had awakened in me, especially now that she was lost to me forever. "I'm a longstanding member of that place. One of the longest."

"No fucking joke. That's what makes it so sad. Get your head on straight, Fort." He stood to leave, his face a disapproving mask. "We hurt women, but we don't damage women. There's a difference." He went to the door, pausing just before he exited. "Good luck figuring things out."

Chapter Twenty-Six: Juliet

I cried through a two-hour shower, questioning my life, stroking the sore marks on my thighs, berating myself, mourning the betrayal of my trust. Fort St. Clair was so good at turning on the charm, so good at dominance and seduction, but until tonight, I hadn't realized how cruel he could be.

Not just cruel. Dangerous.

Well, I was done with his shit. I blocked him on my phone—for good this time. I took my Gallery uniform out of the bathroom trash where I'd stuffed it earlier, cut off the metal pieces, and fed the rest through my shredder. The machine's rumble was satisfyingly harsh as it consumed the lace and fabric. I shredded the stockings next, determined to stick to my comfy over-the-knee socks from now on. I was left with the collar. *Property of The Gallery.*

Nope. From now on, I was the Property of No One. I cut up the collar and kept the lock to remind myself to keep my heart locked away from all men until, eh, maybe ten years from now. Maybe by then I'd be mature enough to choose the right kind of partner. I put the lock in the bottom of my jewelry box, then changed my mind and threaded it onto a thin black cord and hung it around my neck. I'd wear it every day under my clothes, a constant reminder of the consequences of my trusting, emotional stupidity.

By then it was almost five in the morning. I collapsed on my bed, then jumped to my feet as a knock sounded on my door. Holy shit. I couldn't believe Fort would dare show his face. I clutched the lock in my fist, glad now that I'd decided to wear it. It would be my shield, my badge of courage to repel him.

I opened the door already worked into a fury, ready to unleash hell on the head of my tormentor. Goodluck blinked back at me, holding a large, fuzzy calico cat in his hands. "Are you busy?" he asked.

"No, but..." He moved past me, into my apartment. "I'm a little allergic to cats, boss."

"Good, just a little? Maybe you can take some medicine or something. I think me and Mr. Snail Shell have to live with you for a while."

Maybe it was my rough night, or lack of sleep, but I couldn't figure out what the hell he was talking about. Mr. Snail Shell leaped out of his arms and curled up on my sofa.

"Goodluck, I don't really have room in my apartment for you and a cat."

"I know, I know, I know." He buried his face in his hands. "I know I've been so mean to you, Starcomet. I was angry. I love you and I want you to be happy, so I want us to stay friends, even if you have your weirdo thing with that psycho guy..." He waved a hand, dismissing all that. "You'll always be my Starcomet. Also, there was a small fire."

"What?"

"In my apartment. I put it out, but at the moment my place isn't really habitable, especially for Mr. Snail Shell. You know, I was so into flames and candles, and the fire alarms kept going off, so I disabled them, but then last night I fell asleep in the golden glow of one of those flames and..."

"And what?" I gasped.

He turned around. The back of his long hair was much shorter now, and singed black at the edges.

I stared a moment, put my hands over my eyes, then took them off again. "Goodluck, is the fire out now?"

"Yes."

"Right now, this moment, there's definitely no fire or any candles burning in your apartment?"

"The fire's out, but I think some of the furniture and carpet will have to be replaced. The smoke damage…" He spread his arms with a smile. "It's good that I don't develop prints in there anymore. You're right, it's best to have a studio. If those flammable chemicals had been in the apartment, Mr. Snail Shell and I would be stardust now, wafting toward the heavens."

"Jesus Christ." My horror knew no bounds. Goodluck and his cat would have been ashes, not stardust. "You can't burn any more candles in your apartment," I said. "Not unless you enable the fire alarms and install sprinklers. You could have died!"

And that would have killed me. As much as Goodluck drove me crazy, I loved him like my own child.

"Don't be angry with me," he said, his face crumpling with emotion. "It was scary. I had to figure out how to use the fire extinguisher from the kitchen." He came toward me, and I hugged him, stroking his hair, singed ends and all. "It was so scary, Starcomet, and I've missed you. I don't want you to leave me, or stop working for me. And, plus, I have to live with you for a while."

I sighed, holding him, feeling some of last night's angst bleed away. This was one person in my life who wasn't afraid of emotion. "You can stay as long as you like," I said, suppressing a sniffle, probably from Mr. Snail Shell's dander. "But right now, I have to sleep. I really have to sleep this minute. I've had a long night."

"Me too," he said. "Let's get some rest."

I walked down the hall and collapsed on my bed, and a moment later, I felt Goodluck's weight beside me. He pulled the covers over both of us, and I thought, *all right. Whatever.* I was just happy to be Starcomet again. A moment later, Mr. Snail Shell jumped between us, curling into a ball by Goodluck's face. I sighed and went to my bathroom to take an allergy pill.

"Where did you find that cat?" I asked on the way back.

"I didn't find him," he said, scratching his ears. "He found me. He walked into my apartment a couple months ago and that was that. He climbed five flights of stairs to get to me." His expression sobered. "You know, it was his meowing that woke me during the fire. So I only lost half my hair, and he didn't lose any at all."

"What a good cat. I guess both of you are lucky." I turned onto my side, plumping the pillow against my cheek. I could feel the lock shift under my sleep shirt, nestling between my breasts. My nipples still felt sore. They'd been hurt just hours ago, although it seemed worlds ago now.

"You know what?" I said. "You were right, friend. You were right about Fort St. Clair and me and relationships. I'm not going to see him anymore."

"What did he do to you?" His eyes softened as he studied me. "You've been crying."

"I needed to cry."

Goodluck made a distressed sound. "What did he do to you? Are there more...bruises?"

"Just emotional ones. He left me, but I'm thinking now that it was for the best, and I want to apologize for the things I said to you, and the fight we had."

"Fights are part of life's growth process." He reached out to touch my hair. "You know what they say. A whale's cry can make the brightest rainbow tremble."

I bit back a laugh. "Is that what they say? I don't think anyone says that but you."

"Well, people should say it. People should speak the truth, always. If they did, our world would be a much better place."

"Agreed." I trailed my fingertips across the top of Mr. Snail Shell's long fur. He wasn't triggering my allergies too badly, and he *had* saved Goodluck's life. "You're welcome to stay here while your apartment gets fixed," I said. "I think I'm actually going to go somewhere. You know, travel to some exotic location and work remotely for a while."

"Travel where?"

"I don't know. Somewhere that's not here, just for a few weeks. If you needed me, you could reach me by phone or email, or ask your agent for help."

"Or my decorator, now that my apartment's wrecked. I asked him to come over this evening. I'm thinking about rebuilding with a new color scheme, reds and oranges, my apartment rising from the ashes. Literal ashes."

"But no candles." I reached to take his hand. "The world needs you."

He smiled at me, so much caring and openness in his gaze. I let go of his hand and closed my eyes, pretending to go to sleep. It was that, or keep looking at him and start to cry.

God, why had I ever imagined things would work out with Fort and me? We were nothing alike. He was cool and slick as the steel face of a watch gear, and I was a flailing, roiling mess of emotion. If I had a match in this world, it would be someone equally crazy, like Goodluck Boundless. I'd fallen for Fort, yes. He'd thrilled and excited me, and showed me how hot passion could burn, but loving him was a mistake.

Exhaustion overtook me, and tears came, too. I turned on my other side so Goodluck wouldn't see them, wetting my pillow as I drifted into sleep.

Chapter Twenty-Seven: Fort

I managed to ignore the feelings of loss for an entire week. I threw myself into work, into organizing some new ad campaigns, except that memories of Goodluck's ad campaign dogged me by the hour. I took a trip to the Bahamas, thinking to lose myself in luxury, but every voluptuous, seductive woman I saw there reminded me that Juliet was my fetish, my fantasy, with her bright eyes and expressive mouth, and her responsive body.

I returned to New York, miserable with craving and lust.

I swore I wouldn't stalk Juliet, wouldn't linger in the area of the Black Wall or stake out her front door, but I did those things before the second week was out, and that's how I knew she wasn't coming home in the evenings. Goodluck was coming in and out of her apartment, but she wasn't. Maybe she'd taken a vacation, the way I had, or maybe she'd left New York altogether in some effort to forget the debacle of our relationship.

On the three-week anniversary of leaving her at The Gallery, I asked Devin to meet me for drinks. We hunkered down at an Irish-themed pub near the airport, watching Euro league soccer over our beers.

"You look like hell," Devin said, once the waitress left. "Have you been sleeping?"

"No."

He raised his glass in a taunting gesture. "That's what happens when you can't get into The Gallery anymore. Everything breaks down."

"Nothing's broken down," I said, sounding broken down as hell.

He replaced his glass and scrutinized me with his light blue eyes, eyes that missed very little, especially since we were longtime friends.

"I warned you," he said.

"Shut the fuck up."

We sat in silence for five minutes, drinking and watching the game, occasionally looking around the bar. I used to look around bars to measure women's attractiveness, to gauge submissive potential as they grew drunker and let their guard down. I used to look for party girls and sluts. Now I was looking, pointlessly, for Juliet, for someone sweet and unique and emotionally confrontational. I was looking for what used to be my nightmare. It was time to admit the reason why.

"I want to get back together with Juliet," I told Devin. "I mean, I'd like to try...try to work things out between us."

"Are you drunk, or just spouting stupid ideas for the fun of it? Either way—"

"I'm not drunk and I'm not joking. I need to see her again, see if there's anything that can be salvaged."

"Then go see her." Devin leaned away from me, like my neediness might be contagious. "You know where she lives. Go knock on her door."

"She's not there, hasn't been there in a while. Maybe she's moved."

"Have you tried calling her?"

"I'm blocked."

"Contact her through her boss?"

"He won't talk to me. When I asked where she was, he yelled something about whales and rainbows and told me to leave her alone."

Dev took a deep drink of his beer, avoiding my eyes. I could still read his thoughts loud and clear. *If she's moved out of her apartment and blocked you, you should probably leave her alone.*

"I've changed," I said. "I'm not that guy who left her at The Gallery."

Devin snorted. "You're still that guy. I'm looking at you, and you're still the same guy. A little hornier, perhaps. Too bad you were banned. Nona was asking about you last Saturday."

"Fuck Nona," I said with a flare of temper. "I've changed, and that's an example of why, because I don't fucking want Nona. I don't want anyone but Juliet, and I'm about to lose my fucking mind because she blocked my number and she's somewhere I can't find her, and I don't know if she's okay or if she's a fucking mess—"

Dev held up a hand. "Listen, Fort. If she needed you, if she wanted you, she'd let you know."

"No, she wouldn't, because she doesn't realize I've changed."

"Holy shit, you're a fucking butterfly come out of a cocoon, is that it?"

"Yes, that's exactly it."

Our voices had risen in the crowded bar, drowning out the soccer commentator's excitable drone. We ignored the surrounding scowls, returning to our drinks. I tore pieces off the edge of a napkin, working up to the reason I'd asked him to meet me here.

"Dev," I finally said. "Is there any way you can, I don't know... Use your airline connections to find out where she is?"

His eyes widened, and he laughed. "My *airline connections?*"

"Your father owns the largest airline in the world. Don't you have access to airport computers and travel records, maybe rental car records?"

He shook his head. "Not really. They encrypt that shit. You'll have to go higher than me, friend. Know anyone at the CIA? If you say she's a terrorist, they'll find her for you real quick."

"It's not funny." I scowled at him. "I need to find her."

"Why?" He sat back in his chair and fixed me with a look. "You had her and decided you didn't want her. She was too much for you, and you left her. The romance is over, and I doubt she'd have you back."

"I lied to her." I admitted it through clenched teeth. "I said I didn't love her, but I think I do."

"You *think?*" He shifted forward again. "Jesus, you're an idiot. I knew you loved her that night you dragged me to that fucking art opening. Why else would I go to some wacko artist's show, except to see the woman who finally captured Fort St. Clair's heart?"

I took a deep drink of my beer, subduing the urge to pound my head against the scarred wood tabletop in front of us. "It doesn't matter now. She won't believe me if I tell her that I...I need her."

"That you love her," he said in a mocking tone. "You might as well get used to saying the words, especially if you want her to give you another chance. That one's going to want to hear it all the fucking time."

"Don't roll your eyes," I snapped.

"Are you going to tell her you love her all the fucking time?" he snapped back at me. "Are you sure this is what you want? Because I won't let you hurt that woman again."

"What are you now, her protector? You?"

His harsh blue gaze came near to incinerating me. "Yes. You know how it is, Fort. I just want you to follow the rules."

I collapsed back with a sigh. "I don't know the rules in this case. I don't know what the fuck I'm doing, but I need her in my life, so I'm going to have to figure this out."

Devin watched me for a moment, then rolled his eyes to the sky. "Go home and pack your shit, idiot. I know where Juliet is. I know because I flew her there a couple weeks ago, after she came to me for advice on where to go."

"Juliet came to you?" I asked in disbelief.

"Yeah, she trusts me for some reason. Maybe because I helped her when you had a lame-ass breakdown and lost your shit."

"Did you... Did she...?"

He laughed, loudly this time. "Did the two of us hook up? Not a fucking chance. She's in love with you, too." He drained his beer and banged the glass down on the table with a frown. "I don't know exactly where she is, but I can fire up the jet and take you as far as the airport she flew into. If you really want her, you'll have to find her yourself."

"I'll find her."

"You better be worth her love," he said with lingering threat in his voice. It would have scared me if I wasn't so sure of my feelings. "You better treat her right this time. Only the good kind of hurt."

"Only the good kind of hurt," I agreed. "Let me know when you're sober enough to fly. I'm going home to pack."

Chapter Twenty-Eight: Juliet

I stretched and looked at myself in the mirror, my pale cheeks caressed by Tuscan sunlight. The old woman who ran this bed and breakfast said I was too pale, and always tried to feed me the "very freshest milk." I suspected it might have come from the goats who roamed her small farm, so I declined. She also gave me "virgin's water" to restore my eyes, which were often more red than blue these days. I didn't know where the "virgin's water" came from but I splashed it in my eyes anyway.

I studied them afterward, squinting in the mirror. Was my vision clearer? Were my eyes more open than they'd been before I came to this rural Italian paradise?

I wasn't sure.

I made my bed and picked up the beaded sandals I'd bought in Cascina's artisan marketplace, now that the March rains had let up. I stuck my head out the window to gauge the weather. The morning chill had worn off, and thin wisps of clouds blew across an otherwise sunny sky. Later, I'd stroll down the path to Santo Stefano, a nearby hamlet where theoretical physicists scanned for gravitational waves and astronomical anomalies. It wasn't potential energy, but extraterrestrial phenomena.

I wondered if Fort knew anything about gravitational waves.

Even an ocean away, he affected me, his gravitational waves buffeting my soul. I thought of him mostly at night, in the dark and stars, as I fingered my engraved-lock necklace and wondered where we'd gone so wrong. During the day I explored museums and sat outside cafes, becoming one with my sun-drenched surroundings, trying to reinvent myself just as Goodluck was reinventing his apartment. Reds and oranges, rising from the ashes...

I walked down the hall to Signora d'Averio's rustic kitchen and accepted a breakfast of tea and cranberry-walnut scones. They tasted fresh and warm.

"Oh, Juliet," she said in her thick country accent. "Someone has come. I told him—" She gestured aggressively. "I told him wait outside."

"Who is it?"

"I don't remember name. Someone who asks for you. I wouldn't let him in. He has...dark eyes."

For a moment, just a moment, I'd let myself imagine that Fort had come for me, that he'd realized he loved me after all and couldn't live without me. But my visitor couldn't be Fort, because his eyes weren't dark. They were hazel-gold, intense as the sun outside. I didn't know who else it might be. Devin didn't have dark eyes either, and I hadn't met many local men. I'd kept to myself since I'd come here, nursing my wounds, thinking about love, and why my relationships always went wrong.

"He's out there, out in the garden," she said, gesturing vaguely to the distance. "I send him away?"

"No, it's all right."

I picked up my sandals and crossed from the kitchen to the large, open foyer of her country house. I could see her visitor through the window, see dark, curling hair and a physical stance I remembered.

My breath caught. Fort was here.

The gravitational waves had brought him after all. I remembered how dark his eyes could look when he frowned, and understood why Signora d'Averio had perceived them that way. Even from a distance, I could see his serious expression.

I stood where I was, staring out the window, trying to figure out my feelings, trying to figure out the breathless hatred and excitement I experienced at the same time. Even though he'd devastated me and ripped my heart out, I'd wanted him to come and admit that he was wrong, and that he cared for me despite all evidence to the contrary.

I walked outside, conscious of each step I took toward him, conscious of the many ways I'd changed, and the ways I hadn't changed at all. I still wanted him to love me. My heart still surged with emotion when he turned to me. Our eyes locked.

"What are you doing here?" I asked. "How did you find me?"

I sounded a little heated. He looked defensive, or worried. He clasped his hands together, looking me up and down. "Devin flew me as far as Pisa. After that...well, I visited hotels and art galleries, and asked questions in bad Italian until someone could tell me where the wild-haired American woman was."

I put a hand to my unstyled mop. "How persistent of you."

"Are you still angry with me?" he asked. "I deserve it. I shouldn't have come, but I couldn't stay away."

It was my turn to rake my eyes over my ex-lover. He seemed achingly at home in the rustic surroundings, with his ebony hair and olive-toned skin.

Signora d'Averio stuck her head out the front door and yelled something in Italian. I waved to let her know I was okay. She waved a hand and disappeared, as I thought, *Am I really okay?*

"I'm glad to see you," I admitted, "although I don't want to be. You've always made me feel things I don't want to feel."

"Juliet..." He sighed, his eyes narrowing a little. "Right back at you. You make me feel too much. But I'm here anyway, because I need to talk to you."

"Well..." I pointed down the shaded path to the signora's vineyards. "I was just going to take a walk."

"Can I come with you?"

"I guess."

We set out, potential energy turned to kinetic energy. He asked polite questions. How long had I been here? How many people had I met? Did I plan to leave and visit other areas of the world?

The first two questions were easy, but the last one made me realize just how untethered I'd become. Was I going to stay here? Go home? Go somewhere else and hope it was as idyllic as this place? Was I going to fall in love with someone in another country, considering my job and my friends were back in New York?

"I don't know what I'm going to do," I said.

I looked sideways at him, at long legs and strong arms beneath a white linen shirt. His strength and stature reminded me of his power and the way it had changed me...at least for a little while.

"Why are you here?" I asked. "Why did you make the effort to find me after the way you left things?"

"Because I don't like the way I left things. I was horrible to you, and I never told you how sorry I was. That's partly because I couldn't deal with what I'd done."

We walked a while longer in silence. I found myself unable to raise my eyes and look him in the face.

"Here's the thing about me, Juliet," he said, reaching to pluck at a bush as we passed. "I suck at trusting women. I'm terrible at relationships. I have a really hard time...making myself vulnerable. I want everything safe and predictable."

"Like clockwork," I murmured.

"I know. It's fucked up. See, when I was growing up, my parents got divorced, and it was so acrimonious, so hateful, that I decided I'd never be like them. My first few relationships... Jesus, I went all in. I exposed myself and gave them everything, only to be used for my money, or accused of being abusive because of my kink. I started to believe after a while that I was abusive, that I was a rich, selfish asshole, this person they accused me of being."

He stopped and turned to me, and now I could see that his eyes were dark, so dark, as he relived these past hurts. "But I wasn't a rich, selfish asshole. I wanted to love them, but my relationships became these ugly things, full of hurt and accusation and emotional drama. I had to stop trying. I had to put the walls up and stay in control."

I studied him, not knowing what to say. I felt bad that he'd been scarred by his parents' angsty divorce, felt bad that he'd gotten mixed up with women who hurt him. But at the same time, I wouldn't compromise on the love and connection I craved. "I'm sorry you went through that," I said. "It helps me understand you more."

"But it doesn't fix us. I know."

My breath blew out in a long, slow gust. "Do you want to fix us?"

He nodded, regarding me with a pained expression that looked more fearful than hopeful. "I miss you, Sparkles. I think of you every day. I think of your eyes, your voice, your laughter. Your bravery and strength.

Even your emotions, that vast repertoire of expressions that transforms your face from moment to moment." He chuckled, and reached to touch my cheek. "I'm watching them now. I miss them. I miss the way you made me start feeling things again."

His hand dropped away as tears rose in my eyes. "I'm afraid now to be emotional around you," I said. "It makes you close down."

"It did. It still might. But I don't want you to hide how you feel." He came closer to me, cradling my head against his chest. His heartfelt confessions had opened some hopeful part of myself that I'd locked shut. *Maybe...maybe the two of us...* I was crying because I wanted it so badly, and because I was scared he wouldn't be able to change.

"I don't know if I can trust you again," I said. "I want love. You can't have me if you won't love me." I touched the front of my shirt, feeling the outline of the lock. "That's not negotiable, not anymore."

"I want to love you."

"Wanting's not enough," I said, but he held up a hand to cut me off.

"You have to think about it from my point of view, Juliet. Here's me, terrified of grand and dramatic emotion, determined not to get involved with anyone I can't control. There you are, standing against the side of a building, completely unable to care for yourself. What drew me to you? Why did I reach out to you rather than walking away?"

"I don't know. The socks?"

"Your fucking socks." He sighed, taking my hand. "It didn't take long to realize you were bad and dangerous, that you were everything I was careful to avoid...but at the same time, I found myself more and more attracted to you. The more I felt, the more I resisted. The more I pushed you away. But I didn't want to push you away."

He stepped back and pressed his fists to his eyes, his mouth set in a grim line. I saw it then, the emotion struggling to get out. I tried to pull his hands from his face but he held them there. "What are you so afraid of?" I asked.

"Getting hurt."

Funny, that a sadist's greatest fear would be getting hurt, but I understood. He'd been hurt—traumatically—by the first few women he'd opened his heart to. His solution was to never love again, to never give up control. But...

"There's no room for control when it comes to love," I said. "Love isn't like watches. It doesn't keep perfect time."

"Holy shit." His breath came out in a whisper. "I know." He lowered his hands and gazed at me, his eyes sparking with anxiety. "Remember when you asked to try things my way? To try sado-masochism and fetish? I promised we could start slow, build trust?"

I nodded, remembering that weighty conversation. "You didn't start that slow, though," I reminded him. "You wouldn't let me have a safe word."

"I know, because I think I can control everything. I need to control everything to protect myself."

"Yet you wouldn't let me protect myself."

He shook his head. "You didn't want to protect yourself. That's how you are, that's why you scared me so much." He took a deep breath, reaching for my hand again, tracing my fingers. "You were willing to try things my way, with no reservations, no distrust, no fear."

"There was a little bit of fear."

His fingers closed around mine. He brought my hand to his heart and held it there. "You asked me why I came here. Juliet, I came here to ask if you'll let me try things your way this time, so I can learn how to...how *not* to protect myself. You were so open to me, you gave me everything. Now I want to give that to you."

I stared at him, confused. "You want to be my submissive?"

"Oh God, no." He let out a laugh. I could feel his heart beating against my palm. "I want to fall in love," he said, then shook his head. "I'm already in love, Sparkles. I need you to teach me how to do it the right way."

"Oh."

We stood across from each other, connected only by my hand against his warm chest. I realized I didn't want to travel anywhere else, or fall in love with anyone else. They would be strangers, and this man was already well known to me, complex and guarded as he was. Could I teach him how to love? God knew how much courage it took him to ask.

"I'm not giving you a safe word," I said, narrowing my eyes in a warning. "You might end up getting hurt, because love isn't clockwork."

"I know, you taught me that. Juliet...please..."

He took my hand between both of his. His palms were sweaty. The cool, collected playboy was sweating it out in the Italian countryside for a woman who scared him to death. That had to be worth something. I let go of his hands and placed my palms against his shoulders, measuring his solid breadth and the power of his intentions.

"Okay," I finally said. "I'll teach you how to love, so this doesn't end in drama and sadness. We'll respect each other, bond and grow together, and make each other happy." I gazed into his eyes. "Do you believe me?"

A smile dispersed the concerned lines of his face. "I wouldn't be here if I didn't believe."

Then he grabbed me, hard, and clasped me against him for a deep, reuniting kiss.

Chapter Twenty-Nine: Fort

Did u find her yet?

Yes, Dev, I found her.

And....????

She's lying next to me. I can't text now.

You can't text in a good way, or a bad way?

...

C'mon Forsyth. Don't leave me hanging

...

Fort....?

A good way, I texted. ***Everything's good right now. Perfect. See u when we get home.***

I switched off my phone, even though he was typing another text. Dev could wait, New York could wait, everything could wait. Now that I was in love, I wanted to revel in it for a while. I rolled closer to Juliet in our narrow bed and buried my face against her neck, breathing in the scent of my future. Potential energy transformed to kinetic energy.

Two clock gears, finally fitted into place.

EPILOGUE

Six months later

I stood on my toes, without recourse, without a safe word, gingerly sinking back into the black butterfly chair in my lover's secret dungeon. "Ow, ow, ow," I whispered.

"Hush. Don't make me get the bigger one."

Fort had settled into a routine of using the "big" or "bigger" dildo for the butterfly chair. The big one was extremely uncomfortable to take up one's ass, but the bigger one was a monster, only used for punishments. Like if a maso-submissive was whining and complaining too much.

"I'm sorry, Sir," I said. "It's just... It really hurts."

"That's a good thing. Sit all the way back."

He waited while I eased down, seating myself on the jutting shaft. When my ass cheeks finally contacted the chair, I sighed and laid back, taking deep breaths, squeezing on the width inside me as I acclimated to the feeling of being stretched.

"Good girl," he said, his eyes bright with approval.

It was Saturday night. Now that his ban from The Gallery had been lifted, we could have gone there, but he didn't want to.

I didn't want to, either. I was exactly where I wanted to be.

Well, not *exactly* where I wanted to be. I moaned as I shifted on the lubed phallus. "How long will I have to..."

He put a finger over my lips. "Enough. Don't make me gag you."

"I'm sorry, Sir." I bit my lip, trying not to talk so much. We were still working on that.

"Hold up your wrists for me," he said.

I obeyed, knowing I was about to give up all control of my body. Or rather, his body, the body that belonged mostly to him. I still used my body to work for Goodluck, to move around in the city, but I'd come to think of my body as Fort's, so it was only on loan while I was away from him. When I returned home, when we were together, I was his. He loved me, just as he promised.

And he hurt me, but we both liked that part.

He held my left hand, turning it over against his palm. "We'd better take this off before we get started."

I'd been wearing a watch since shortly after we'd returned from Pisa, a timepiece that rarely left my wrist. Goodluck might not like watches, but I treasured mine.

Fort unbuckled the thin, black leather band, the watch face reflecting the stark light in the ceiling above me. The face was clear, just a thin sheet of glass, so all the miniscule working parts inside the watch were bared to the world. Fort had designed it for me, a promise to be open with me, to connect even if his inner workings were complicated. The fact that the style became a runaway bestseller, the season's most coveted accessory, well, that was wonderful. But not as wonderful as the symbolism of that watch around my wrist.

He placed it on a shelf, near enough that I could keep an eye on it. Even when he took it off my wrist, I didn't want it out of my sight.

"Okay, Sparkles." His rough voice thrilled me. "Arms by your sides."

I couldn't see his face as he leaned down to fasten my wrists into cuffs at each side of the chair, but I imagined he wore the dangerous, assessing look I'd come to know well. He moved behind me then, and I squeezed on the shaft inside me as I heard him undressing. He reappeared at my side, yes, wearing that look—and nothing else.

"Are you ready?" he asked.

Maybe. Probably. "Yes, Sir," I said aloud.

He knelt in front of me, a pair of sleek, black, over-the-knee socks in his hands. "Then let's get you dressed."

He held my gaze as he gathered the first sock and pulled it onto my toes. He smoothed the thin cotton up my legs, over my calves, then up over my knees where they ended in a line of embroidered flowers. Sometimes there were bows instead, and sometimes sewn-on jewels. I hoped the flowers meant he was in a romantic mood.

"How does that feel, baby?" he asked. "Are you getting ready for me?"

"Yes, Sir."

He started putting on the other sock. "After I hurt you, where does my cock go?"

"In my ass, Sir, because I'm a maso-slut."

He smiled, giving the second sock's cuff a playful tug. "You are, aren't you? Thank God."

He spent a few minutes pinching and twisting my nipples. It hurt so much worse than wearing clamps. At least clamps only gave one burst of pain before my nipples settled into numbness, but with this type of play, the pain went on and on. When I moaned for a break, he slapped my breasts instead, making me squirm on the unforgiving shaft in my ass. My hands were cuffed, so the fists I made were useless to push my tormentor away.

"Do you want more?" he asked. "Or would you like to move on to your caning?"

My ass clenched and my legs trembled. "You just caned me last week."

"Oh, no. Don't you want the cane?" He started unbuckling my cuffs, not really sounding all that sympathetic. "How about a strapping instead?"

I studied him, wondering what the catch was. "A strapping and what else?" I asked.

"A strapping, with a strap. Because I'm a kind sadist, I'll let you choose between that and the cane."

"You're not really a kind sadist." I whimpered as he lifted me from the chair. The shaft slid out of my ass, leaving me empty, yet full of dread. He was still going to fuck me there, after he did something hurty, because he liked me to be all opened up with pain.

"Okay, not a kind sadist," he admitted. "But I'm a sadist who loves you. So you get to pick: cane or strap?"

"I'll take the strap, Sir." Was there any question? Strappings were much easier to handle. They stung and they were painful, but they didn't feel like your ass was being slashed to ribbons by slices of fire.

"The strap it is," he said, leading me to the St. Andrew's cross. "Of course, since you chose the less painful option, I think I'd better use some naughty cream too."

My eyes went wide, and a flush heated my cheeks. "But you didn't say—"

"No, I didn't say, but you don't have a choice if I decide to do mean things, do you?"

I moved my hands behind me to cover my butt. Naughty cream was a pepper-based compound he rubbed into my ass cheeks to intensify the heat of a spanking. Even after the spanking, the burn from the cream lingered, sometimes for hours.

I mashed my lips shut so I wouldn't get myself in trouble by begging for a reprieve. He was already screwing a punitive attachment into the X-frame, a short, rounded bar perpendicular to the frame that I had to straddle. Of course, it was placed in such a way that any slouching or squirming resulted in uncomfortable pressure against my pussy.

When he was done, he stood back, gesturing to the rack. "You know what to do."

I swallowed another whimper and fitted my stomach and thighs against the wooden structure. The bar pressed between my pussy lips as I straddled it. Fort checked to see if it was snug enough, then tsked. I was so wet.

"I think you liked my idea about the naughty cream," he said.

"No, Sir. Please—"

He swatted my butt, parted my pussy lips, and ratcheted the bar up another notch. "I can go higher if I need to," he said. "I can force you onto your toes."

I shook my head, for all the good it did me. Any movement pressed my tender pubic area against the hard bar between my legs, and once he applied the stinging cream...

I took deep breaths as he strapped me down tight. Wrist cuffs made my arms reach high, ankle cuffs spread my feet below. *Ow, ow, the bar, my pussy...*

He bound my stomach against the front of the cross with a belt around my middle, cinching that tight as well. His cock poked against me as he worked, but he wouldn't take me yet, not until I was tearful and marked.

He stepped back, taking a few moments to appreciate my helplessness as I stood in my bonds. I was pinned to the cross like a butterfly, my pussy hurting now, instead of my asshole. I leaned my head back, feeling my loose curls slide across my shoulders. I heard the snick of a cap and the rustle of a latex glove. Lube? God, I wished it were lube. No, it was the stinging cream.

He applied it right in the middle of each cheek, small smears that he rubbed in with gentle fingers. The first time he'd done it, I'd thought, *oh, this is nothing*. Now I knew better.

He put the cream away and took off the latex glove, then produced the strap, giving each of my thighs a series of slaps while he waited for the cream to heat on my skin. Each slap made me jerk, pressing the bar against my slit. My clit felt swollen and hot—and not all from pain. I bucked against the front of the cross as the heat increased, but I couldn't touch my clit to anything, which was by design. I'd receive no relief until the punishment was through—and if I didn't take my punishment well, I'd receive no relief at all, no orgasm permitted. Too horrible to think about.

My ass was heating up in earnest now, and Fort commenced strapping me on my burning bottom. I cried out at each stroke, then twitched and tensed in agony as he made me wait for the next.

"Oh, God," I gasped, bouncing on the bar. "It hurts. It hurts."

But it wasn't enough for it to hurt, not for either of us. He strapped me until I squealed, and then screamed, and then broke down in tears of supplication. It wasn't that the strokes got any harder or more unbearable. No, it was just that they continued falling, and my ass got hotter and hotter, and I couldn't move or escape or do anything but beg and cry.

Whack. Pause. *Whack.* Pause. *Whack.* Please, please, please.

I bobbed on my toes, ignoring the ache in my pussy, wishing only for this to end so I could get away. When my begging tapered off and I broke down to only crying, he relented and put the strap away. He pulled my hair back, nuzzling my tears.

"Does your ass burn now, baby?"

"Yes," I sobbed. "Yes, Sir." The strapping had ended, but the naughty cream ensured that the sting went on and on.

"I'm going to let you go now. Tell me the rule."

"No touching my bottom."

"That's right. No matter what. You don't want that cream getting on your fingers because it might end up somewhere very, very bad. And if it ends up somewhere bad on me, what happens to you?"

"The chastity belt," I whispered.

"That's right. The chastity belt, and no orgasms all week."

He undid my bonds and I clasped my hands in front of me with the effort not to reach back and soothe the sting. If I could paint what my ass felt like, it would literally be an entire canvas of flames. "I hate the naughty cream," I said, wiping away my tears. "I really, really hate it."

He smiled at me. "I know, baby. That's why I use it a lot. Now, let's get you to the table so I can fuck your ass. Go on. Crawl up there. Lie on your back."

Our sex table was a re-purposed medical table with attachment points of just about every type. Tonight, he pulled my arms up and cuffed them over my head. It was merciful, because then I couldn't lose control and try to rub the pain off my ass. My waist was buckled down near the other end of the table so my ass hung off the edge, the better for him to fuck me. My legs were left flailing in my flower-cuffed socks. So much for romance. He gripped my thighs and held them open, his heavy cock falling down against my sore pussy.

"I bet you'd like me in here," he said, slapping his cock against my folds. "You want my cock in your nice, wet pussy?"

I lay helpless as he pressed halfway in. My clit zinged to life, ready for his touch, ready to come. I bucked my hips, but he only pulled back out. "It would be too easy for you to come like that," he said. "When are you allowed to come? When's the only time you're allowed to come, baby?"

"With something in my ass," I said, sniffling.

"Yes, that's our rule, isn't it? Do you want to come?"

I nodded. *Yes, yes, yes.* My ass burned. My clit throbbed. I needed release, needed all this pain to come together and make sense.

"Your little clit makes it too easy for you to come, doesn't it?" he asked, his eyes alight with sadistic challenge. "It's so sensitive. We'd better take care of that so you can focus on having your ass fucked, don't you think?"

These were all rhetorical questions. He was the only one who got to answer. He opened a drawer in the side of the table and took out one of the small, biting clit clamps I'd come to dread.

"I know you don't like this," he said as I squirmed. "But it's better to learn to come from Sir's cock in your ass, instead of clitoral stimulation. You want to be a good little maso, don't you?"

A tear slipped down my cheek. "Yes, Sir. Please..."

"Please what, baby?"

"Please hurt my clit so it won't help me come while your cock's in my ass."

"Okay," he said. "I think that's a great idea."

My hips bucked as he applied the clamp to my tender, teeming nub. All pleasure fled, replaced by sharp pain, but there was another sensation taking over me. He lubed his cock and spread some lube around my asshole. The cold, liquid slipperiness contrasted with the heat burning my bottom.

"*Owww*," I said. He pressed the head of his cock against my hole, and while I'd learned to stay open for him, it was still hard to let him in without tensing first. His hands tightened on my knees, pushing them back, spreading them wide. It made the penetration feel even more invasive. I hid my face in the side of my arm.

"No, Juliet. Look at me."

I opened my eyes and obeyed, sighing as he pressed deeper.

"Does that hurt, baby?"

My voice quivered in a sob. "Yes, Sir. It hurts so bad. It burns. It aches."

"Oh, no," he said, in a voice that meant *oh, yes*. He pressed deeper, sliding along the lubricant-eased passage, filling me to the hilt, then tilting my hips and forcing himself deeper. He braced his hands on either side of me and arched over my body, bumping his hips against my thighs, riding me, forcing me open for his pleasure. Even in the clamp's metal grip, my clit responded, throbbing to life again. I yanked at the cuffs as Fort leaned over me, rubbing his rough, stubbled cheek against my temple, breathing in my lust and fear. "You know why I hurt you, Sparkles..."

"Yes, Sir. Because you l-love me. And I submit to you because I love you."

He licked my lips, then licked my tears, kissing them away. "It's wonderful how that works, isn't it? We fit together, you and me."

Like clock gears in a platinum setting. Like the engagement diamond I wore on my left hand that never came off, even during scenes. I twisted it as my fingers scrabbled in my bonds. All our past hurts and disappointments were forgotten, or at least pushed away to make room for a new connection, a new freedom to love.

"Look at me," he insisted. I did, my eyes alight with pure, unconditional desire.

A Final Note

I hope you enjoyed this first book in my new Dark Dominance series. Please remember that practicing BDSM without a safe word is best attempted in the realm of fantasy (like my fantasy BDSM club, The Gallery.) Any real-life BDSM interaction requires a relationship of the deepest trust.

If you enjoyed Fort and Juliet's story, I invite you to read some of my other intense BDSM contemporaries, like my award-winning Rough Love series. You'll find those blurbs below. You should also sign up for my mailing list so you'll know when the next Dark Dominance books come out. I plan to write two more standalone stories, one for Devin and one for Milo. Devin's is next, and of course, Fort and Juliet will return for brief appearances as they enjoy their happily ever after.

Many thanks to my beta readers on this story: Carol, Doris, Lina, and Audrey. Thanks also to my editor Kyla at Missed Period Editing for the spit and polish. Your efforts are so appreciated. A final thank you to my readers who waited so patiently for this book. You're what it's all about!

Coming Soon:
Book Two in the Dark Dominance Series
Deep Control

Not all fantasies are safe, sane, and consensual. Welcome to the world of The Gallery...

Devin's a pilot and playboy, as well as a Gallery Dominant known for his sadistic desires. Ella is a famed physicist whose quiet intelligence masks a depraved longing for pain. When the two connect in a foreign dungeon, neither knows that one of them will soon save the other's life.

From such dramatic beginnings, a mutual friendship grows, along with a daring D/s relationship. Is their play merely sensual, or do their feelings run deeper? Within the opulent walls of The Gallery, Devin and Ella explore ever-expanding limits and test the boundaries of trust...

YOU MAY ALSO ENJOY
THESE EDGY BDSM ROMANCES BY ANNABEL JOSEPH

THE AWARD-WINNING ROUGH LOVE SERIES

There's rough sex, and then there's rough love. The challenge is learning the difference...

Chere's a high-class call girl trapped in a self-destructive spiral, and "W" is the mysterious and sexually voracious client who refuses to tell her his name. Over the span of four years, their tortured relationship unwinds by fits and starts, encompassing fear and loneliness, mistrust, aggression, literal and figurative bondage, and moments of excruciating pain.

But there's also caring and longing, and heartfelt poetry. There are two deeply damaged people straining to connect despite the daunting emotional risks. When he slaps her face or grasps her neck, it's not to hurt, but to hold. His rough passions are a plea, and Chere's the only one so far who's been able to understand...

The Rough Love series is:
#1 *Torment Me*
(Winner—BDSM Writers Con Best Dark Erotica Novel—2016)
#2 *Taunt Me*
#3 *Trust Me*

THE CLUB MEPHISTO SERIES

Club Mephisto... Molly is a 24/7 slave dedicated to serving her Master. When business calls him away on a weeklong trip, he arranges to leave her in the care of Mephisto, the owner of a thriving local BDSM club. Molly is both excited and scared to be given over to Master Mephisto. His power and mysterious intensity have long compelled her from afar.

She finds herself immersed in a world of strict commands, pervasive sex, and creative torments. Over the course of a week, Mephisto strips away privileges Molly took for granted, and forces her to understand and acknowledge the depths to which she can be made to submit. But a surprising conversation the last day threatens Molly's worldview, as does the strange closeness that develops between them. As the time of Master's return draws near, Molly finds herself deeply and inexorably changed.

Note: this BDSM fantasy novella depicts "total power exchange" relationships that some readers may find objectionable. This work contains acts of sadism, objectification, orgasm denial and speech restriction, caging, anal play and double penetration, BDSM punishment and discipline, M/f, M/m/f, M/m, orgy and group sexual encounters, voyeurism, and limited circumstances of dubious consent.

Molly's Lips: Club Mephisto Retold... If you've read *Club Mephisto*, you know the story from Molly's perspective. Now, prepare to relive the experience from Mephisto's point of view in this gripping novella.

When Mephisto's friend Clayton is called out of town on business, he agrees to look after his slave for the week. But Molly isn't your average slave. She and Clayton share a serious, full time dynamic. Mephisto feels a weight of responsibility he isn't used to, and worse, an intense attraction to Molly, the partner of his friend.

Mephisto is determined to sublimate his inappropriate desires and provide a challenging and instructive week for the devoted slave. He subjects Molly to orgasm denial, speech restriction, scenes of erotic torment, even an orgy where she is made to service his friends. Along the way, he experiences unfamiliar jealousy, and deep cravings to possess her himself.

Throughout the week, he is also haunted by persistent questions. Is she happy being a 24/7 slave? Or is there another Molly trapped beneath her submissive, surrendered gaze?

Burn For You... When Molly loses her longtime Master, she feels lost, angry. Confused. She's unsure of her future, even her calling to the BDSM lifestyle. She knows her Master always intended her to go to his friend Mephisto next, but their emotionally—and sexually—fraught history is still a confusion of desire and fear in her mind.

Mephisto wants to help Molly, but he doesn't want to force her into service she's not sure she wants. He owes it to Clayton to help her find happiness, but how? Molly and Mephisto advance and retreat from one another as they try to untangle their complex feelings. More and more it seems their tense standoff will only end one way…

Note: this 63K-word erotic romance novel contains consensual BDSM play, Master/slavery, sado-masochism, anal play, objectification, caging, and other consensual activities which some might find offensive.

The Comfort series

Have you ever wondered what goes on in the bedrooms of Hollywood's biggest heartthrobs? In the case of Jeremy Gray, the reality is far more depraved than anyone realizes. Brutal desires, shocking secrets, and a D/s relationship (with a hired submissive "girlfriend") that's based on a contract rather than love. It's just the beginning of a four-book saga following Jeremy and his Hollywood friends as they seek comfort in fake, manufactured relationships. Born of necessity—and public relations—these attachments come to feel more and more real. What does it take to live day-to-day with an A-list celebrity? Patience, fortitude, and a whole lot of heart. Oh, and a *very* good pain tolerance for kinky mayhem.

Comfort series is:
#1 *Comfort Object* (Jeremy's story)
#2 *Caressa's Knees* (Kyle's story)
#3 *Odalisque* (Kai's story)
#4 *Command Performance* (Mason's story)

About the Author

Annabel Joseph is a NYT and USA Today Bestselling BDSM romance author. She writes mainly contemporary romance, although she has been known to dabble in the medieval and Regency eras. She is known for writing emotionally intense BDSM storylines, and strives to create characters that seem real—even flawed—so readers are better able to relate to them. Annabel also writes non-BDSM romance under the pen name Molly Joseph.

You can follow Annabel on Twitter (@annabeljoseph) or Facebook (facebook.com/annabeljosephnovels), or sign up for her mailing list at annabeljoseph.com.

Made in the USA
Columbia, SC
07 October 2017